Resurrection

Resurrection

Mark A. Daniel

Prologue

She ran frantically through the dark forest, fleeing the terrible thing that seemed ready to fall upon her at any moment. The darkness of the forest was broken only by the occasional glimmer of the half-moon through the limbs of the tall pine trees that covered the east Texas countryside. The cold night air dried her lips and needles of numbness covered her face. But she did not notice these things. Her mind was focused only on her escape. Adrenaline flowed freely in her body as she fled the terror that had only moments before been sleeping the deep sleep of the ancients.

But now, that terror was awake.

Her heart was pounding loudly in her ears, and she took in deep and fast breaths of the icy air. She did not know where she was running, just what she was running from. She could still hear the chants of those who would survive this night. By now they were far behind her, yet their voices seemed to fill the air above her, a beacon of sorts for the evil that pursued her. The forest seemed endless. She knew she was losing ground, but she also knew it made no difference. It was too many miles to civilization. And only the coyotes and the buzzards would hear her screams.

Then it was upon her.

1

East Texas - 1993

1

Lying in a small heap on the concrete floor of the shed were the tattered and almost unrecognizable remains of a potbellied pig. Jack Macon was sure which of his pigs this was since he could see a small piece of the pig's tail bearing the unmistakable white ring that was only Sammy's. Most of Sammy's blood was splattered about the walls of the room. Jack's tools that still hung in neat and orderly rows on the western wall were colored a deep red. Much of the dried blood was also smeared across the floor.

Jack looked around the shed, expecting to see some trite word or phrase scrawled on one of the walls, perhaps in the pig's blood. But there were no words. There were, however, some strange lines and shapes that he decided were probably symbols of some kind, or perhaps this was nothing more than a Rorschach manifestation.

"See the butterfly, Jack?"

But he saw no butterflies here. He did, however, see the little patterns of light at the periphery of his vision that only came with rage. And there was rage-a-plenty in Jack's head. Even so, unless you knew the man, you wouldn't see the rage. His face was stony and looked emotionless. But his large hands were balled up into fists, his fingers white with the pressure.

He walked very calmly to the pile of flesh that used to be one of his best breeding pigs. Too much was missing, both flesh and entrails. Jack could only guess what had happened to the missing pieces, and the image made him momentarily nauseated. But the nausea passed, and Jack looked for his shovel. Only the cool fall morning kept the flies from covering the awful mess.

As he dug a small pit behind the barn, he decided it might be best to leave the remains where they lay. The smell would certainly get worse, but if he buried Sammy's remains, the police would tell him he should not have. It wasn't a dead human, but there might be clues here that Jack didn't see, at least not yet.

He left the small shed and walked back to the covered pen where the remainder of his pigs rutted about as if the loss of Sammy, Pots, and Sally meant only more food for themselves. He did another head count just to be sure that Pots and Sally had indeed been taken. There were only nine pigs. Last night, there had been twelve. He turned away from the pen, a look that might be mistaken for mild frustration on his face. He looked across the yard to another, larger shed. The shed was made of aluminum panels but painted red in the tradition of the classic barn. Inside was Jewel. Jewel had been his father's horse for fifteen years. She had been Jack's now for three years, since his father died. The barn had been built especially for Jewel, and she had lived most of her life in the field it rested on. On the far side of that field, about a hundred yards away, stood the house Jack had grown up in. Now it was empty, still a part of Jack's property. From across the field, it looked dead.

Jack walked across the dirt yard to the back door of the barn, his hands still balled tightly into fists. His heavily muscled forearms rippled as the pressure in his hands shifted across his fingers. As he approached the barn, his right hand finally opened.

He reached forward and threw the latch on the door. The barn was never locked, but there was a small pin that normally held the latch firmly shut. Jack had added the pin after Jewel had figured out how to push the door open from the inside. Now the pin dangled at the end of its small chain. It was not in the latch, although Jack had put it in the night before.

Jack paused for a tense moment before opening the door. He listened, but there were no sounds coming from inside the barn.

At first, he hoped against all hope that they had not stolen his horse. He pulled the door open. And then he wished they had stolen her.

Instead, they had put a crude muzzle on her filled with old towels and cloth so that she could not be heard. Then they had done terrible things to her. Jack could not imagine what those things had been, but the remains were worse than gruesome.

It was bad enough that her blood marked the walls of her barn and had soaked the hay that had been her bed. It was bad enough that her belly had been cut open and her guts lay strewn across the floor in front of where she now lay.

The most terrible thing of all was that she was still breathing. Jack's face remained stone-cold as a tear fell from his eye. He looked one last time at his suffering friend. Then he returned to his house and got his rifle.

2

Carrie Price stood at the front counter of the Smith County Sheriff's Department with fire in her eyes. The short, round man across the counter was patronizing her. He smiled the smile of someone who might be trying to explain something complex to a child, and his eyes ran up and down her shapely body when he thought she wouldn't notice. It was infuriating.

If she had come here because of a speeding ticket or some other petty citation, she might have used his archaic attitude and her stunning looks to her advantage. But she was here because her sister had disappeared without a trace three days earlier, and it seemed that absolutely nothing was being done. She was already worried beyond belief and exhausted from the stress, and now this man on the other side of the counter was adding one more volatile emotion to the pile. She was sure that if the man dared to call her sweety, or any other demeaning diminutive, she would certainly find herself locked in one of the small cells in the back of the building with the officer's eyeballs still in her hands.

"Look," she began. If the man had known Carrie, he would have recognized the red flag that this little word sent up. "I've been in here every day since my sister disappeared, and you've handed me the same line of puckey every time." She knew harsher words, and used them on occasion, but she also knew that some measure of restraint was in order, lest she kill all hopes of cooperation. "I haven't seen or heard from my sister in three days." She held up three fingers for emphasis. "And I can't find anyone who has. Now I've told you guys everything I know, and you're not telling me squat. This is my sister we're talking about here; I have a right to know what you're doing!"

The insipid smile melted slowly from the officer's face as Carrie threw her small but sharp darts.

He shifted uncomfortably. His eyes dropped from hers. "It's like I told you, Miss, we're working on it, and we can't divulge the details of our investigation."

"So, there is an investigation?" Carrie asked with obvious yet subdued sarcasm.

"We're doing what we can," the man answered, his eyes not meeting hers.

"I want to know what you've found out so far. Is that so much to ask?"

The little man would have lost his patience with someone less attractive. Instead, he simply stopped patronizing her and began speaking to her as an adult, as if this were some kind of punishment. "Quite frankly, ma'am, it *is* too much to ask. When we look into things like this, we have to keep what we know to ourselves. If we go around telling citizens what we know, word can eventually get back to the wrong people, or worse, to the press and then to everyone. If there is foul play involved, we want the perpetrators to be very comfortable that they've gotten away with their crime. They're more likely then to stay put and less likely to muddy up the investigation."

Apparently, he hoped that using words like "perpetrators" might intimidate her, perhaps get her to back off a little.

"Are you saying this was a kidnapping?" Carrie quickly concluded. This woman caught him off guard. She drew extremely quick and accurate conclusions from his seemingly casual speech. "Not at all, ma'am. I'm simply speaking in general terms." Still, his eyes wandered below hers, looking up only from time to time to make a point, then quickly away.

"Well," she continued, "in general terms, I hope you guys can find something out soon. I get this strange feeling that you've decided that she left on her own and will call from Rio in a week or so. I want you to know that whatever Terry was into, however strange it might have been, she still wouldn't have just gotten up and walked away without telling anybody where she was going. I just hope she does turn up somewhere, and not floating in Lake Tyler a week from now when the guy who has her decides he's had his fun."

With that, she turned from the desk and stormed out. The fat little man had begun to respond again, but before the words came out, she knew what they would be. Certainly, he was going to assure her that they were doing everything they could to find her sister, and tell her to just sit back and let the police do their job.

At first, she had placed her faith in the police. Then she had lost that faith. Three days was a mighty long time when every waking minute was focused on her sister, and her nights were haunted by dreams of where Terry might be.

Carrie was sure that her sister's disappearance was a direct result of her recent interest in the occult. Terry hadn't talked about it to any of the people at her office or at school, but Carrie had found out, nonetheless. She had seen the things in her sister's apartment that had suggested involvement, and once when Carrie had called her sister's apartment, the answering machine had malfunctioned and given her all of Terry's messages. Some of them were quite bizarre. Carrie knew her sister had been involved in something dark, and she felt strongly that it was this darkness that had claimed Terry. Maybe she had gotten involved in something serious and had decided to get out—and maybe getting out wasn't an option. Terry was impulsive, but she also knew when she was getting in too deep.

Carrie had told all of this to the police. But they had done nothing. She was not going to just sit back any longer.

3

James Lorimar did not know that this night he was a doomed man. In fact, he was whistling.

James was driving his company-provided Plymouth Sundance down an old farm-to-market road that had recently been repaved. The indicator light on his car phone was blinking as he passed slowly out of cellular coverage. This happened often on sales calls that took him too far from civilization, or at times like this when he was simply driving through the barren portions of east Texas, and there were many such times.

On the seat next to him was a book that lay open to almost its center. The exposed pages revealed a series of small towns with names that were typically Texas: Edom, Moore Station, Coffee City. Most of them had populations of less than one thousand, and all of them had at least a Baptist church and a Dairy Queen.

The open book was an atlas of Texas roads, and its attention to detail, at least as far as roads were concerned, was formidable. This very book had saved James Lorimar hundreds of hours of driving time, revealing to him the back roads and shortcuts normally reserved for locals.

But tonight, it would cost him his life.

He almost missed the dirt road that he had been looking intently for during the past ten minutes. He drove past it and would have continued had it not been for the small wooden sign that had, "Boy Scout Camp" painted on the face of it and an arrow pointing toward the road. The map showed the road as a dotted line that ran for about fifteen miles before changing to a solid line and then meeting with another farm-to-market road about twenty miles to the south. The key explained that the dotted lines stood for unpaved roads and suggested confirming the condition of the road with the locals. James had found in the past that these roads were always in good enough condition to drive on, though some of them did get quite rough. He figured this one would save him almost an hour. What he didn't know was that he was turning about one hundred feet too soon. The rocks crunched under his tires as he turned onto the road. There were no streetlights out here and there was an eerie mystique that always accompanied these back road journeys. The sky seemed infinitely black and deep, and the stars were like grains of sand cast upon an eternal canvas. It was a cool night and even with the heater running, James felt a chill run down his spine.

He followed the rough road for several miles. The map indicated that it would be twenty-five miles before he finished this shortcut, but it didn't indicate all the twists and curves he was encountering. Nevertheless, he drove on.

Then, about fifteen miles down the rough road, he came to the bridge.

He had never encountered a bridge like this one, and he felt his balls crawl up inside him as he approached it. It was only as wide as one lane of the road, and there were no guard rails. It had been raining heavily the past week and the river was at its banks. The water was at best only six feet beneath the bridge. He held his breath as he drove onto it.

His mind raced with the awful possibilities. He might drive off the edge and flip into the river. Even if he just slipped off the edge and stayed on the bridge, he would be stuck for who knew how many hours or days before somebody came along.

"Shit, shit, shit," he said to himself as he crossed. He leaned slightly forward in his seat, as if this would ensure he would not stray off the bridge and tumble into the moving and presumably icy water.

But then he was across, and the relief was tremendous. There was a rush of post-danger excitement, and he felt the satisfaction of his success.

Suddenly, there was a small wall of stone to his right. Behind the wall was a steep hillside. Then he was driving uphill, and the ground to his left dropped away. The road began to wind about again. Once again, he had little more than one lane in which to drive.

James finally realized this could not be right. He was going to have to backtrack and take the long way to Tyler after all. The images of the terrible bridge flashed through his mind. He was not looking forward to encountering it again. He looked to his left. The edge of the road was jagged, and he could see where the ground sloped away, but could not tell how deep the ravine was. He was going to have to keep driving until he found a place where he could turn around. As he drove, the narrow road continued to climb and wind. He drove slowly and carefully, looking as far ahead as his high beams would allow for a change in his situation.

Then, as he crested the top of another small hill, he saw the large house off to his left.

The building was large and the side facing him had a series of openings that looked like windows, though there was no reflection of his headlights, as if none of the windows had glass in them. It was not lit at all and looked to be abandoned. Nonetheless, it frightened him. Most of the building was obscured by the large stone wall that seemed to surround its front. He felt as if he had stumbled onto someone's secret hideaway. Perhaps it belonged to one of the Texas/Louisiana drug rings. He watched carefully for any signs of danger. Out of instinct, he reached over and hit the switch that brought down all the locks in the car.

He drove on until the large wall surrounding the compound was on his left. To his right, the small stone wall continued, although there was no longer a hillside behind it. Just over the small wall was a field that, as far as he could see, was no more than dirt and small trees. Still, there was nowhere to turn around.

Ahead of him was an open gate. Beyond the gate was a large, circular driveway. He could see no alternative other than to drive through the gate and around the driveway. As he approached the gate, he could see that the driveway would take him uncomfortably close to a large, covered walkway that seemed to lead only to darkness. A good five feet of the driveway was obscured by this darkness that even his passing headlights did not seem to penetrate.

He passed through the gate and into the yard. Old and eerie statues filled the courtyard that the driveway encircled. As he drove past a few of them, an irrational fear took hold of him and he decided that he did not want to drive around the whole driveway, especially if it was going to take him so close to the building. He looked for a good spot to turn from the main path, then drove into the courtyard, which was made of firmly packed dirt and rocks. Once, it had been landscaped, but all those plants had died ages ago. He pulled into the courtyard as far as he could, then backed up onto the driveway. He did this one more time until he was turned completely. Then he headed back for the gate, a sense of false relief creeping into his brain.

It was a short drive to the gate, but as he approached, he could tell immediately that something was wrong. When he'd entered the courtyard, he had passed through an opening between two large stone columns. Now there was an iron gate closed across that opening. He had not seen the black iron gate swinging shut, nor had he heard the noise, but somehow it had shut, and he was trapped. His heart began again to race as he wondered how this had happened, and how he was going to get out.

Then the lights came on.

Bright white lights flooded the courtyard, and suddenly there were half a dozen men and one woman where before there had been only shadows. Two of them had guns. The rest were just standing back, observing.

James held his foot on the brake and revved the engine. One of the men was standing between him and the gate, but he was not armed, and James decided rather quickly that he would have no problem running the man down.

Then he heard an explosion and saw that a hole had appeared in his windshield. His right shoulder burned, and he knew instantly that he had been shot. The man who had fired the gun stepped in front of the car, about twenty feet away, his gun pointed directly at James's head. He stood there staring at James. James wanted to simply run the man down and race through the gate, but there was another man to the right who also had a gun. It, too, was pointed at his head. Then he worked out a solution.

He looked one last time toward the gate. Then he ducked in the seat and let up on the brake. He sped forward, aiming as well as he could for the iron gates. He heard two more shots and then a heavy thud as the man who had stood in front of his car was struck and thrown into the courtyard.

He misjudged the entrance by only a few inches, but it was enough to bring the car to a sudden stop as it struck one of the stone pillars. The impact threw James forward and his head glanced off his car phone and struck the radio firmly. The impact wasn't enough to knock him unconscious, but he was dazed for a few moments. By the time he had figured out again where he was, the armed man whom he hadn't hit appeared at the passenger window pointing his gun at him.

James reached for the shift lever in the hopes that he could throw it in reverse and take another shot at the gate, but then there was another explosion, and the burning pain was in his left leg.

"The next one goes through your head!" shouted the man outside his car. Then two more men appeared at the driver's side, though they were not armed. "Turn off the engine!"

He reached slowly over to the keys and switched off his engine, which was rattling loudly from the damage that had been done in the collision.

"Now sit up slowly and keep your hands where I can see them!" James didn't keep a gun in his car, but wished now that he did. He sat up slowly, his arms raised over his head, his injured shoulder screaming out at him as he did.

He followed the man's instructions carefully, keeping an eye open to possible escape. It looked as if he had been right—he had stumbled onto a drug operation of some kind. They probably thought he was a federal agent or something like that. Either way, they probably wouldn't let him go any time soon. The man signaled for him to get out of the car.

James reached down and popped open the lock and emerged slowly. He didn't want to alarm the nervous-looking man into firing.

He walked in front of the man carrying the gun as he followed another of the men to the front entrance that had seemed so dark and foreboding. The rest of the small group dispersed at the entryway. James did not see where they went. Even now, with the courtyard brightly lit, it seemed too dark under the stone canopy that covered the final ten feet of the walkway to the door. They walked up the stone steps and into the building together.

It had been chilly outside. When they stepped into the house, it was only a little warmer. As they stepped through the doorway, the lights outside went off again. For a few seconds, James could not see anything as his eyes adjusted. As he stumbled forward, the pain ran around the sides of his wounded leg. The bullet had gone clear through the leg but had not broken any bones.

When his eyes finally adjusted, James could see that the inside of the house was also constructed of stone. His dress shoes clicked loudly against the floor that had once been shiny polished marble but was now faded and cracked. The only light was provided by candles that were set in holders near the floor about every ten feet. A cold breeze made the flames dance and cast eerie shadows on the dark walls. He could see where paintings had once hung, but where now remained only lighter patches of wall and the holes that had been drilled to hang them.

About every ten feet, between each candle and the next, was a doorway. Most of the doors were closed, though some lay sideways off their hinges. He looked into a few of the rooms where the doors were not completely closed, but the rooms were dark. He would have thought they were abandoned too, except that he could hear muffled noises coming from them. His wounded leg pained him as he followed the man in front. He'd stopped asking questions and bargaining when he realized nobody was listening. His offers and pleas fell on deaf ears, or ears that were instructed to remain deaf.

He followed the man until they came to a set of double doors that were closed. The hall continued for about ten feet beyond them before ending at another door. The man reached forward and knocked firmly. At first, there was no answer, but the man stood still and waited, nonetheless. Finally, the left door creaked slowly open. This room was lit more brightly than the hallway, though still without electricity. James could smell the odor of expended kerosene and felt a little warmth coming from the room.

Standing before them in the doorway was a young girl. She looked to be about fifteen. Her hair was long and black, and looked as if it had not been washed in a very long time. She wore no shoes, and the pinkness of her feet was buried beneath several layers of dirt. She wore an old dress that draped loosely from her shoulders and covered her clear to her ankles. The dress was torn, revealing skin in many places, some indiscreet. It hardly excited him considering the repulsive condition of the girl and the distraction of his pain.

"We've got someone who drove up here," the man explained to the girl. She looked at James with dull eyes that stayed glued to his. He wanted to look away, but there was something darkly inviting about those eyes. "I think Darius will want to talk to him."

The girl stared back at the man who was speaking. At first, she just stood there. Her head wobbled a little while she did. James wondered if this might be from drugs. He was beginning to think that he might like to have some of those drugs himself as his pain increased. He felt light-headed both from the loss of blood and from the strange situation he found himself in.

Finally, the girl stepped back into the room. She left the door open, and the man leading James pushed it the rest of the way and stepped into the room. James stood where he was for the moment, then felt the gun in the small of his back and heard a voice whisper, "Move." It seemed odd to him that the voice would be a whisper, but then it seemed to better fit the atmosphere than a normal tone of voice might have.

James entered the room. It looked like it might have been a small library at one time. There were bits of broken furniture that looked very old, though worthless because of their condition. There was a dead and empty fireplace on one wall, and a picture that had been left behind still hung over it. The picture was a painting of a wild countryside with rolling hills and abundant wildlife. The painting was cracked and faded. It looked like it might have been a representation of what once lay outside these walls, perhaps a hundred years ago.

Apparently, he lingered over the painting too long, because the man walking behind him gave him a shove. His left leg took a jolt as he stumbled forward, and he cried out. James followed the man in front of him to another set of doors on the opposite side of the room. The man stood looking at the doors. He seemed suddenly unsure that this was the right direction. Then he looked back at the girl, who now lingered near the dead fireplace.

"Is he busy?" he asked.

The girl smiled. It was just her mouth smiling, however, not her eyes. "Why don't you open the door and find out?"

James heard the man curse the girl under his breath before turning back to the door. He stood a moment longer, then put his slightly shaking fist up tentatively and knocked.

At first, there was no answer. The man who had knocked seemed to grow more nervous with the silence. Then a rough and raspy voice came from the other side of the big wooden doors.

"What do you want?" it said simply.

The man cleared his throat. "We've caught someone snooping around. I brought him to you."

Again, it was silent, and the girl moved slowly from the fireplace to James's side. She looked him up and down disinterestedly, as if sizing him up for some task or other. Then she suddenly leaned forward and licked the side of his face.

James recoiled from the gesture. Her tongue was rough and felt dry, and her breath smelled like rotten flesh.

Then there was a shuffling sound followed by a loud *click*, and the door opened slowly. The girl stepped quickly away from James, as if she didn't want to be seen near him by the man on the other side of the door.

A man appeared before them. He did not look very old, maybe in his late twenties or early thirties. But he looked very tired, as if most of his life had passed out of him. James still thought this was probably because of hard drugs. It looked as if this kid had been mainlining speed every day of his adult life. His face showed battle scars that should have been exclusive to a man thirty years his senior. He was a tall man, but he was not fleshed out. The man was not exactly skinny, but more formless and skeletal. But there was something very formidable and frightening about him, nonetheless.

The man looked him over. His eyes were cold and distant, yet there was some kind of pleasure buried deep inside them. James knew that this pleasure came from some dark knowledge of what was going to happen to him. Perhaps they had torture in mind, perhaps they would simply shoot him. But somehow, those eyes told him that he would not be leaving this house alive, not unless he was able to escape.

"Very well," the man said. His breath, too, was rancid. "Put him in a holding room and watch over him carefully. This should take care of our little problem." He looked James over once, then returned his gaze to the man who stood before him. "Well done," he said.

James finally spoke. "They'll come looking for me, you know," he said.

The man stared at him in silence. James felt a cold chill run through his body. It seemed to come not from himself, but from this man's eyes. "I think not," he finally said. "You are lost, and no one searches these roads. Whatever wrong turn you made was a very unlucky one, sir." Then his mouth spread into a wicked grin that showed his yellow and slightly crooked teeth. "But you will be put to a quite glorious use, sir. And if we are successful, your life will not have been extinguished in vain." The smile widened and the man retreated into his chamber.

As he did, James looked into the room and caught a glimpse of something that seemed both dark and horrible.

Then he was struck on the back of his head and saw no more.

2

1

Carrie had waited long enough. The police were not giving her any satisfactory answers, so she decided it was time to get some on her own. She considered hiring a private investigator like the people in so many television shows did, but there were only a few agencies in the city of Tyler, and they had failed to gain her confidence over the phone. She supposed that the really good investigators were probably making the bigger money in Dallas, which was about a hundred miles away and home to over a million people. Tyler was much smaller than that, with a population of about sixty thousand. The investigators who did hang around in Tyler were probably there only because they couldn't make it in Dallas. Carrie wasn't about to hire a second-rate investigator to bumble around and tell her no more than she could learn on her own. Likewise, she didn't think she could afford the cost of getting one of the Dallas firms to take on a Tyler case. She decided to just look into things herself, then make the calls to Dallas as a last resort.

The day after she had made her frustrations known at the Smith County Sheriff's Office, Carrie began her own research. She got off from her job at the rose gardens around five o'clock, then drove across town to her sister's old apartment. The drive felt odd to her and brought back recent memories. She had taken this very route on several occasions when she would join her sister for an evening of shopping or lounging around and watching movies. Despite their differences, there always seemed to be time to simply enjoy being together. They had some similar interests, and it was these they concentrated on and discussed most of the time. From time to time, they would wander into a subject on which they had serious disagreements, such as abortion or religion. Then the evening would often end in bad feelings. Now Carrie was sorry that their last evening together had ended badly. Now her memories of her last evening with her sister would be memories of bad feelings and sharp words.

But that was only if her sister was dead.

Only as these thoughts ran through her mind did she realize that she had begun to give up on finding her sister alive. Already she was preparing herself for the search not for her sister, but for the cause of her death. This realization brought a sinking feeling to her stomach and a tear to her eye.

Carrie drove eastward on Loop 323 to Broadway, then headed south, away from downtown. She passed the mall, which was within walking distance of her sister's apartment, then she turned onto the road that led to the apartment complex. As she turned, she could see the familiar green sign of the apartment complex that seemed to imply in her mind a comfortable place, perhaps only because she had gotten used to visiting it. But today there was no comfort here for Carrie, only turmoil. She drove into the complex and headed to the back row of apartments where her sister's unit was located. She parked her Thunderbird next to a big black Oldsmobile Cutlass that looked like it was about ten years old and had a big dent in the front right fender. Carrie walked around the building to the front door of the unit. There was yellow tape across the door that warned against entry. The police department had placed it there a couple of days earlier. Already the black words across the yellow tape were a little faded, and it seemed to be another reminder that little or nothing was being done. Carrie heard the voices of some people approaching and hurried across the concrete walkway to the door across from her sister's unit. She stood as if waiting for someone to answer. At first, she thought the two women who appeared were walking toward the apartment she was standing in front of, but then they headed up the stairs that led to the second level. After they had entered their apartment, Carrie returned to the door of her sister's unit. She removed a fingernail file from her handbag and cut the yellow tape where it crossed the door jamb. Then she dug in a side pocket of her purse and produced a key. Terry had given her a key to her apartment about two months earlier when she had gone out of town for a week. Carrie took care of Terry's apartment and her cat, Taylor, while her sister was away. Terry hadn't asked Carrie to return the key, and Carrie had forgotten to give it back. Now she was glad for this.

Carrie opened the door slowly, almost expecting that someone might be inside waiting for her. Then she heard more voices approaching, so she entered quickly and quietly, closing the door silently behind her. As she looked around the room, she immediately knew that something was wrong.

As wild and unpredictable as Terry had been, she had always kept her apartment in order. All her pictures and trinkets were always where they belonged. But things did not look right, and they did not look like Terry had rearranged them. Carrie supposed that the police had moved some things around while searching for evidence, but it was more than this, Carrie thought as she looked, trying hard to pinpoint what was wrong.

She walked across the living room floor to the small couch that was actually a loveseat. Carrie owned the couch that went with the set. She had paid only a hundred dollars more for the set than she would have paid for the sofa alone and had then given the loveseat to her sister. Terry had then immediately spent another hundred getting it recovered to her taste. That was two years ago. Above the small sofa hung a three-part painting that was a peaceful sunset scene at an anonymous beach. Terry had always wanted to see a real southern California beach but had never had the chance.

There she went again, thinking of her sister in the past tense. But the more it happened, the more it seemed to be the truth. Inside, Carrie knew that her sister was dead. It was not because Carrie was pessimistic in general, but more a feeling that an important part of her was gone in a permanent way. She hoped against it, but inside, she knew her hope was in vain. As she inspected the small table next to the sofa, Carrie noticed that there were indeed some items missing. At first, she did not know what they were, then she remembered. Over the past few months, her sister had been collecting some odd pewter and silver pieces. Some of them were very strange-looking, some were eerie, and none of them was particularly pretty. The pieces had been crudely made, probably by hand. They looked like poor models of some ancient Incan or Aztec pieces in theme if not in reality. Carrie had commented on the pieces only once, and that evening had ended in a fight. Then Carrie saw that there was a pattern. Many of the new items that Terry had accumulated over the past two months were missing. Most of the items were things that Carrie had never cared for in the first place, things that did not seem to fit the motif of the small apartment, and that did not really seem to be in her sister's usual taste. The most repulsive of these things had been a hand-sketched picture of a man wearing a black robe standing in the woods holding two silvery daggers over his head. On a table beneath him was an animal of some kind, though the overall theme of the picture had been darkness, and Carrie had never looked at it long enough to see just what kind of animal it was. Terry herself had sketched the picture, and she had hung it in her bedroom. There were only two more of her sketchings on display in her apartment. Most of the time, Terry was shy about her work. But two of her pictures were magnificent, and she had been very proud of them.

Dozens more lay packed into boxes in her closet, some finished, most abandoned, all showing a particular gift for expression. But this picture of the robed man was awful. It was drawn extremely well, but it was too dark. It did not seem to Carrie that this sinister imagery could have come from her sister's soul, and it was a frightening thought that it had.

Carrie walked to her sister's bedroom and looked at the wall across from the dresser. Somehow, she had known that the picture of the naked man would be gone. The two others were still hanging.

Where were these things now? Had her sister taken them with her when she left? Had someone broken in later, or come here with Terry's key and taken them? Had the police taken them as evidence?

Carrie wished she knew. Then she wished again that the police would tell her more. Perhaps their information combined with her insight would solve this mystery. But that wasn't going to happen. It had become quite obvious to Carrie that the police were going to share nothing at all with her for now. So, she would have less to work with than they did.

But she would have more dedication and more insight. Perhaps these two things would get her the answers she needed.

Then she heard a strange metallic rustling that startled her. She looked to her right and saw that it was only the metal blinds that covered a small window. But they had rattled. Then she saw them move away from the window again, slowly. They returned to their place against the wall with another soft metallic sound.

The window was partially open. The blinds had been closed completely, probably by the police. When they had billowed out slightly, Carrie had seen that the window was open. She took a step toward that window, then she heard a soft shuffling behind her.

She turned her head quickly and looked. Her first thought was that it was her sister's cat, but then she remembered that Taylor was at her house. She stood still in the dark room, listening. She stood absolutely motionless for a full minute but heard nothing more.

Then there was a soft thud. Her eyes caught a glimmer of a small object as it rolled from the partially open closet and onto the floor. It was one of the small silver trinkets. This one was a troll-like animal, and it lay on the carpet looking up at her.

Somebody was here. They were in the closet, and they had Terry's missing things. She suddenly felt warm as terror gripped her. For a moment, she was frozen, unsure what to do. Then she turned and fled from the room.

As she did, she heard the closet door opening the remainder of the way. This forced a scream from her, and she hurried to the front door, trying desperately to get out of the apartment before the shadow from the closet caught her. She could hear padded footsteps as she slid on the tile entryway and fell to her knee. She grabbed the doorknob and turned it without getting up, pulling the door back and open. The door brushed her leg as she opened it, and she put her hands on the cold tile, pushing herself up and out of the apartment. She didn't look back as she ran, but she saw the blinds rustle as she passed them.

She ran past a couple on the way to her car. They must have seen the look of terror on her face because they looked immediately behind her, as if to see what it was she was running from. She didn't notice them but continued instead to her car. She fumbled with her keys, anxious to get in and get away before she was confronted by whoever had been in her sister's apartment.

Carrie got into her car and started it. As she did, she watched for anybody who might come running suddenly toward her car. As the engine roared to a start, a man came walking casually around the other end of the unit. He was a tall man wearing sweats and gloves. It seemed too warm for gloves, and this worried Carrie. She took a good look at the man; in case it was a face she needed to remember. That was when she noticed he was doing the same to her. Was he trying to remember her face too? His was dark and hard. His body was tall and lean. As she pulled quickly away, she watched the man, who followed her gaze. He stopped walking toward her car, but she could see him staring into her rearview mirror as she drove away. Was he memorizing her license plate number?

She felt the terror of the incident course through her veins. But she felt something more. Had the man who had been staring been the one in her sister's apartment, or was he just a gawker? Carrie had gotten used to gawkers—it came with the coarse brown hair and soft complexion. If he wasn't the one who had been in the apartment, had she been seen? Now she was at a terrible disadvantage. She had found out some things of value, but she would need time to figure out what it all meant. In the meantime, she had possibly put herself in a terrible position. If she had been seen, perhaps she, too, would become a target.

But a target of whom or what?

As she drove toward her home, her mind raced with the possibilities.

2

The big old '57 Buick Roadmaster, which had once been restored to beauty but had since become faded and worn again, rolled southward on Highway 110 toward Mount Sylvan. It had made the same trip the night before, only then, it had carried five people and a trunk full of knives and bowls. Tonight, it carried just two young men. The driver was named Raymond, but now that he was a member of the Family, he was known simply as Night. He had three teeth missing, which caused him to sound juvenile when he talked, though almost nobody said anything about it anymore. The passenger was Mickey. His new name was Thor. He was the more nervous of the two.

"I can't believe you left it," Raymond said. It was the third time since they had turned off the interstate that he had said this. Each time, it made Mickey sink a little lower.

"I heard you the first time," Mickey responded. He'd said nothing until now.

Raymond took his eyes away from the road to throw Mickey a glare. "You better watch yourthelf," Raymond warned.

Mickey wanted to say more but decided against it. He knew he could defend himself against Raymond if he had to, but Darius would frown on the bloodshed.

"If you're lucky, it'll thtill be there. If ith not you might as well kith your ath good-bye."

Raymond was referring to the knife. The knife was very ornate and plated with pure silver. But it was not the silver or the fine handwork or the antique nature that made the six-hundred-year-old knife valuable, but rather what it could do. More than once, Mickey had seen what it could do. He had seen it again last night. That knife seemed to cut through flesh as if it were cutting through paper. The skin and body seemed to part magically before it, even before the blade actually touched anything. The knife sang with anticipation of the kill and had a hunger of its own. Last night, they had used it to sacrifice a pig and slaughter a horse. The pig had been killed for ceremonial purposes; the horse had been just for fun. They had taken two more of the small pigs back to the compound with them for future ceremonies. Darius had been pleased with this. But then his pleasure had faded suddenly. Nobody had even said anything about the knife. Nobody had even known it was missing. But Darius knew. Mickey had felt the heat of Darius's anger in his head. He had been worried that he would suddenly drop dead from that brain heat. He had seen that happen to someone before. But Mickey had been spared, though only because he was the one who had to go back and get the knife. Mickey hoped that retrieving the knife would be enough to save him.

Mickey had been in charge of the knife, but both Mickey and Raymond had used it. Mickey thought Raymond had kept the knife and brought it back. Now he wondered if Raymond had left it on purpose.

Mickey began to grow more and more nervous as they approached the place where the ceremonies had been held. They would have to park the car away from the house and walk up to it. There would be even more danger tonight since any sounds they made would probably bring out the owner of the house.

"What if the polithe came out here today and found it?" Raymond taunted.

"Then Duke will have it. We'll just get it from him."

"If Duke had it, don't you think Dariuth would have it back by now?"

"No."

Raymond stared ahead at the road and grinned. He loved putting the squeeze on Mickey. Tonight, he was squeezing big time, and there was more to come.

Raymond drove to the driveway of the big house and parked the car on the shoulder of the road behind some trees. The house was at the end of the long driveway, about eighty yards away.

"Okay," Raymond said, "go get it."

Mickey looked nervously at him. "What are you talking about?" he asked, his voice showing his disbelief. "Aren't you going to help?"

"Hell, no!" Raymond exclaimed. "I'm not the one who lotht it. Frankly, I don't even care if you find it or not. It'd be kind of interetht-ing to thee what happenth to you if you don't find it."

"Get out of the fucking car and help me," Mickey demanded. Raymond just smiled.

Mickey pulled the handle on the door. When it popped open, he reached over suddenly and punched Raymond in the mouth, then he stepped quickly out.

The smile left Raymond's face. His first instinct was to pull the gun he was carrying and blow Mickey away. Instead, he just watched as Mickey slammed the car door and headed toward the barn. He waited until Mickey had walked about halfway, then quietly got out of the car himself. Raymond opened the trunk and retrieved something that was wrapped in a large blanket and headed quickly up the driveway.

3

Jack was lying in his bed, only half asleep. He had been lying awake with the lights off for three hours. The events of the day kept replay-ing in his head. The police hadn't done much of anything. They had taken a few pictures and asked him to tell his story a number of times. Then they had told him that it was very unlikely they would catch the criminals based on this incident alone, but that his information would be helpful if there was another similar occurrence. Jack had asked if this kind of stuff had been going on a lot lately, and the officer quickly responded in the negative. But Jack knew better. He had seen the stories that appeared from time to time on the back pages of the *Tyler Courier Times*. And that only accounted for the incidents that the newspaper had found out about. Nobody from the paper had contacted Jack, so they probably didn't know about what he had been through. He wondered how many more incidents like his there had been in the Tyler area, including all the ones that never made it to the press. The whole thing had made him nervous again. He felt those strange feelings that had only visited him a few other times in his life, most recently when he had walked in on a robbery at a convenience store in Van. That time, he had been shot once in the arm before the robber fled. The feelings that came to him now were helplessness and anger. In more magnitude than the robbery incident because this time, he felt more violated. Who were these people? What right did they have to do these things to his animals? Over and over, the picture of the dying and mutilated horse had come back into his mind. It was a picture that would haunt him at night for weeks to come, or at least until another, more intense picture took its place. Then there were the markings. Symbols had been left on the walls of both the shed and the barn. They were not symbols with which Jack was familiar, but they made him uncomfortable, nonetheless. He wished now that he had possessed the presence of mind that morning to take pictures of the markings before the police had cleaned them from the walls. And that seemed odd, too. Why had they done that? Why hadn't they left the symbols and cryptic messages for him to clean up? It made Jack wonder if perhaps this was a very big problem for the sheriff's office, and they were doing their best to keep it a secret. All these thoughts and images kept Jack awake until two in the morning. Then his eyes were only half open as his thoughts became jumbled with his dreams, and he began to drift to sleep. Then he heard a loud noise and his eyes opened wide. His heart began to beat fast and hard, and he could feel the rush of the adrenaline in his veins. Last night, he had slept through much more noise, but tonight, his mind had become an alarm waiting to go off, and something had just tripped it. He lay still, listening carefully for more noises. Then he heard it again. It was a thumping sound, like somebody was striking the side of his house with a small bat. It was not a loud sound, but it carried through the timbers of his home. His heart still racing, Jack rolled over and opened the top drawer of his nightstand beside the bed. He reached inside it and removed his .357, which he kept handy for such a time as this. He walked quickly but quietly to his window to look out. When he drew the curtains, the rod fell from its holder and the curtains tumbled to the ground. This always happened, and he swore at himself for not having fixed it yet. He looked out the window. At first, he saw nothing, but then he could see that there was a dim light coming from the base of the door to the small shed where his pig had been slaughtered. It was not bright enough to be coming from the light bulb inside the shed, and it hinted at motion as if it were a flashlight.

Somebody was in the shed. Maybe more than one person.

Jack debated what to do. He decided that he would call the police, then guard the shed so that nobody got away. If it looked like they were going to leave, he would turn on the light that illuminated the outside of the shed and tell them to stay put. If they tried to get away, he would shoot. Maybe he would even kill one of them. He did not look forward to this, but his anger had a good enough hold of him that he thought he could do it. He made the phone call, then he hurried to the closet and put on his coveralls. It would take the police about ten minutes to get to his place if they had a car at the station. In two minutes, he was dressed and downstairs. He traded the .357 for his hunting rifle in the case by the couch. He stood at the front door with his deer rifle in his hands. He opened the door slowly. It creaked as it opened, and he felt a chill run down his spine. There was no way that someone inside the shed could have heard that sound, but at that moment, Jack was sure he had been heard. When he had the door open, he looked at the shed. The dim light was still moving around inside it. On the wall beside the doorway was the switch that turned on the lights. Inside the dirt yard were two telephone poles. At the top of each pole was a light with a halogen bulb. The shed was about fifty yards away from the front door, an easy shot with this rifle. Jack sat and waited. In the silence of the cold night, his ears began to ring as he listened carefully to the shuffling sounds coming from the shed.

Then somebody shouted.

"HEY!" came a call from somewhere nearby. It had come from his right, toward the road. Then suddenly there was a loud crash, and the door of the shed came open,

Jack reached over quickly and flipped the switch on the wall. Immediately, the shed was illuminated, as was the man emerging from it. The man looked terrified, and he headed for the road.

"Hold it! " Jack shouted from the doorway. But the man continued to run. "Stop, damn it, or I'll shoot!"

His words had no effect on the fleeing man. Then Jack realized he was not angry enough to kill this person. Instead, he aimed over the man's head and fired a warning shot.

His shot made a strange echo. The running man fell to the ground and rolled forward. Then he stood again and continued running, only now he had acquired a limp. Jack knew he had fired too high to have wounded the man, and he tried to understand what had happened.

Then there was another shot. The sound came from the end of the house, in the same direction that the voice had come from. This shot put the man down, but not out. The man struggled on the ground, unable to get up.

Then Jack heard footsteps running away. He could see only a shadowy figure as it fled through the night toward the road. On the ground at the edge of the dirt yard, the man continued to roll around in pain. It was all happening too fast, and Jack was lost in confusion.

He heard a car start and speed away, though no headlights were ever turned on. A moment later, he heard the sirens.

Jack sat down on the front steps and kept his eye on the writhing man. He couldn't tell if it was someone he knew, but he doubted it. He figured that later he would get a better look, probably at the police station. He supposed that wounding the man would probably have been a good solution, though he couldn't understand who else had thought so, and he wondered if wounding him was all the mysterious party had been aiming for.

As these thoughts ran through his mind, the red and blue lights of a county police car lit the trees at the end of his driveway. The deputies inside made a quick assessment of the situation and drove across the grass to the fence surrounding the dirt yard. Then one of them got out of the car, climbed over the three-foot fence, and carefully approached the writhing man. The man's movements were becoming much more subdued and changing gradually into more twitching than writhing.

"Call for an ambulance!" he heard the man call back to his partner. Then the deputy looked in Jack's direction. "If you're over there, Mr. Macon, could you please come out into the light, and leave your weapon behind." It was more a command than a question.

Jack left his rifle on the porch and walked across his grass to the gate of the dirt yard. As he became visible in the light, the deputy spoke to him again.

"Were there any more?"

Jack looked quickly at the shed. He hadn't even thought that there might be more of them, perhaps still hiding in the shed.

"One ran off, I think. There may be more in the shed."

The deputy looked at the man on the ground quickly and decided that he wasn't a threat. His partner was still on the radio, so he ran across the yard to the shed, motioning with his hand for Jack to back away again. He checked the shed out, but there was nobody in it. Then he walked to the small gate and motioned again, this time for Jack to come to him. The two men met at the open gate.

"It seems we may have something to work with now," the man said. "Thanks for leaving him alive."

The county deputy was a big Black man. Jack looked up to his eyes, and Jack was a few inches over six feet himself.

"I didn't shoot him," Jack explained.

The deputy looked a little surprised. "Then who did?"

"Someone who was hiding at the south end of my house. They ran off after firing a second shot."

The deputy looked back at the wounded man, who had finally stopped moving at all. Would he live? Probably. The wounds were bloody, but they weren't in vital areas. They were certainly painful wounds, no doubt painful enough to move a man to unconsciousness.

"Why don't you come over and take a look at this guy, see if he looks familiar?"

Jack followed the deputy to the bloody body at the edge of the dirt yard. The man was unconscious now and lying on his side. The deputy rolled the man over with a boot so that Jack could see his face more clearly.

The face was that of a young man. He didn't strike Jack as having a criminal face, if there was such a thing. Nevertheless, it was not a face he recognized, and he told the deputy so.

"Well," the deputy responded, "take a good look at him, because he may be the key to figuring out the mess that took place here last night." The deputy did not look familiar to Jack.

"Were you here this morning?" he asked.

"No, but I heard about it. Quite a mess. One of the worst. And the horse too, that was a shame. I raise a few horses myself. There was no sense in it at all."

Jack sensed a chance to learn a little more. "So, there have been other things like this going on?"

"Oh, a little here and there. It's been worse lately, but I'm not supposed to get into any details. Ongoing investigation, you know."

"Of course," Jack replied. He had heard that several times the previous morning. At least this man had been willing to confirm that there was more of this going on. Then Jack noticed that the deputy had a slight but gentle smile on his lips. It was a smile that said, "If you bought me a beer, I'd tell you all about it, and boy is it a story." It was a friendly smile, the only one he had seen all day. Jack looked at the deputy's name tag. All it read was Williams.

"Ben," the man said.

"Huh?" Jack said.

"Ben Williams." The man held out his hand. "Nice to meet you, though I wish the circumstances were more pleasant."

Jack grabbed Deputy Williams's hand and shook. It was a firm hand like his own, and it too seemed to exude goodwill.

He had a feeling that before these men left, he would have some more answers.

In the distance, there were once again sirens, though this time they were from the ambulance that was coming for the wounded man.

Deputy Williams turned to Jack and took a look at the man's wounds. "Got to do a little work here," he explained. "The paramedics get pissed off if we just let them bleed."

Jack smiled a little himself and watched as the deputy tended to the intruder's wounds.

3

1

Raymond drove south on Highway 110 instead of north. He was not going back to the compound. Instead, he was heading south and east, toward New Orleans.

As he drove, he reached under the seat and removed a lumpy roll of black cloth. He unrolled the black cloth and the shiny silver knife fell out onto the seat. Even in the darkness, it shone. He picked it up with his right hand and looked up and down the blade. It was a wonderful piece of metal. It made him want to stop on his way out of town and cut somebody up. He wasn't going to go out of his way to do this, but perhaps if the opportunity simply arose...

2

Darius stood in a room lit only by candles. He spent most of his time in this room, regarding his Queen.

Lying in a glass case in front of him was the fallen goddess. Her hair was dark black and flowed to her shoulders. Her eyes were closed, but he knew that they were deep green, and he remembered them as they once were. Her skin had once been olive, though in death, it had grown pale and cold.

The coffin was plush, its interior made of dozens of red satin pillows. Candlelight added a soft illumination to her features, which seemed to hint at life. Darius knew that life had to be inside her, somewhere. He had seen its glow from time to time. The wonderful power of her glorious days had left her in death, but some of it had remained and was waiting only to be awakened—of this he was certain. It had come to him in his dreams. Hanging on the wall above the head of his Queen's coffin was a painting. In this painting, she stood in the woods holding her hands toward the heavens. Her eyes were wild and hinted at tremendous power. She was surrounded by the wildness and the power of nature. This was the Queen he had once known. This was the Queen he waited for now. He knew she would return, if only he waited for the right time and did just the right things. He was sure that she could be resurrected. He had seen a resurrection once before of a much less powerful person. He had watched his Queen bring back a dead companion, the leader of what had been a dark and powerful army. Darius knew that his own power was far less than hers had ever been, but he relied on what power remained within her slowly decaying body to aid him in his efforts. He didn't have the ability to bring any person back from the dead. But his Queen was no mere mortal. He had tried before. He had tried five times over the past three years. It was almost time to try again. But now he sensed that another time had come. It was a time he regretted as it meant the loss of a Family member. It was a time he looked forward to as it meant the thrilling rush of the Power.

Darius stood from his chair. He was tall and thin and deceptively looked frail. But the Family had taught him to be strong. He had seen what the Power could do in its full glory, and he yearned to return to those days. He remembered all the things that he had learned and seen back then. He knew that alone, he could never bring his new Family to that former glory, but with his Queen alive, anything was possible. He took one last glance at her lifeless body. Then he turned and left the room.

3

Raymond pulled over into the small gas station and tried to pump his own gas. The old Buick guzzled gas, just as all the cars made in 1957 did. But the gas did not flow. Then he saw the small sign over the pump that informed him that all gasoline sold after ten o'clock at night had to be paid for in advance. Apparently, this was to stop people from simply filling up and driving off, as he had intended to do. He was both insulted and infuriated by the sign, and he glanced into the small station, where a pair of unsure eyes looked back.

"Turn it on!" he shouted to the girl who watched him.

"You gotta pay first!" she shouted back.

Apparently, she had been taken advantage of before by those not wishing to pay for their fuel. She was just some arrogant bitch, Raymond thought, who got her kicks out of telling people they had to pay first. Well, tonight she would be made to pay for her arrogance. Raymond reached behind himself and patted the back of his pants as he headed toward the small shop. Then he threw his hands up as if he had left his wallet inside the car. He walked back to it and opened the door on the passenger side. He leaned over and unfolded the shiny knife, which he quickly tucked inside his jacket. It seemed warm in his hand, as if anxious to be put to work. He felt his heart beginning to beat faster in anticipation.

Raymond closed the door and walked again toward the small store. The girl had kept her eyes on him. Did she suspect something? He watched carefully to be sure she did not pick up the phone. He put a smile on his face, but her face remained expressionless. Hers was a plain face, neither pretty nor ugly. He tried his best to look as unthreatening as possible. He pushed the door open, and a small bell confirmed his arrival.

"Hi there," he said to the girl. She looked about twenty. "They got you working here all alone tonight?"

"I've worked nights here since I was fifteen," she explained. "It's my dad's place."

Raymond reached back and took out his wallet as he approached the counter. "Ithn't it kind of dangerouth?" he asked with mock concern.

"I've only been robbed twice in six years, and I knew the guy both times."

Raymond pulled a ten from his wallet and placed it on the counter with a grin. "But I gueth you've had people fill up and drive off?" he asked.

"Only strangers," she answered as she stepped to the counter and picked up his bill.

Raymond turned away from her and grabbed the knife from inside his jacket. It still felt warm in his hand, and it began to hum softly as he pulled it out. He turned back to face the girl. She had taken the ten-dollar bill and was facing the panel of switches next to the counter that turned on the pumps. She did not look at him for a moment, her concentration focused on programming the ten-dollar amount into the small computer. Raymond looked at the girl for a second, then he leaned forward and drew the knife through the air. One moment he was preparing to cut the girl, and the next he was holding the knife out past her. At first, he thought he had missed her and sliced only the air. She looked toward him with surprise, and for a moment, she did not know that she had been cut. Then, as she turned toward him, blood began to flow from the neat slice that ran through her mid-section, about four inches deep at her stomach. Blood was followed by intestine and what remained of her late-night snack of chilidogs and chips.

Raymond felt his heart pounding with the excitement of what was happening. He looked at the girl's face as she looked down at her erupting stomach. She drew in a breath to let out a scream, but the expansion of her lungs pushed out more guts and blood, and she collapsed to the floor. Within ten minutes, she would be dead from the loss of blood, most of which was spreading from her awkwardly sprawled body.

"That'll teach you, bitch." Raymond put the knife back into his jacket. His right hand shook with excitement, and he cut his jacket as he slid the blade carefully into the padded pocket. The knife was sharpest when wielded by a hand intent on maiming and slicing. Now, at rest in his jacket, it was no sharper than a good hunting knife. He jumped over the counter and slipped in the spreading blood. He caught himself on the counter, then walked carefully to the cash register that was next to the pump computer. After he emptied out the cash in the register, he cleared pump one and turned it on. He had worked long enough in a gas station himself to know how to operate the machine. He looked one last time at the dying girl. Her wound lay open, and he could see what guts remained inside her. They undulated as if they were themselves alive. His ten-dollar bill lay bloody on a small mound of upper intestine by her neck. He decided then that it was a shame he had not spent more time here, perhaps getting her to perform for him some before killing her. He pursed his lips in a frown at not having thought of that earlier. But the kill had been good anyway.

He leaped back over the counter and ran out to the big Buick, and he filled its tank before getting in and driving away.

4

There were few times when Darius left the compound. One of those times was when there were ceremonies to be performed. Tonight, it was cold, and there was a light drizzle falling. The twenty members of the Family who lived at the compound were gathered in a small clearing in the woods about a mile south. They were surrounded by tall pine and oak trees. On some of the trees, there were torch holders that had been found in one of the waterlogged basements of the compound. They encircled the small clearing, which was man-made. The fallen trees had been used for firewood. The flames on the torches danced in the light rain. They gave off a thick black smoke as they burned. The kerosine-soaked and tar-covered cloths on the end of the torches still burned in the wetness, though the light they cast into the clearing was much less than usual. Usually, the moon provided the light needed for the ceremonies. Tonight, it was well hidden behind the heavy clouds.

In the center of the clearing was a small object that looked like a poorly constructed table. It was actually an altar made of rough wood. On the edge of the altar were a white cloth and a brass chalice. A terrible squealing came from time to time from the base of the altar. A small pig at the end of a rope cried out occasionally at its unfamiliar surroundings. It cried out for its companions, which were twenty miles away.

Nineteen members of the Family stood around the altar in a semicircle. They stood about four feet from each other and about twenty-four feet from the altar. Each wore an old-looking red robe and held a red unlit candle. In the center of the circle, next to the altar, stood the young dark-haired girl named Misty. Nobody but Darius knew if this was her real name or her given name, and nobody but Darius knew where she came from. To everyone else, she was a mystery. She belonged to Darius in many ways, and as such, she was feared by the members of the Family. They tried to avoid her whenever possible. When they had to deal with her, she was treated with almost as much respect as Darius. She knew this and used it to her advantage.

Misty walked around the semicircle with her candle and used it to light each of the candles held by the members of the Family. The candles lit readily, despite the rain, as if eager for the ceremonies that were coming. As Misty lit the candles, another Family member named Lot extinguished the torches.

When Misty and Lot had finished, Darius entered the circle from the north. He, too, wore a robe. His robe was black and did not fit him as well as it should have. It was a little too short. Only Darius knew why. This robe had once belonged to his Queen. Until she returned, it belonged to him. In his left hand, he held a long red candle that was also lit. The candles burned brightly enough to light the faces of all the members as well as the altar. In Darius's right hand, he held a long silvery knife. It was a good knife, but it did not cut magically as did the knife he normally used, and it was nowhere near as old. But it had been used by his Queen in the early years, and as such it was magical to him.

The members began to chant as Darius slowly approached the small altar. The chants were made up of words with which Darius had grown quite familiar and he mouthed them as he approached the altar, though he did not speak them. When he arrived before the altar, he raised his head and let out a terrible shout that silenced the members. A white cloud of steam came from his mouth into the cold night air as he called out. Then the only sound was the patting of the raindrops as they hit the ground and the branches of the trees around them. After a moment of silence, Darius began to chant.

As he chanted, Misty pulled a long spike from under her robe. She walked to a point about ten feet from the altar and looked at the ground. The leaves and debris had all been cleared away from this area, and she dropped to her knees and began to draw. The symbols and shapes she drew did not come from within her, but from Darius's memory. He had taught her these shapes, and there were places within the inverted star that looked incomplete or out of place. But there seemed nevertheless to be power in the symbols. She could feel it tingle in her arm as she drew. Darius's eyes lost their dead look and took on a lively glow as she drew the symbols. The candles burned brighter.

Then there was the gentle breeze. It did not come from the woods, but from the small clearing itself. It was a soft yet cold breeze that ran in a counterclockwise circle and seemed to weave between the members and run across their faces, though the flames of the candles did not move. A light dust began to flow. The golden-colored dust was dry and did not come from the floor of the woods, but simply seemed to be drawn from the air around the Family members.

The member standing nearest to Darius approached the side of the altar where the pig had been tethered. The member loosened the pig from its collar and picked it up. Then he walked to the altar, where he held the animal by both its front and back hooves. The little creature squealed in protest and wriggled furiously in the member's hands. But the member was a strong man, and he held the small pig firmly in place while Darius stood opposite him, chanting a few last mysterious words as he raised the ornate dagger over his head.

In his mind, Darius pictured the traitor. In his mind, he dealt out the justice due him. This image was passed into the minds of the members who watched and now hummed a monotone tune.

As Darius thought his thoughts of retribution, he brought the knife down into the soft belly of the small pig. He cut quickly with the experience of hundreds of such cuts, and in moments he was holding the beating heart of the creature. The pig let out one last terrible squeal after the heart had been removed, then fell still. As Darius held the

pumping heart before him, he chanted more words, and it became hot
in his hand. He took the chalice and held it under the heart, letting the
blood run through his fingers and into the brass cup. When the blood
slowed to a trickle, the heart suddenly burst into flame in his hand.

His lips parted and a hideous grin came to his face. There had been
a time not so long ago when these things did not all go as they should
have. But over the past year, he had seen more of the symbols and
remembered more of the old chants. The power had grown within him,
just as it had begun to awaken within his Queen.

He held the chalice out toward the members of the Family, then he
raised it to his lips and drank.

5

Raymond looked at the clock on his dashboard. It was almost four
in the morning. He was approaching the small town of Colmesneil. In
about an hour, he would be on Interstate 10, heading east. Tyler was
over a hundred miles behind him now, and the farther away he got, the
safer he felt.

But inside, he knew nowhere was really safe.

He drove down the dark state highway, which wound only slightly
as it took him a little to the east and a lot to the south on his drive to the
interstate. He drove fast, though he slowed down when he was within
a mile of any town, regardless of the size, and whenever he spotted any
oncoming cars. He didn't want to be pulled over by the police tonight.

When he got to New Orleans, he would sell the knife to the underground. A knife with the history of this one would bring a premium
from any number of cult groups. And he would be dealing with the big
ones that had been around and had the cash. Any group that knew of
Darius and who he had been before, and who knew of his Queen and
how she had used this knife would give anything to have it for their own.
It carried with it a tremendous history and would certainly empower
whichever group was willing to pay the highest price.

Raymond heard a strange noise. He did not recognize the noise,
so he listened intently as he drove. The big old car produced a lot of

road noise, so it was difficult to hear much more than the road running under the tires and the wind rushing past the windows.

But then he heard it again. It was a low humming sound. At first, he thought that something had gone wrong with the car. Then he smelled the smoke and looked at the seat next to him. The smoke was coming from the black cloth that covered the silvery knife.

Raymond reached out instinctively for the knife. He fumbled underneath the cloth for it, afraid that some harm was coming to it. But just before he touched it, he realized nothing was wrong with the knife. He tried to pull his hand away, but his middle finger brushed the handle, and then it was too late.

He felt his hand grip firmly around the handle of the silver knife. He tried to open his hand and let it go, but as he did, he saw the shiny blade as it emerged from the black cloth and headed upward. He pulled quickly off the road, hoping that he could use his free hand to stop the ascent of the blade. But before the car came to a stop, the blade had found its way into his leg. He cried out and covered the deep wound with his left hand.

The car continued off the road and slid into the slick mud of the shoulder before plowing over an old, rotted fence post and carrying rusted goat-wire ten feet into a muddy field. His headlights lit the wet field and cast just enough light into the car that he could watch the blade as it moved through him. It burned as it moved, and he saw the flesh part just a moment before the blade came to it, just as he had seen before, though only on other people. Now he tried frantically to stop the ascent of the blade as it tore through his pants toward his crotch. He covered his privates with his left hand, but the blade neatly lopped off his fingers as it also split his testicles and cut a neat slice across the top third of his penis.

He screamed out again as blood began to soak his tattered jeans and drip onto the floorboard of the car. He pushed himself back into the seat, as if he could avoid the cutting and carving knife as it made its way through his abdomen, slicing open his stomach and bursting his appendix. He heard the seat behind him tear as the blade cut through it as well on its way upward. He looked down one last time at the burning, ripping blade as it headed upward, took a sharp left, guided by his own defiant hand. His mouth hung open in terror, but now there was no scream. He watched as the blade cut between his ribs and pierced his heart, which exploded, splattering blood onto the dashboard and windshield in front of him.

Then, finally, his hand released the silver knife and dropped into the gaping wound in his lap. His eyes remained open and stared blankly at the muddy field before him.

About an hour later, a black Cutlass pulled up behind the big Buick, which was still idling. A tall, thin man got out of the driver's side and ran to the Buick. He opened the door and leaned inside just for a moment before racing back to the Cutlass with something shiny in his hand.

4

1

Carrie Price awoke to the telephone. She rolled over in her bed to face the night table where her lamp, phone, and clock rested. The numbers on the face of her digital clock read 3:36. Who in the world was calling her at three thirty in the morning? She let it ring while she worked herself up to being able to think just a little more clearly, hoping that perhaps it would stop ringing before then. But it continued to ring. She turned on her small lamp and lifted the receiver at the tail end of the sixth ring.

"Hello," she said in a voice that was groggy at best.

At first, there was no response. Carrie thought, *Great, a crank call at three thirty in the morning*. Then a soft and shaky voice came across the line. "Who is this?" it asked.

"What?" Carrie responded, not sure yet whether to hang up. "Is this Karen?" the voice asked.

"You have the wrong number," Carrie answered, and was about to take the phone from her ear and replace it in its cradle when the next thing the voice said stopped her.

"Are you Terry's sister?" it asked.

Carrie was silent for a moment. "Yes," she answered, "but my name isn't Karen."

She had almost given her name but had been able to think clearly enough to keep it to herself. There was no telling the intent of the weak-sounding voice.

"Okay," came the girl's voice, "I just want to tell you that you might be in danger."

"Who is this?" Carrie asked.

"My name's Laura. I was a friend of Terry's."

At the use of the past tense, Carrie felt her throat tighten. Did this mean that the caller knew what had happened to her sister?

"What do you mean 'was'?" Carrie asked.

"I mean she and I were good friends before she disappeared."

"I don't remember meeting any Laura, and I don't remember my sister mentioning anyone named Laura," Carrie explained. "What do you want?"

"I want to help you," Laura explained. "I want somebody to know what's going on, and Terry said you were someone she trusted. I can't trust anybody, but I can't stay by myself forever."

Carrie tried to take in all of what she was hearing. The nervousness in the voice seemed genuine, but this didn't mean that there was no danger here.

"How can you help me?" Carrie asked.

"I'm calling from the inside of somebody's house. I broke in to make the call. I can't go back to my place because they know where I live, and I'm afraid to stand at a payphone for too long. So, I broke into these people's house and used their phone to call you. I want to meet with you somewhere and talk. I want to tell you what I know so you won't get into any trouble. But you might be in trouble already."

"What do you know about Terry?" Carrie asked.

"I don't want to tell you right now; I'll tell you tomorrow."

"Damn it," Carrie called out, "she's my sister. Tell me what the hell has happened to her."

There was no answer. Then there was a click.

"Hello?" Carrie said. There was no response. She slammed the phone down forcefully and began to cry. "Why does it have to be like this?" she said aloud through the tears that began to crawl down her face.

Although "Laura" had not said so, she knew now that Terry was dead. If Laura had some answers, then she would talk with her. But why had Laura hung up, and how would she get in touch with her?

Once again, she felt helpless and angry. She turned the light back out and lay in her bed, her mind racing with turmoil.

She did not return to sleep and when her alarm went off three hours later, she got up tired and red-eyed.

2

Carrie spent the morning in a daze. Her lack of sleep began to catch up with her despite the coffee, and she was preoccupied with the mysterious call the night before. She had thought only for a moment about letting the police know about the call. Then, with some bitterness, she decided this was her private information. The sheriff's office had plenty of information they were not telling her about. She decided she would continue her own investigation and not share her information with the police, at least not yet. In any case, she wasn't prepared for the routine they would give her when she gave them the information. She would feel only more helpless when they gave her that idiotic smile and buried the notes somewhere in the rest of the pile. Besides, if Laura was telling the truth, she didn't want the police to know about her. Carrie wondered all morning how she would get in touch with this girl. She hadn't sounded much older than a teenager, and she'd sounded genuinely frightened. But breaking into someone's home to use their phone? That seemed too extreme, too desperate.

"You've been distracted all morning," Kyle said to her.

Kyle was the tall, blond manager of the nursery. He was always very friendly to Carrie and even asked her out from time to time. Carrie had promised herself she would say yes one of these times, especially after seeing how much effort it took the poor guy to ask, and how crushed he looked after her refusals. Still, she felt no pressure at all from this young man who was her boss.

"I didn't sleep well last night," Carrie explained.

"I hope you're feeling okay?" Kyle said, genuine concern showing on his face.

"Actually, I think I may be catching that flu that's going around," she lied. But perhaps this lie would help cover her lack of attention to her job, as she was sure that inattention would last into the afternoon.

Kyle's look of concern deepened as he took an unconscious step away from her. "Do you need to go home?" he asked.

"I'm not sure I have anything yet," she said. "May just be early cramps or something."

A look of embarrassment crossed Kyle's fair face. From time-to-time, Carrie was simply too frank, though she never carried it to the extreme of indiscretion or vulgarity.

"Well," Kyle said as he backed away, "let me know if you need to take off. I'm sure we can cover for you for a day or so."

"Thanks, Kyle," she said with a smile. Then she thought again of a girl who would be perfect for him.

Carrie looked at her watch. It was almost lunchtime, finally. It seemed as if a whole day had already passed. She wasn't looking forward to the long afternoon. She spent the rest of her morning double-checking the shipments of rose bushes that were headed to southern Louisiana and Texas the next day. It was turning out to be a mild fall, and some of the plants were coming to life much too early. Hopefully, they would be able to move them as either late winter or very early spring plantings.

At lunchtime, Carrie left the office and walked out to her car. She had intended to take one of her dresses to a nearby seamstress for mending, then she would grab a salad at one of the fast-food joints on the loop. As she approached her car, she saw a yellow piece of paper that had been placed under her windshield wiper. It flipped back and forth as a gentle but cold breeze blew across the hood of her car. When she reached her car, she pulled the note out from under the wiper blade and unfolded it. She knew before she opened it that it would be from the mysterious caller who had interrupted her sleep the previous night.

She read the note, which instructed her to take her lunch break at the Corral, a popular barbecue place that was a couple of miles to the south and was always quite busy for lunch. It also instructed her to be certain that she was not followed. Carrie thought that perhaps this was a bit paranoid, but then remembered how she had felt during the hours after the incident at her sister's apartment.

Carrie got into her car and drove southward on the loop until she saw the familiar golden sign and loaded parking lot of the restaurant. She parked her car in the fourth row from the front door. As she walked to the restaurant, she glanced at her watch. It was probably going to have to be a long lunch today. She was grateful that she had a boss who was forgiving as well as infatuated.

When Carrie entered the restaurant, she began to look around. She didn't see anyone who seemed to be looking for her, so she had the waitress seat her and informed the girl that she would be going to the salad bar. She waited in her seat for a minute, but nobody approached her, so she decided to get her lunch. Carrie got her salad and sat down. When she was about half finished, a young girl did step up to the table. At first, Carrie thought it was one of the servers. When she looked up at the girl, she knew this was not the case. The girl looked worn out and ragged. She didn't have any makeup on, and streaks of dirt colored her cheeks. Her clothes might have been nice if they had not been both soiled and torn. There was evidence of a recent cut on her left cheek.

"Are you Terry's sister?" the girl asked. It was that same timid voice from the night before.

"Yes," Carrie answered. "You must be Laura."

The thin girl looked around the restaurant nervously, then sat down across from Carrie. Carrie saw those eyes as they looked wantingly at her salad. Carrie put her fork down and pushed the plate across the table.

"I'm done with this, if you'd like some," she said.

Laura looked up at Carrie with a sorrowful gaze. Then she picked up the fork and began eating. Though she tried not to eat too fast, Carrie could sense the eagerness with which she was consuming the food. In her mind, she began to trust this girl.

"So, what can you tell me about Terry?" Carrie asked. Laura took another bite and swallowed most of it before responding.

"She was really involved in this cult," she explained. "That's where we met." She forked a small tomato and popped it quickly into her mouth.

"Is she still alive?" Carrie asked.

Laura chewed on some more greens and looked up at Carrie. Her eyes told Carrie what she waited to hear from her mouth. "She started to get worried about things," Laura continued. "Both of us did. We decided that we wanted to get out." Laura gave up on etiquette and continued to eat while she spoke. "There was another girl, Tess. She was going to go with us."

"Go where?" Carrie asked.

"Out of the cult," Laura explained. "Maybe to Saint Louis or something. We had to leave Texas if we got out, "she said. "There are too many people involved around here. They'd find us for sure." Suddenly, she took another nervous look around the restaurant. "So, we were all going to leave together, only Tess wasn't really ever going to leave. She was telling Darius our whole plan, and he put a stop to it all."

"Who's Darius?" Carrie asked.

Laura finished off the salad and put down the fork. "He's the guy who's running this whole thing. You see, there's this big old stone house up near Mineola. I don't know if he owns it or what. He stays up there all the time, and so do some of the members of his group. But most of them don't live up there."

"So, what happened to my sister?"

"Well, like I was saying, Tess was ratting on us. One night, when we were all up there, Darius had a couple of his guys lock us up in one of the rooms. He kept us in there for a couple of days. Then one night, they came and got Terry. They put her in a white robe and took her away."

Frustration showed on Carrie's face. Was this it? Was this all the girl knew? "So, she's still up there somewhere?" Carrie asked.

Laura looked down at the table for a minute, then back at Carrie. "Well," she began, "I've only seen the white robe one other time, about six months ago. They used it on a girl who had run away from home and had come to the home of one of the cult members. She was his cousin or something. That guy got quite a promotion for bringing her in because it was getting close to time for the big ceremony and they hadn't found anybody yet."

"Anybody for what?" Carrie asked. She sensed what the answer was, and she dreaded what it meant.

"Every few months, when the moon is right or something, Darius holds a big ceremony in the woods. He brings out this dead girl that he calls his queen and puts her on a big table thing. Then he does a ceremony." Laura looked down again and hesitated. Carrie did not interrupt her. "Anyway, they do this thing where they sacrifice somebody and put her heart in the dead girl's chest. I think that Darius hopes this will bring the dead girl to life, but it never works."

"My God," Carrie gasped. "They cut Terry's heart out?"

"I think so," Laura replied, her eyes turned down again. "That's when they use the white robe, on the person getting sacrificed. And I know it was about time for the ceremonies again."

Carrie stared into the air beyond Laura. She had prepared herself to hear that her sister was dead, though she was not prepared for the details of how it had happened. As much as she resisted, she could not help but visualize her sister lying in a bloody heap with her chest torn open. Where was she now? Was she lying in some unmarked grave in the woods? Was she rotting under the forest floor with no one to put flowers on her grave?

Laura's expression said she knew it was not the right thing to say, but her hunger forced her to ask Carrie if she could take her plate back for seconds at the salad bar. Carrie did not answer, she simply nodded as she continued to stare into space. As Laura filled her salad plate, Carrie sat alone and her mind whirred. A thousand thoughts came into her head, making only a jumble of nonsense. She did not cry; she was too shocked and disoriented for this. But later, when she had calmed down, she would cry again for her dead sister. When Laura returned, Carrie finally withdrew her distant gaze.

"Do you know how to get to this place?" Carrie asked.

"What place?" Laura said.

"The old stone house where the cult lives."

"Sure," Laura answered as she continued to eat. She was a thin girl with sharp features, but she was eating like someone twice her weight. "But there's no way I'm going back there. They'd kill me."

"Well, now I know enough to go to the police," Carrie said. She knew that it was too big now to handle on her own.

"No!" Laura shouted, her voice carrying throughout the restaurant. Again, she looked around nervously to see who had noticed. "No way," she continued, "you can't tell the cops."

"Why not?" Carrie asked.

"I know one of them is in this thing, and there might be more."

The shock showed on Carrie's face. "You mean there's a police officer in this cult?"

"At least one," Laura confirmed. "Who knows how many more."

"But why?" Carrie asked.

"Because one of them really believes all this stuff about Darius's queen and the new order when she comes back to life. I know for sure he's a cop because I heard someone say she'd seen a badge and a radio in his car. But he's the only one I know about for sure. But if he found out where I was, then he'd come after me. If he finds out what you know now, he'll come after you too. And we can't be sure he's the only one."

"Do you know his name?"

"Nobody goes by their real names. I think that's in case someone like me gets away. They called him Michael, but that's not his real name."

Carrie sat and thought this over. She knew now where her sister might be, and who her killers probably were, but she couldn't do anything about it. Maybe she could tell the FBI or the state police. But they would undoubtedly involve or at least inform the local authorities. And

Laura hadn't said whether this cop was city, state, or county. But if she told the police that one of their own was involved, couldn't they find him and stop him based on Laura's description? Perhaps. Perhaps not.

"We've got to find someone we can tell," Carrie said.

"I know," Laura answered. "That's what I kept thinking. There were only two people I could think of, and you were the first one. I was hoping that if we got together, then you might be able to help." Laura looked nervously around again. "Or at least I wouldn't be completely alone."

"Does anybody know where you are?" Carrie asked.

"No," Laura answered. Her eyes seemed locked on some distant object, and her voice was fading. "My folks live in Missouri, and I don't have any family here." Her final words were almost a whisper, and her eyes were still glued to something or someone.

Carrie glanced to her right, in the direction that Laura was staring. At first, she saw nothing unusual. Then she saw the man. It was the tall thin man she had seen staring at her in her rearview mirror at her sister's apartment. This had to be the man who had been hiding in Terry's closet, the man who had come after her once already. Had he followed her here? Or had he followed Laura? It didn't matter. Now they just had to figure out how to shake him.

"Don't stare at him," Carrie said. This brought Laura's eyes back to hers.

"Do you know him?" Laura asked.

"I saw him once at my sister's place, when I was checking things out. Do you know who he is?"

"He was looking for me, I'll bet," Laura said with disdain. "I stayed there for a couple of days."

"Who is he?" Carrie asked again.

"I'm sure he's a Family member, but I never saw him at the compound."

"He's part of your family?" Carrie said with confusion.

"No, I mean a member of the cult. It doesn't really have a name, so people in it are just called members of the Family."

"Well, as long as we stay in busy areas, we'll be okay," Carrie said, not sure she believed it herself. Laura had finally stopped eating. Her plate held a few pieces of lettuce and some cheese she had left. Apparently, she had finally gotten her fill.

"Let's go," Carrie said, standing as she spoke. Laura looked up with frightened eyes.

"Where?"

"Just come with me. We'll get in the car and then we'll talk about it."

Laura looked again at the thin man. Now he was looking back at her. Her eyes grew wide as she stood, looking away as she followed Carrie. As they reached the exit, she looked back again, but the tall thin man was nowhere to be seen.

"Shit," Laura whispered under her voice.

Carrie walked out the door with Laura close behind. Laura kept looking back at the door to see when the man came out, but he never did. Laura followed Carrie to her car. She kept looking over her shoulder, waiting for the man to come out of the restaurant. They got into the car and Carrie drove out of the parking lot, onto the loop. As she did, she noticed a late model black Cutlass pulling out behind her. She knew she had seen it before but could not remember where. The dent on the right front fender was the distinguishing mark.

Laura noticed Carrie's concentration on her rearview mirror, so she turned to take a look. "Oh, my God," she exclaimed, "he's following us."

The windshield of the big black car was tinted too dark for Carrie to be able to make out the face of the driver. She assumed that Laura knew what she was talking about. Then she remembered where she had seen the black car. She had parked next to it the day she'd gone into her sister's apartment.

"Lose him!" Laura shouted.

"He won't do anything to us in broad daylight," Carrie explained. "Not in all this traffic, with all these people around."

"What are you going to do?" Laura asked.

"I think the safest thing to do right now is go shopping."

"What?" Laura asked with obvious incredulity.

"We'll head to the mall. It's just a few miles down the road here. It's a very public place, so it's relatively safe. When we get there, I'll call the police."

"I already told you," Laura said, "we can't go to the police."

"He won't know whether I'm calling them or not," Carrie explained, "and I don't imagine he'll stick around to find out."

Laura sat and considered the plan. It seemed flawed, but she couldn't think of a better one.

Then there was a loud popping sound, and the car began to rattle. Laura, who was already on edge, almost hit her head on the top of the car when she stiffened at the noise.

"What was that?" she asked in a panicky tone.

"I don't know," Carrie answered. "But I hope we can get to a service station or something before it stops us."

The car began to stall out, and she took a quick glance at her gauges. Then she noticed that the needle on the temperature gauge was approaching the red line, and the rattling noise was getting louder.

"Come on," Carrie coaxed her car. Under normal circumstances, she would have stopped to avoid doing any further damage to the car. But these were not normal circumstances. She slowed down some, but the needle on the temperature gauge was still rising, and the rattling was continuing to worsen. Then the car began to cut out badly.

"We're not going to make it," Carrie said as the car began to slow on its own. She turned at the first opportunity, pulling into the parking lot of a hardware store. She was able to get the car halfway to the building before it died. Laura turned to look at the same instant that Carrie again checked her mirror. The black car had followed them and was now only a few feet from their rear bumper. It had come to a stop. The door on the driver side opened and the tall thin man got out. He had put on a cap and sunglasses, and he was wearing thin leather gloves.

"We've got to run for it," Laura exclaimed. "He'll kill us."

"Stay inside the car," Carrie said as she locked the door with a flick of her index finger.

"He's not going to kill us, not here. There are people walking around in this parking lot constantly." As she said this, a tall muscular man walked by Laura's window. He seemed oblivious to the impending danger that faced the two girls but confirmed Carrie's point. The tall thin man walked slowly up to Carrie's window. He stood there for a minute before leaning down and looking in at her. He was smiling a broad, insincere grin. Carrie noticed a long deep scar running down the right side of his face and halfway across his neck. She could not see his eyes through his dark glasses. Steam rose plentifully from the hood of her car. The man tapped on her window, as if he expected her to simply roll it down. Carrie surprised Laura by pushing the button that lowered the window, though she only dropped it a couple of inches.

"Having a little car trouble?" he asked Carrie.

"Yes," she answered curtly.

"Mind if I take a look?" he asked her.

She didn't answer. Instead, she stared at her reflection in the man's glasses. His smile did not fade. He moved back from the window and walked to the front of her car, where he stood waiting.

"What is he doing?" Laura asked.

Carrie didn't answer. Instead, she reached down and pulled the lever that released the hood. The man quickly found the latch and pulled the hood open, as if he knew exactly where it was supposed to be. A few seconds later, he walked around the side of the car holding something that looked at first like a snake. Then Carrie recognized the dangling piece of rubber and fabric.

"It seems your fan belt has broken," the man said as he approached the window. "Which is quite odd, since it looks almost new."

Carrie did not answer. Instead, she continued to stare into the man's glasses, trying her best not to let him see just how frightened she really was.

"If I were to guess," the man continued, "I would say that it had been cut, perhaps by someone who is trying to scare you. Would you say this is a good guess?" The belt continued to dangle in his left hand. His grin remained.

"I'd say that somebody should probably leave me alone, before he finds himself in jail."

This caused the man to break out into laughter. It was a harsh bray that hurt Carrie's ears. Laura was pressed against her door, trying to melt away from the whole scene. When the man suddenly stopped braying, he put his face up close to the window. Carrie did not back away.

"If you want to go on with your life, you'll forget you met this girl and let her out of your car. She'll come with me, and I'll forget who you are. I have nothing against you, even if you are a snoopy bitch. You may be curious, but you are certainly no threat."

"Don't let him take me," Laura pleaded.

"Don't let him take me," the tall man mocked in a high-pitched voice.

"I don't believe you," Carrie said, "and even if I did, I wouldn't just hand this girl over for you to kill."

The man's smile faded. "Maybe you don't understand me," he said. "If you don't hand her over, you'll both end up like your sister."

At the mention of her sister, Carrie lost her poker face. The fear and rage both showed.

The man's smile returned. "Or perhaps we'll just cripple you for life. It would be fun smashing your legs and arms, and then having my way with you." His grin grew to show his small yellow teeth.

"You son of a bitch," she said. "You son of a bitch." It's all she could think to say. At that moment, she wanted to be somewhere, anywhere away from this man. On the other hand, she wanted to jump out of the car and pound the man's head in with the tire iron in her trunk.

She reached forward suddenly and laid into her horn. She pushed down firmly and did not let go.

The man's smile faded into a smirk, and he ran his long and slimy tongue up the glass before dropping the broken fan belt and shouting over the horn, "You'll be more than a little sorry, missy." He started to turn and walk away, then he added, "I can't wait to get hold of those legs." He held his hands out as if her legs were in them and rocked them back and forth. Then he turned and walked back to his car.

Carrie watched him get into his car. When he did, she let up on the horn. She watched him leave the parking lot and waited until he was out of sight before she got out of her car.

"Just stay here with the doors locked," Carrie told Laura.

"Okay," she said, her eyes still wide.

Carrie picked up the broken fan belt and walked into the hardware store to use the phone.

5

1

Jack Macon was repairing the damage to his fence when a car pulled into his driveway. It was not a car he was familiar with. From time to time, he would have customers who came directly to him to buy his fine show pigs, but they were usually referrals and they always called first. His mind went back immediately to the odd events of the past few days.

He stood and faced the approaching car. His grip tightened around the big pliers he was using to tie off the tightened portion of the fence. The car pulled up to his house. A moment later, someone got out of the passenger side and began walking toward him. It was a young girl of about twenty. She looked dirty and weary, and she had walked almost all the way up to him before he recognized who it was.

"Laura?" he said tentatively.

"Hi, Jack," she said.

Jack relaxed his grip on the pliers and walked over to his young niece. "Laura, what happened?" He knew that someone else had gotten out of the car and was also approaching, and he took a quick glance upward to see if it might be his sister. It was not. He looked back at Laura, his eyes still asking the question.

"I've gotten into some trouble," she explained.

"You're a mess," he said. Then he looked up at the woman who was coming up behind Laura. This time, he noticed that she was a beautiful young woman. His eyes relaxed some, and he immediately wondered if he perhaps looked rugged, or just messy.

"This is my friend, Carrie," Laura said.

Jack nodded at the lovely woman and removed the glove from his right hand. "Very nice to meet you," he said.

Her eyes met his as he greeted her. She offered her hand to his and he held it gently for a moment, then let it go. Hers was a warm hand, even on a cool and cloudy day like today.

"Nice to meet you," she repeated to him.

His eyes remained on her pleasant face a little longer than they should have, then he looked back at his niece.

"What happened?" Jack asked.

"We probably ought to talk about it inside," Laura said.

"Well, you know your way around in there," Jack said. "Go on in and make yourself at home. I've got one more strand to tighten here, then I'll come in."

"Okay," Laura answered. Then she led Carrie to the house.

Carrie followed Laura to the front door of the big home. It was a tall, two-story home with a colonial look. It was a large rectangular prism, and was sided mostly with wood, not brick. Most of the homes in Tyler were brick. This one looked nice in a newly painted white. White was the right color for this house. Carrie guessed correctly that it had always been painted this color.

She followed Laura into the house. When she stepped in, she found herself at the edge of a large living room that stretched out to her left. She guessed from the furnishings that Jack was probably married, which was a shame, considering his good looks and charming manner.

"I'm going to wash up some," Laura said as she disappeared into a small hallway that led to a set of stairs.

Carrie took a seat on one of the two couches. She picked the one that looked comfortable as opposed to ornate. It was angled toward a television, so she supposed this was the couch meant for sitting on. The nicer of the two couches had a solid cherry frame that was highly polished and looked more like a decoration than a piece of furniture.

Carrie eyed the furniture and layout of the living room as she waited for Laura. She heard water running and figured that Laura had decided to take a shower. It was a good idea. Then she heard heavy steps, then a delay of a couple of seconds before the door came open. Jack walked into the house in his socks, leaving his dirty shoes on the porch.

"Can I get you something to drink?" Jack asked as he headed to the kitchen.

"No, thanks." Carrie watched him walk down the small hallway. A moment later, Jack came into the living room with a glass of apple juice and sat in a big old chair that looked like it was fifty years old. It squeaked loudly as he settled into it, but once he was in it, she saw that it fit him.

"You here alone today?" Carrie asked.

"I'm here alone every day," Jack replied. Then he took a drink. "It's just me in this place. Me and my pigs."

A slight smile crept onto her face, which she quickly stifled. "What do you do?"

"I raise potbellied pigs right now. This spring, I'm going to get some worn-out cows and a good bull and do some profitable breeding." The chair creaked again as he leaned back. "I just do a little speculative work in livestock of one kind or another, whatever I think might be profitable."

"I was raised on a farm," Carrie explained. "And I swore when I left that I'd never do it again." She noticed Jack's expression change slightly. Was it disappointment? "But after putting up with city life for the past seven years, I've about decided that country living isn't so bad after all. I'm getting tired of the hassles, and the traffic."

"I know what you mean," Jack explained. "I only spent my college years in the city. By the time I had my degree, I was ready to get back here."

"Did you grow up here?" she asked him.

"Yes," he replied. "The house I was born in is at the other end of my property. My mom and dad lived there until they passed away."

"In a way, that's nice, to have roots like that I mean."

"It's all I've known," Jack answered. "But it's been good to me."

They continued with the small talk for another half hour, discovering little things, each party becoming more interested in the other. Jack liked the way Carrie smiled, and she seemed to be somehow elegant yet down to earth. Carrie liked the way Jack spoke with his eyes, and the confidence that was not arrogance his voice projected. Laura finally appeared. She looked clean, though she had put on her old dirty clothes again. Carrie thought Laura looked plain, yet pretty. Jack looked at this girl whom he had not seen in almost a year, even though she'd been living in Tyler for the past two and a half. Jack invited Laura to join Carrie on the couch. She sat down and the room was silent.

"So," Jack began. "What in the world has been happening with you?"

Laura paused, took a deep breath, then told Jack her story. She started with her involvement in the cult in the summer and told about the ceremonies and sacrifices. As she spoke, there was a spark of realization on his face. Laura told Jack about the man who ran the cult, and the dead woman he kept in his room. She told him about the compound and the people she had seen there.

"Darius really believes that he will be able to resurrect the dead girl," she explained, "then she will lead the Family to some grand plan, though I'm not sure just what that plan is." Laura told Jack about her friendship with Terry Price, and how Terry and she had decided to get out of the cult. She explained how she thought that Terry had been killed, and how she herself had escaped. Jack noticed that Carrie looked down and closed her eyes as Laura talked about Terry. Then Laura told Jack how she had spent the past three days hiding from these people who seemed to be everywhere. She explained how she had gotten in touch with Carrie.

"Why didn't you come here sooner?" Jack asked.

"I didn't want you to tell my mom. And I didn't have any way to get here."

"You could have called me," Jack said with some anger, "and I would have come and gotten you."

"I was afraid to drag anybody else into this," Laura said. Tears came into her eyes. "Please don't tell Mom," she pleaded. "She'd flip out. She'd come down here right away, and I don't want to get her involved in all this."

Jack had always been close to his sister, though they had grown further apart since her move to Kansas City twelve years back. Laura had always been somewhat of a rebel, though for the most part, she had been able to stay out of trouble. Until now.

"You're an adult," Jack said to her. "If you want your mother to know, you can tell her yourself." He wanted to let his sister know what had become of her daughter, but he had always stayed out of what he considered to be internal family matters. "But I really think you should give her a call, in case she's been trying to get a hold of you or something."

Laura thought it over. "Okay," she said, "but I'm not going to tell her what happened, or where I am."

"That's your decision," Jack said, his eyes showing his disapproval.

Laura was silent for a moment. Carrie looked shaken to Jack. He supposed it was because she was thinking again about what had happened to her sister.

"So," Laura finally said. "What should we do?"

Jack felt the expectant eyes upon him. Was he supposed to have the answers? There was so much more to this than he had suspected.

"I know a police officer," Jack offered. "He's a county deputy. He might be able to help us out."

Laura looked panicked. "No way," she said. "I told you the cops were in on this."

"You told me somebody said that they saw a cop. I would be surprised if it goes beyond that. What we really ought to do is just call the police and tell them what you know. I imagine this 'cop' is a fake. And if he is a cop, they'll still lock him away with the rest of the crazies."

"I don't know, Jack." Carrie had come out of her sad silence. "I've given the police a lot of information, and they just seem to be sitting on it."

"Carrie," Jack said, "I'm sure they're doing everything they can. It just always seems to be going so slowly to those on the waiting end. I know. I've been there."

"I really feel like it's more than that," she explained. "I keep thinking back to the things missing from my sister's apartment, and I can't help but shake the feeling that somebody from the police department took them to cover something up."

"I seriously doubt there is anything to worry about," Jack said. "And if there is, I think this cop I spoke with the other night isn't involved. He seemed very friendly, and he was willing to talk to me a little about the cases like mine they had run across."

"What do you mean?" Carrie asked.

"I lost some of my pigs a few nights back. It was some strange sacrificial thing, I think. The guys came back the next night, too. We got one of them."

"That's probably my fault," Laura explained, her eyes looking at the living room floor. "I told them when I first got there that they could get some pigs here for their ceremonies. I'm sorry, Uncle Jack."

"It doesn't sound to me like there's nothing going on with the police then," Carrie said.

"What makes you say that?" Jack asked.

"It just sounds strange to me that no progress has been made, and that the officers are afraid to get close to the case. Maybe they've been warned off by other officers."

"I doubt that," Jack said. "I just think this guy I spoke with was particularly superstitious, and he was spooked by the thing. He may know one or two other guys in the office who feel like he does. I imagine that's all it is."

Laura sat up. "I don't know if it's the best thing, but this guy sounds like he might be okay."

"Laura," Jack said, "I think everybody in the sheriff's office is okay. But if it'll make you feel better, I'll call up this guy I spoke with and get him to come over. He should be able to help us get a hold of the right people."

"Okay," Laura agreed nervously.

Jack looked at Carrie. "Sounds okay to me," she agreed.

2

Deputy Ben Williams arrived at Jack's house that evening, after his shift was over. Jack had left him a message at the station and the deputy had called him when he got off his patrol.

Jack introduced Deputy Williams to the two women, then took a seat on the couch with Carrie. Laura sat in another chair which also faced the couch. Jack started the conversation.

"Laura here has been involved in a group of some kind that I think might be tied in with the things you and I talked about last night."

"Oh?" Deputy Williams said with some interest as he looked at Laura.

"Laura," Jack said, "why don't you tell the deputy here what you told me."

Laura again told the story of how she had become involved in the strange cult, and how she had seen these animal sacrifices take place. As she described being held in the room with Terry Price, the deputy's eyes widened. His face showed incredulity when Laura suggested that people were being sacrificed.

"Did you actually see somebody get sacrificed?"

"No," Laura said. "I avoided those ceremonies. I think that they knew I did, and maybe that's why they started watching me."

"But you're sure it happened?" Ben asked.

"Positive."

"Unbelievable."

Jack shifted in his chair. He had found himself watching Carrie's face as she became involved in the story again. Then she caught him looking. It embarrassed him a little, but then she smiled.

Jack looked back at Ben. "Laura says there was a rumor that a police officer was at this compound."

"Did you see him?" the deputy asked Laura.

"Yes."

"Describe him to me."

"Well, he was kind of short, and he had really black hair." Her eyes went to the ceiling as she tried to remember what the man looked like. "He wasn't fat or skinny, just average."

"How old do you think he was?"

"Oh, maybe forty or so."

"Did he have any distinguishing marks? Any scars or anything like that?"

"No," Laura answered, "none that I could see. But he did limp a little when he walked."

Ben's eyes grew narrow, and he leaned forward slightly. Jack could see that this last piece of information had struck some kind of chord with him.

"Did he talk with an accent?"

"Not really, he sounded like people up in Kansas City. He didn't really sound like he was from here."

"Did he laugh strangely?"

"I don't remember hearing him laugh."

"Did he smoke a lot?"

"Yea," Laura answered. "He had a cigarette in his mouth every time I saw him."

"What brand?"

"I don't know."

Ben looked away from Laura and pursed his lips.

Carrie turned to face him. "It sounds as if you might know this guy."

"I might," Ben answered.

"So, he really is a cop?" Jack asked.

"I think so. I think he might be a detective in my department."

"A detective?" Jack asked. Then it suddenly struck him. "Is it the detective who's in charge of the case we talked about last night?"

Ben looked at Jack. Jack knew the answer to his question.

"I can't be sure, but it sounds suspicious."

"So, whoever assigned him to the case is in on it, too," Carrie deduced.

"Not necessarily. Nobody really wanted this case. It was a dead end at best. The first guy was getting spooked, didn't want to handle it anymore. Jacobson volunteered."

Laura spoke. "But it doesn't mean that there's other cops in on it?"

"I find that difficult to believe," Ben said. "Most of those guys were brought up around here, like me. They're good cops. Most of them have been on the job for at least seven years. And they all seem pretty stable, except for Jacobson. He always did seem a little odd to me." Deputy Williams leaned back. "But I can't think of any other deputy who would be interested in joining a cult. And certainly not the sheriff."

Laura objected. "But they could be bribed. It's happened before."

"I don't imagine fifty bucks would make the sheriff look the other way."

"They have a lot of money," Laura explained.

"How much is a lot?" Jack asked.

"Enough to buy off cops," she said. "Sorry," she apologized to Ben. "I hear that there's a safe in Darius's bedroom, that he keeps all the cash in. I hear that there's supposed to be something like a million dollars in it."

"A million?" Carrie asked. Her voice showed her disbelief.

"That's what I heard," she said.

"Where would they get money like that?" Ben asked.

"These people are nuts. But it's not just scum of the earth. There's doctors and lawyers involved, too. There's one guy who comes to the compound in a Rolls. There's money around, and they give it to Darius."

"All for the purpose of bringing some dead girl back to life?" Jack asked.

"I suppose they give money because they believe Darius, that his Queen will come back and that she'll be powerful. I would think that they are giving him money because he needs it to run things, like bribing cops. And because if she does come back, they want to be in good with her and Darius."

"What do you think, Ben?" Jack asked.

The deputy sat thinking for a moment. "I don't know."

"So, there could be other cops involved," Laura said, "and payoffs and stuff."

"Sure, I suppose it's possible." Ben shifted uncomfortably. "But I still don't think it's likely."

Carrie turned to the deputy. "But possible enough that precautions should be taken."

"Sure, you should always take precautions. But we've got to trust someone, or we won't get anywhere with this."

Jack had an idea. "Could we go to the press with this?"

Ben thought about that suggestion for a second, then raised his eyebrows. "Sure, but they'd want to check it out carefully before printing anything. They've been burned already on a couple of these cult things. They always snoop around our offices to try and confirm their stories now before going to print. I've seen them not print a couple that were true simply because we did a good enough job of acting like their information was bogus, and they couldn't get any other confirmation. If they started snooping around the office, and there were dirty cops in there, we'd be in trouble. And if the press couldn't get any cooperation from them, they might send a reporter or two up to that compound."

Laura raised her eyebrows. "That might not be so bad."

"But if they went to us first, and they probably would before wasting any time driving to this compound, and if there were dirty cops who found out, the reporters would be expected at the compound."

"So?" Laura said.

"So, then that might put them in danger too."

"But then the story would get out," Laura said, "and we might be able to do some good."

"Not if the people they send up there don't come back. From what you've said, these people aren't beyond murder to protect their cause."

"But if they didn't come back," Laura argued, "then the paper would get more involved."

"And who do you think they'd contact first?" Ben asked. Laura knew the answer. They would go to the police. "And," Ben continued, "if there are cops involved, there might be people at the paper involved, too. That may be why the paper seems to miss some of the stories. And the ones they don't miss never show up on the front page."

Then Laura remembered talking to one young man who had boasted that his uncle was a bigwig at the *Tyler Courier Times*, and that he had let him write a story from time to time. She figured then that the guy was just trying to get her to get in the sack with him. He had succeeded and she'd thought no more of it. Until now.

"We can try to get the Dallas paper out here."

"Good luck," Carrie said. "They might get someone to look into it with a phone call to the police, who will tell them that there's no story. They've got enough news to cover in Dallas and Tarrant Counties alone to fill two papers every day. The last time they printed a story on the front page about Tyler was when the mayor got busted for accepting payoffs from that drug ring."

For a moment, the room was silent while they all considered their options.

Jack finally spoke. "I think maybe we should tell the paper anyway, anonymously so that if there is a connection, we won't be revealed. Then if that falls apart, we won't be involved in it."

Jack looked at each person. Nobody raised an objection.

"Okay," Ben agreed. "But that won't get us anywhere."

"But it can't hurt," Jack reiterated.

Carrie began thinking again about her sister. "Then we can go up there and get evidence ourselves, maybe bring in the state or federal cops."

Laura sat up straight. "Wait a minute," she said with some panic, "I don't want to bring this thing down. I just want to get away from it."

Jack had similar feelings. "We're not qualified to get into this, Carrie. It's way too big for us."

"Then who?" Carrie asked, anger flashing in her voice. "Who's going to do it?"

"I've got a friend in the state troopers office," Ben offered. "I might get him to look into it for me. Maybe he'll help us out."

"What if he's dirty too?" Carrie asked.

"He's not," Ben answered. "I've known him since the sixth grade. My mother still has tea with his mother on Sundays, after church. This guy's a good guy, too smart to get involved in this crap and too honest to take a payoff."

"But why can't we do something in the meantime?" Carrie asked.

Laura looked frantic. "Like what? Snoop around up there until somebody finds you and then end up lying on a table with a knife stuck in your chest? No way. Whatever happens, I want out of here."

Jack turned to his niece. "I'll get you out of here, no matter what we decide to do about this here. I'll put you on a bus home tonight if there's one going out and you're ready to get on it."

"Hell, I'm ready," Laura said. "I've got everything I'm taking with me right here."

"What about your belongings?"

"There's no damn way I'm going back to my apartment. They're waiting for me there. I'll just leave everything for now. You can send it up to me when this all blows over."

"Sure," Jack agreed. He could see that Laura just wanted to go home, and as soon as possible. "Why don't you go make some phone calls and see when the next bus leaves? And give your mother a call."

Laura looked around at everybody, almost apologetically. But she had been in peril long enough. There was no more fight left in her—she was just ready to go home. By this time tomorrow, she would be safe, in her old bed. Her mom was going to rag her out, but she would almost welcome it. She would stay there for a while. Then she would start over. She stood and went to the kitchen to use the phone.

"Now," Jack said to Deputy Williams, "you can talk things over with your trooper friend. I'll write a note to the newspaper. You get back to us and let us know what you find." He looked at Carrie. "Are you going to be able to wait for the deputy before jumping into anything?"

"Sure, but not forever." She was silent for a moment, but Jack could tell she had something more to say. "I'm not sure I'll feel very comfortable being alone until then."

Jack had a solution in a second. "You're welcome to stay here if you'll feel safer." He paused, a look of slight embarrassment on his face. "I mean, you're welcome to stay at least for the weekend."

"I think I'd like that," Carrie agreed. It wasn't just her attraction to Jack that made her want this. She really didn't want to be alone, and she felt like Jack's place might be a good location for several reasons. If she stayed with one of her friends, she would still be in the city. She wanted to get away from that. Somehow, Jack's place felt safer. It was like a fortress to her. It would also give her an opportunity to discuss more options with this man, who seemed to have some good ideas and a level head.

"Can you come back to my place with me and help me get a few things?"

"Sure," Jack agreed.

Ben jumped in. "Take Carrie's car. That way, if you are spotted and they run the plates, they won't come up with anything about you, Jack."

"Right," Jack agreed. It was a good suggestion. Otherwise, he would probably have taken his truck and given away Carrie's hiding place. "It'll be easy to see if we're being followed on Highway 110, and I know the back roads here good enough to lose anybody."

"Okay," Ben agreed. "Carrie, you stay here at least for the weekend. If we don't have anything by Monday, then maybe you can stay here a little longer. If you two decide to do anything, please run it by me first. Maybe I'll be able to help." His eyes looked back and forth between Carrie and Jack for a moment. "Quite frankly, this thing scares the shit out of me. I don't know who these people are, or what they're really up to. But I've seen and heard a lot of strange things in my life." Ben looked around for a second, as if to make sure nobody was listening in. "I've heard a little about this cult in New Orleans that got pretty big a few years back. Some of my cop friends over there said they found a big open theater sitting in a field north of town. Said it had been used for some big ceremony. Somebody had built and used it on a pretty fast schedule. Best they could tell, something had gone wrong. There were signs of some kind of disruption, including casings from a nine-millimeter pistol, and blood on the top of the stage. Everything else I heard about the mess was pretty much just rumor, but some of it was pretty scary stuff. I think things had gotten much bigger than anybody suspected." He paused. "Nobody is quite sure what happened to that group." He shifted uncomfortably again. "There are things about this group that scare me, things that sound a lot like this group from New Orleans. If they're connected somehow, I hope to God we can put a stop to it before it really gets going. Otherwise, we may have one hell of a big problem."

Jack watched his new friend intently. He could see loads of emotion in his face. "You think they're connected?"

"I think it's possible. And New Orleans is only a six-hour drive from here."

"And you know more?"

"I have suspicions."

"We've got time," Carrie said.

"All I have is rumors. I've given you too much speculation already. What we need here is facts."

Jack looked at Ben, whose face revealed he was struggling. Whatever the deputy knew or had heard, it had to be pretty horrible. It was obvious that they wouldn't hear anything that evening.

"Whatever you can tell us that might be of help," Jack said to Ben, "please let us know."

"I think I've said too much already," he said, standing up. Carrie watched him stand. "You're not leaving, are you?"

"I'm going to head over to my buddy's house before it gets too late. If I can borrow your phone, I'll give him a call first."

"Sure," Jack said as he too stood. "As soon as Laura gets off."

Just then, Laura walked into the room. "Are you leaving?" she asked Ben.

"I'm going over to my trooper friend's house to see if I can do any good."

"The next bus doesn't leave until six in the morning," Laura said to Jack.

Deputy Williams walked past Laura and into the kitchen to make his call.

"Carrie's going to stay here for the weekend," Jack told Laura. "We're going to run into town in a minute and get her things."

"I think I'll stay here," Laura said.

"Wouldn't you rather be with us?" Carrie asked.

"No way," Laura replied. "You guys might run into our friend again. At least here, I'm safe." She looked at Jack. "Just show me where the guns are kept and lock the doors when you leave."

"Sure," Jack agreed. Then he got his coat and put on some shoes.

Deputy Williams emerged from the kitchen. "I got my friend's wife. She says he'll be home by nine o'clock. I think I'll head home first, then go over there in an hour or so."

"Okay," Jack said. "Give us a call if you find out anything important."

"Sure," Ben agreed.

Jack thanked his new friend as he walked him to the door. Then he said goodbye to Laura as he and Carrie left for town.

After they had gone, Laura went through the house and made sure that all the doors and windows were locked.

Just in case.

6

1

The room was damp and cold. But Darius didn't notice. He had learned not only to tolerate darkness and cold, but to thrive in those elements. Candles were set about his room, and they cast a dim glow that did not penetrate the deepest corners. These corners remained dark and seemed to hide waiting spirits.

Darius wasn't the name his mother had given him—it was his Family name, and it was much stronger than "Dirk." That name, his original one, didn't seem like one that commanded respect. It sounded too much like "Jerk" or "Dork," which he had, of course, been called in his school days. Before The Thing happened. Before Saul's first kill.

Darius sat and stared again at the pale yet beautiful face of his Queen. She looked so restful to him. In life, she had never been so restful. Then she had been powerful. He could see hints of that power under the features that claimed to him that she was only sleeping. She was his sleeping beauty. But he could not wait one hundred years for his beauty to awaken. Tonight, it was again time to try the ceremony of the resurrection. Tonight, his followers would gather in the forest and recite the now-familiar chants and dance the familiar steps that would bring his Queen to life. Perhaps tonight was the night she would rise. He felt that this was so.

But he had felt this way before. There were times, most often just after the failure of these ceremonies, when Darius began to doubt his power. He wondered what had become of his former self. There were three who had originally been blessed with this ancient power, and

Darius had been blessed the least. Saul, his friend since childhood, a man now dead, had been wonderfully blessed. But the Queen had put Saul to death years ago, at the height of his glory. It was neither for haughtiness nor challenge that she had put Saul to rest. Saul had made plans to leave the Family and live in a foreign country. When he had performed his last task for the Family and was prepared to leave, the Queen struck him down. She had done this with much sorrow, but had done so at the request of Cole, the only man who had ever told her what to do since her empowerment. This man who controlled her had not been blessed by any measure of power, other than his influence over the three who had been blessed. In those days, Darius had seen Cole as a wonderful leader and had hung on his every word. Now as he looked back, Darius saw this man only as a power-hungry fool, a man who had controlled the three of them by default. It was Cole, not Regina, whom Darius blamed for the death of Saul. Cole had been present when the three had received their powers. In a way, he had been responsible for getting that power for them. But then he had taken them from their rightful youth and led them down the path that had ultimately meant destruction. They had seen him as their leader. But now, Darius knew this man had been a fool. Darius did have power, but his Queen had been the cornerstone of that power. She alone had controlled the destiny of the Family.

And then she had been killed.

At the height of her power and her purpose, she had been killed. The ceremony that would have brought them all the greatest and most pervasive power had been near its glorious climax when somehow it had all come to a sudden and horrible end. The Family had scattered. Only Darius remained. And when the time was right, he traveled to the remote graveyard where his Queen had been laid, and he retrieved her body.

Saul was dead. Cole had disappeared. But his Queen would return. Then she would be in control. Cole would not be there to control her. She would be an uncontrollable fury and she would reign without mercy. Then the former glory of the Family would rise again, and all would be made to tremble.

Darius pondered the years that had passed. He wondered again what would become of those years that remained. Many nights he dreamed of the return of his Queen. They were glorious dreams. In these dreams, she fulfilled his desires to be a part again of something great, something that transcended humanity, that soared above and looked down upon it. And he knew she would return. He hoped again that it would be tonight. But if not tonight, then soon. But if not soon, he would persist. She would return to him someday.

Darius walked to the large closet in the far corner of the room. It was dark there, but he knew where the important things were. He removed his black robe and looked it over. This robe had once belonged to his Queen. It would be hers again.

2

James Lorimar sat in another cold, dark room. A shackle surrounded his left ankle. A chain ran from the shackle to the wall, where it disappeared into a solid mass of stone. His left leg was numb. At first, it had just hurt from the gunshot wound. Then it tingled for several hours. Since yesterday evening, his whole leg had gone numb. By now he would have been reported missing. But nobody knew where to look. His wife would certainly have missed his call on the first night, though he was not always known to call in, and he didn't always stay at the hotel where he had made his reservations. He thought back to the way that Sharon had always hounded him about not being specific about his travel plans. It worried her when he was on the road, and she didn't know exactly where. But he had always liked to travel at his own pace, without a schedule, and without being accountable to anyone for his whereabouts, especially his wife. This time it had all backfired on him, just like Sharon had said it would someday. In the back of his muddled mind, he could hear his wife harping at him, "I told you so. I told you that you could get into trouble, and nobody would be able to find you."

If James was lucky, Sharon had reported him missing some time yesterday. Even so, she didn't know exactly what his schedule was. But his customers and his secretary did. But even with his schedule in hand, they would only be able to estimate his location within thousands of square miles. He knew that even if they found the place where he had last filled with gas, and they would know this from his last credit card charge, this would still give them an area that they could not cover by air in less than a week's time. He didn't think he would have that long.

He grabbed his numb leg again, hoping for some kind of sensation. There was none, and the leg felt oddly soft. As he felt along the leg, he heard a squeak, and something ran quickly across his hand. Then he found the place where the small rodent had been gnawing at him. He felt the small pit and the fluid that seeped from it. Then his stomach tightened, and he heaved nothing.

The numbness in his leg seemed to cover a larger area now than it had since that morning. And there was a bad smell that frightened him even more. His stomach felt tight. His captors had left him a bucket that contained putrid water, but there had been no food since his capture two days earlier. Since then, he had heard many strange sounds and seen glimpses of faces through the partially open door. Last night he thought he had heard the squealing of pigs. Every so often, the same face would appear at his door, as if checking to see if he was still alive. But inside his room, it was completely dark. He could not be seen. He could not even see himself. And until now, he hadn't even been aware that part of him was being eaten.

The thought again made him retch, and he held his stomach tightly as he shivered. Sweat beaded on his forehead, and at that moment, he decided that his chances of surviving were poor at best.

3

Laura looked at the clock again. Carrie and Jack had been gone an hour already. It seemed longer than that. She wondered why they weren't back yet then remembered that the trip to Tyler was about twenty minutes each way.

She sat on the couch, facing the big window that looked out into the front yard of her uncle's house. She had drawn the curtains because it made her feel more secure. Normally, she would have been walking around the house, exploring the closets and cupboards while the stereo blasted. But the house was silent except for the ticking of the big grandfather clock. Laura simply sat and stared in the direction of the big window. In her hands, she held a small-caliber pistol that she had dug out of a drawer in her uncle's gun cabinet. She wasn't sure exactly how to use it, but she felt safer holding it in her hands.

The ticking of the big clock seemed to make the wait even longer. She looked around the big living room at the items that decorated it. She recognized many of the more solid-looking older pieces from years ago when they had belonged to her grandparents. They bore fond memories. With the memories came the smells of freshly cooked bread and the images of Papaw playing silly games and always teasing.

Laura was seven years old when her mother moved to Kansas City. Laura had only seen her Papaw three times since then, the last when she was still only eleven. He died when she was sixteen. She felt a loss more for the man she had never really known than for the one she had. Her grandmother died when she was thirteen. She'd had no other grandparents. Her father left when she was six, and her memories of him were muddied and distant.

She heard something. It was faint, but it sounded like a grinding sound, though one she didn't recognize. Her hand tightened around the gun as she turned to her left. She listened carefully, but the sound was gone. She sat very still, trying to hear more.

Then there was the sound of a latch being thrown and by the time she figured out what was happening, the window was open. Someone was coming for her. She could not see the window that had been opened, but she knew from the sounds that it had, and she knew that the intruder was inside the house. In an instant, she ran across the room for the front door. By the time she got the door unlocked, she could hear heavy footsteps rushing through the house. She could feel the panic as it tightened around her throat. Her head felt hot, and it seemed to tingle.

She threw the door open and ran out of the house, pulling the door shut behind her. She ran wildly, heading first toward the barn, then deciding she would have a better chance if she headed for the highway. Jack's truck was parked in the driveway, and she headed for it, praying that the keys would be inside.

As she got about halfway to the truck, she heard the door of the house as it came open. She looked over her shoulder to catch a glimpse of her pursuer. The image did not surprise her, but it did terrify her. It was the tall thin man. He looked quickly around the yard before spotting her. She couldn't help but notice that he was smiling.

Then she remembered that she had a gun. She turned quickly and pointed it at the man, who was still about sixty feet away. As she faced him, she saw that he had no weapon, and she watched as his eyes widened and he tried to turn and go back to the house. The grass was too slippery, however, and he slid to the ground with an "ugh" escaping from his mouth on impact.

Laura pulled the trigger. The hammer rose and fell on an empty chamber. She knew that the gun was loaded—she had seen the bullets inside the magazine that had only been partially inserted when she first picked the gun up. But the gun was not firing, and she did not know that she had to pull back on the top part of the gun in order to slide the first bullet into the chamber. Instead, she kept pulling the trigger of the double-action semiautomatic weapon, which refused to fire for her.

The man got to his feet and made it back into the house. Laura decided to keep the gun, since it was better than nothing. But the man had heard the clicking sounds, and he knew that the gun was no longer a threat. Instead of coming back out the front door, he waited. He listened as Laura got into the truck. He had pulled the main wire off the distributor cap before entering the house, and knew that once she was inside the truck, he would have her.

Laura ran the rest of the way to the truck and looked into the window. The keys were in the ignition. She felt a load lift from her shoulders as she opened the passenger side door and jumped inside, pulling it shut behind her. She slid over to the driver side and turned the key. As the engine turned over, the tall thin man appeared again. She reached quickly to her left and fumbled around before locating the power lock. She flipped it down, but it was too late. The engine continued to turn, but it wasn't starting. She held the key in place and watched as the man threw the door open. She hoped that the truck would start, and she would be able to pull away in time.

But then she knew it was too late and she let go of the key to pick up the gun again. She pointed it at the man's head, but this time, he didn't even flinch. Instead, he lunged and grabbed the gun and her hand. She screamed out as he did this and she tried to pull away, but the man had a strong grip, and she could not pull free.

"You silly bitch," he said to her as he pulled at the gun. "You may fool me once, but you'll never fool me twice."

With that, he yanked the gun from her hand, twisting her finger in the trigger guard as he did. The pain ran up her finger and into her hand as she pulled it free. Then she turned to open the door and get out of the driver side. First, she forgot it was locked, then she popped the lock upward and pushed the door open. As she did this, the tall thin man pulled back the slide on the little pistol and popped a bullet into the chamber. Laura heard this sound and knew that the gun had now become lethal. She waited for the man's hand to wrap around her leg or neck as she leaned to get out of the truck. But he did not. Instead, he waited until she was out of the truck before firing a shot into her back.

The bullet hit high and right, piercing the skin and tearing through the muscles around her shoulder blade. The impact threw her off balance and she fell forward onto the asphalt, catching herself with her right hand as she fell. When her hand hit the ground, the pain in her back grew and spread to her side and her chest. She felt a burning inside, and it was hard to breathe.

She got back up and ran for the corner of the house away from the man and the truck. Her sudden movement surprised the man, and he could not get a clear shot until she was away from the truck. He fired again as she rounded the corner of the house, and she felt another burning sensation, this time in her left calf.

She stumbled again, but this time she didn't fall. Her adrenaline kept her mind off the wounds that should have had her lying on the ground unconscious but instead urged her to flee. She ran up the side of the house, looking for a place to get away from the man who was now armed, and no doubt in pursuit. She heard another shot as she ran through the freshly turned soil of a flower bed and under the cover of the back porch. She tried the back door, but it was locked. She had locked it. She cursed herself. The man was approaching again—she could hear his steps as he came down the walkway toward the covered porch. Then she found the reason that the dirt in the flower bed had looked so fresh leaning against the side of the house.

As the man appeared around the corner of the porch, she swung the rake, hitting him squarely in the face. He hadn't even seen it coming and the sharp tines tore into his cheek, the top of his nose, and his right eye. The man fired a shot as he fell back, but it missed Laura by several feet. The bullet exploded a small hanging pot. A pound of dirt and a small ivy plant showered Laura's back. The man held the gun in front of him as he lay on the ground, figuring that the girl would come after him with the rake. He held his left hand to his wounded eye and felt the blood running through his fingers. The pain was terrible, but he kept his left eye open and looking ahead.

Laura started around the small post that marked the corner of the porch, but then she saw that he still had the gun and she ducked back. As she did, he fired another shot that missed her head by inches. She heard the bullet whiz by her right ear as she pulled herself back. Then she heard the sounds of the tall man as he scrambled to get up. The burning in her chest grew, but she did not put down the rake, and she knew she could not run now. It was too far to the other side of the porch, and her leg was beginning to throb with pain. Instead, she stayed just around the corner of the porch, the rake held firmly in her hands.

Then the man appeared again. This time he knew where she would be, and he aimed the gun at her and fired.

But the slide was open. The last bullet had not gone all the way into the chamber, and the slide had jammed halfway. Had he looked down at the gun for a second, he would have seen it. But he had been too intent on getting the girl, and the pain and the blood pouring from his eye had distracted him.

A second after the gun refused to fire, the rake came down once again, this time hitting him mostly on the forehead. The last prong on the right grazed his remaining eye, blinding him momentarily. He tried to back away from Laura, but he ran into the corner post as he did, and Laura advanced on him, hitting him on the top of the head. He heard the loud ringing and felt the blackness of unconsciousness creeping in. He tried to fight it off, but then there was another impact. He wasn't sure exactly where it was, but his jawbone sent a shock wave through his skull that sent him to the ground, out cold.

Laura watched as the bloodied and blinded man stumbled back away from her and fell to the ground. She wondered if she had killed him. Then she decided that she should make sure.

As she approached the body, she began to cough. The attack was sudden and violent. The coughing sent tremendous pain through her chest and her right shoulder, and she dropped the rake. She felt the warm wetness on her chin and reached up to wipe it off. Her hand came away covered with blood, and the coughing began again.

Then the pain seemed to explode in her chest, and she fell backward to the concrete of the porch, her back against the corner post. The pain seemed to radiate from her chest and cover the entire upper portion of her body. The violent coughing returned, and it was becoming difficult to breathe. The hole that had been torn in the top of her right lung grew larger as she moved, torn open by the bone fragments that had come from her scapula. The blood from the torn muscle and her punctured liver flowed into the open hole, filling her lung.

She slid down off the post and onto the concrete porch and spat up more blood, her body trying desperately to clear out the wounded lung. Then she was unable to breathe in and the coughing was replaced by spasms. Her chest heaved and contracted, and blood continued to flow from her mouth,

The world around her seemed unreal now. The pain faded slowly and was replaced by images of colorful lightning from her oxygen-starved brain.

Finally, all the pain left, and she felt herself slipping off into the final, most painless state.

7

1

Carrie and Jack loaded the last box into Carrie's car. The sun had disappeared, and the sky was streaked with purple and gold. Under different circumstances, it might have been romantic. Under the current circumstances, it was frightening. It would be dark soon. And with the dark came the fears of what the night might hold. These fears were strong in Carrie, but they pulled at Jack too.

Carrie decided on getting a few more things than she had originally planned. As they had driven to her house, she'd begun to think that it might be wise to gather enough things for a stay that could go beyond just the weekend. There was no telling what they might dig up in the next two days. If it was anything like what she had experienced with Laura, then she wouldn't want to be spending any time alone at her place. She had been alone for several months now. For a moment, she wished she hadn't broken up with Jeff at the end of summer. But then she remembered all the reasons that she had, and that wish quickly dissipated.

She hardly knew Jack, but already she trusted him. She supposed part of the reason she did was that she needed somebody to trust right now. But there was more. Jack struck her as an honest man, one who might be honest to a fault, His smile seemed genuine, and he didn't talk down to her like most men did. It seemed as if most men felt that since she was beautiful, she must also be stupid. And he did not stare. When he spoke with her, his eyes looked into hers, but they did not crawl all over her body. She had gotten so used to the latter that at first, she thought that Jack simply did not find her attractive. But after spending just a short time with the man, she realized it was because he respected her. This impressed her tremendously. So, she trusted him, perhaps more than she should, but if there was any time to take such a chance, it was now.

"I think we've got more in your car than we left in the apartment," Jack said with a smile.

"I'm sorry," Carrie replied. "I didn't mean to bring so much stuff."

"I wasn't complaining," Jack said quickly. "It just reminds me of how my mother used to pack when we were going to my great uncle's for a week. She took practically everything we owned, including her favorite rocking chair. We had to take two vehicles just for four people because of all of the stuff Mom had to bring."

Carrie smiled at the story, then got into her car.

Then she remembered that Laura was back at Jack's house, and that they had been away longer than they had told her they would be. "I ought to call Laura before we go," she said, "just to let her know we're okay."

"Okay with me," Jack agreed. "Do you want to go back in, or use a payphone on the way back?"

"I'd rather go ahead and call from here. I'll bet she's worried crazy. I should have thought of this sooner."

Jack got out of the car to follow Carrie inside.

"I'll only be a minute," she said. "I'll be okay. You stay here and watch the stuff."

"You sure?" Jack's eyes showed his genuine concern, his hope that she wasn't just trying to prove that she was brave.

"Positive," she answered. "Just tell me your phone number and stay in the car. If I'm not out in five minutes, come in with your guns-a-blazin'."

Jack grinned at Carrie's poke at his lifestyle and got back into the car after telling her his phone number. He watched her until she disappeared around the side of the building, then he looked around the parking lot again to see if anyone was watching, or if there were any suspicious-looking vehicles. There was an old black van with no windows and Oklahoma tags parked near the end of the row across from him, but it had been there when they arrived. Still, he would keep an eye out to see if it followed them.

A few minutes later, Carrie came back to the car. Jack could see the look of deep concern on her face as she opened her door and got in.

"Trouble?" Jack asked.

"No answer."

"Are you sure you dialed the number right?"

"I tried twice to make sure. She's not answering."

Carrie started the car. As she backed out of the driveway, Jack offered some explanations to ease her worries. But though he was usually upbeat, the look on his face betrayed that he feared the worst.

2

"How the fuck could you let him get in this shape!"

The garbled voice broke James out of his semi-conscious state of shock. A light that seemed brighter than any he had ever seen washed over his body and his face. In reality, it was just a flashlight. But James's eyes had been in almost total darkness for two days.

"The rats have even been eating on him, you stupid shit!" The voice was deep and gravelly. Even so, it seemed as if the man to whom the voice belonged was almost whining, as if afraid of what this meant.

"How'm I spose to know the rats are eatin' him, man? The rats never ate on nobody before."

James lay propped against a cold stone wall. His pants were wet with blood, pus, rot, and urine. All feeling seemed to stop just below his waist. At the point where it disappeared into numbness, there was a line of excruciating pain. This line of pain had slowly worked its way up his leg and now circled the base of his pelvis.

"I'm going to have to talk to Darius about this, and you better well hope he doesn't come down here personally and rip your fuckin' head off." The man talking sounded as if he might be more worried about what was going to happen to *him* when Darius found out.

Then the door slid most of the way closed.

It was silent again, except for the hurried breathing of the man who was left with him.

He wanted to speak, wanted to talk to this man. Maybe he could offer him money. Maybe he could offer him escape from the wrath of Darius. Maybe he could simply find out why they had done this to him, or what was going to happen to him.

But he could do none of these things. He wanted to speak but could only moan.

The light backed away from him some. The moaning sounds frightened the man. As he backed away, he flashed his light across the rotting body of James Lorimar one more time, as if to make sure it had not gotten loose from its chains and decided to come after him.

"Oh, Jesus. Oh, shit."

It was a really awful mess.

3

Deputy Ben Williams sat in a small two-bedroom house belonging to his longtime friend, State Trooper Budd Holloway. Ben had known Budd since the sixth grade. For a few years in high school, they had run in the same crowd. Budd was a good guy.

Budd sat across from him, holding a can of Miller Lite in his big left hand. Budd drank a lot of beer, and he had the gut to prove it.

"You fellas want another burger?" Jayne Holloway called from the kitchen. In the background, the grease snapped and popped as another half-pound of ground beef was dropped into it. The sound and the smells were comforting to Ben, reminding him of Friday nights at home when Mom had made hamburgers for him. Apparently, Jayne knew that Budd would want another one. The question was really intended for Ben.

"I think I'll be fine, Jayne," Ben called back. Despite his answer, he heard another burger drop. Apparently, the question had been rhetorical.

Budd leaned forward. A silent burp that smelled of digesting beef escaped as he did. "So, you think this thing that Jacobson's on is related to that big cult in New Orleans from a few years back?"

"I have to admit, that's been in the back of my mind ever since I saw the first mess those people left." Ben shifted. "Just the way things were cut up and thrown around. The things I saw remind me of some of the stories I've heard."

"These cults probably all act pretty much the same," Budd observed.

"I talked to a couple of people tonight who know more about this."

"How?"

"I met a young girl who was part of the cult for a while."

"Have you told Jacobson yet?" Budd asked.

"I just heard it all a few hours ago. You're the first person I've talked to. I wanted your opinion."

"Why?"

Ben paused, wondering how his friend might take what he was about to say. "Because I think Jacobson might be dirty."

Budd leaned back and took a drink of his beer. "Shit, Ben, you sound like one of those conspiracy nuts. You've been listening to too much of that AM radio crap."

"I don't trust the man."

"You don't trust him 'cause he's a fuckin' Yankee. He talks through his nose, and he only washes his hair twice a week. From what I hear, he's a pretty sharp detective despite the poor hygiene."

"So, why hasn't he gotten anywhere on this thing?"

"Christ, Ben, the guy they had working on this the first time around couldn't get anywhere with it. Sometimes these investigations take time, you know that."

They paused as Jayne brought in two big hamburgers. Steam rose from the hot patties and drifted slowly from the plate.

"Thanks, Jayne," Ben offered. Budd's burger was already on the way to his mouth.

"You bet," she answered. "You let me know when you're ready for another one."

"This is one too many already." He turned to Budd, who was eagerly consuming the first half of his burger. "No wonder you've put on fifty pounds since high school."

"Shefenty," Budd muffled through his food.

Ben ate slowly, his mind more on the discussion than the food. "This girl I spoke with," he said, "she says that they're sacrificing people."

A piece of Budd's burger went down wrong, and he started coughing. The piece came free, and he swallowed hard, his eyes a little wider. "She saw this?"

"No, but she's pretty sure."

"Pretty sure isn't enough for charges like that," Budd argued.

"And she described a man to me who sounds a lot like Jacobson."

"Coincidence."

"Limp and all," Ben said.

"Jacobson's not the only man with a limp."

"And the cigarettes."

Budd put down the small piece of his burger that remained. "Look, man, I don't doubt you or anything. I just don't think that they're sacrificing people up there. I think what we have is some oddball cult made up of a bunch of brainless fools who kill people's pets and give their money to some head weirdo. I think you should call Jacobson from here and tell him what you know, and he'll have the thing solved by tomorrow morning. Did this girl you talked to tell you where this place was?"

"Yes."

"Good." Budd picked up the phone on the small table and handed it to Ben. "Give Jacobson a call now and forget it. He'll be grateful to you, and you'll get brownie points." He paused and looked longingly at Ben's food. "You gonna eat that?"

Ben nodded no and took the phone from Budd. As Budd consumed the remnants of Ben's burger, Ben put the phone down. It was going to take too much time and effort to convince Budd of anything.

"Look, Budd, I just need a little time on this. I want to make sure it's as simple as all that before I pass any information on."

"It's *your* ass," Budd explained.

"They're not gonna know I found any of this out until I tell them."

"You're probably right, but you're being stupid. If I were in your department, I'd be calling the sheriff as soon as you left here."

"But you're not in my department."

"Right," Budd answered, then slammed down the rest of Ben's burger.

"So, you're not gonna call."

"You fellas want some more?" came a voice from the kitchen. This time, there was no sound of popping grease.

"No thanks, Jayne," Ben called back. "It was great." He looked at Budd. "You won't say anything, right?"

"Hey," Budd said, "you're county, I'm state. You do what you want. I'll get worried when we get involved. If it all stays in Smith County, whatever you do is up to you. But if this shit starts bleeding over, I'm going straight to the sheriff."

"It'll be taken care of before that happens," Ben assured him. But he wasn't so sure this was true.

They sat in a silent room now. Ben debated telling Budd more. Budd didn't seem interested. "This girl says that they're worshiping some dead girl's body up there, and these sacrifices are meant to bring her back to life."

"And you believe her?" Budd asked.

"She says she's seen the body," he lied, hoping to get more from Budd.

"I'd say you've got a fairly unreliable source, Ben. You'd better cover yourself good on this one."

It looked like Budd didn't have any more to give. It was time to give up.

"I've got to get going," Ben said as he stood.

"Stay and watch the game if you like?"

"I've got some things to take care of," Ben replied.

"Hell, it's almost ten o'clock. You're gonna work yourself into the ground, just like you did in high school," Budd commented.

"I'm going to be sheriff someday, remember?"

They both smiled and remembered his jokes about being sheriff from their high school days. Ben had always been the straight one.

They walked to the door together. "Just tell me something," Budd said.

"Shoot."

"Who is this girl you spoke with?"

"Just a kid from town. Nobody in particular."

"What I thought," Budd mumbled.

Ben punched his friend on the shoulder. "If I come back here in serious trouble, I expect a little more cooperation from you."

"Of course," Budd said, extending his hand. "You can count on me, bud."

"You're Budd," Ben said as he shook his friend's hand. Another joke from high school, an old and worn-out one.

After Deputy Ben Williams left Budd Holloway's house, Budd went back into the small living room and called to his wife to please bring him another beer.

He chuckled to himself about his friend's wild imagination.

He would have no idea how much trouble he was getting Ben into when he mentioned the discussion to his partner the next morning.

4

Darius looked in wonder at the man lying on the table in front of him. Slim Tom was a good soldier, his finest and most trusted. The man looked awful. Dried blood covered his face. His right eye was shut and swollen; a white fluid still seeped from it. Part of one of his teeth showed through the flesh just below his lip where it had torn through.

Slim Tom had called from a phone booth in Lindale. He had made it that far on his own, then realized he could not come the rest of the way. Darius had sent two men after him and had called for the doctor. Doctor Fleming had been at home, tending to his garden when he got the call. Now he was on his way, and he would arrive soon.

Darius stood and looked. He had already been moved to extreme anger once this night when he'd learned the condition of the man who was to be the sacrifice. He could see places on Slim Tom's face and head where something had pierced the skin and torn the flesh. There was one spot in particular that worried him. It was a deep indentation into the forehead, just beside his temple.

"Are you sure he didn't say anything about the girl?" Darius asked the man closer to him.

"He wasn't saying anything that made sense when we found him, and he went unconscious after we got him into the car."

"But he was talking when you found him?"

"He was muttering."

"What was he muttering?" Darius asked.

The man started shifting on his feet. "I couldn't tell."

"Didn't you think that it might be important?" Darius asked. "Didn't you think that you should listen closely, that he might have something important to say?"

"I was in a hurry to get him here, Darius." The man grew noticeably shorter.

Darius looked back at the man lying on the table. His best soldier. Then he reached inside his oversized shirt and grabbed onto the pearl handle of his prized knife. In one quick motion, he slid the knife out of its sheath and pulled it through the air. It looked as if he was making no effort at all, moving the knife quickly as if he were swatting a fly. The man standing next to him took a step back, fearful of what retribution lay there. But then it was done. The silvery blade hummed as it cut effortlessly through flesh and bone. The man went down, blood pouring from his torn body. It happened too fast for him to scream. His guts parted with his stomach and poured out onto the floor as he fell back. A moment later, the knife was back inside the sheath. Darius had never taken his eyes off the man lying on the table.

"If he dies," Darius said, still looking at the man lying on the table, but speaking to the one across from him, "so do you."

The man standing across the table said nothing but a short prayer that Slim Tom would live.

5

Carrie kept a watch on the rearview mirror as she drove. It was dark now, and there were no headlights following. They had taken the most direct route driving along the loop until they came to State Highway 110. Now they had been on the highway for almost twenty minutes and Carrie could tell they were almost to Jack's place. She had been anxious the whole time, and there hadn't been much conversation. Now as they drew closer to Jack's, her face showed a measurable amount of tension. Jack could see this, and he stayed quiet. There wasn't much he could say to calm her down. The only thing that would calm her down was getting to his place and finding that Laura had indeed been outside or had run to the store. Jack's face showed no tension, but it was there.

Finally, they got to Jack's driveway. It didn't look right. As they approached the house, Carrie noticed that there were no lights on inside the home. In Laura's state of mind, she probably would have turned on every light inside and outside the house. But even the outside light was not on. And Jack's truck was not gone. Jack could see as they approached that the doors of his pickup were open; the driver side was wide-open. The first picture that came to Jack's mind was one of somebody in a hurry to get out of it.

"I don't like this," Carrie said.

"Me neither. Stop here." They were still about thirty yards from the garage door. "Did you notice any cars parked back along the highway?"

"No, but I wasn't really looking."

Jack looked around the yard. It was dark, but he could see unfamiliar shapes. "I'm going to go into the house and see if Laura's okay."

"What if she's not?"

Jack didn't answer. Instead, he opened his door and got out. "Keep the engine running, and the doors locked. Keep an eye on the front door for trouble."

"Okay." The dome light inside the car revealed the fear that had crept into her brown eyes.

Jack walked first to his pickup. He walked to the driver's side, his eyes and ears keen to his surroundings. When he got there, he noticed that the keys were in the ignition. What had happened here? It was very puzzling. He reached behind the seat and felt around for the leather pouch that held a twenty-two pistol he used mostly for shooting snakes and skunks. It wasn't much as pistols go, but it was better than walking into the house completely unarmed. He armed himself and walked around the truck to the front door. When he got there, he saw that it too was not completely closed. Something was very wrong. At that moment, he knew that when he opened the door, he was going to find a terrible, bloody mess in his living room. He pushed the door open, his gun held in front of him. The door revealed a dark and empty entryway. He reached in and turned on the lights. The house was silent.

"Laura!" he called out. There was no response. He stuck his head inside the house and looked into the living room. There was no blood. There were no signs of a struggle. Nothing seemed to be out of place. He called out to Laura again, but again got no response. Had someone come and taken her back to the compound, or had they just killed her? Was she alive thirty miles away, or was she lying dead somewhere nearby?

He walked carefully through the house. Everything seemed to be in order. Then he saw the curtains in the back corner of the utility room fluttering. Laura wouldn't have left any windows open. Jack walked to the window and pulled back the curtains. When he pulled the window shut, he saw the neat circular hole that had been cut at the top of the lower section of the glass, just an inch under the latch mechanism.

Somebody had come in here. Something had definitely happened. But what? And where was Laura now?

Jack inspected the rest of the house. Apparently, they had come and taken her away, and they had done so quickly and quietly. When he finished looking the house over, he walked outside.

As he walked down the driveway, a reflection on the ground caught his eye. He backed up and bent over, picking up the small shiny object. He looked at it carefully. It was an empty brass casing from a .380 automatic. Was it his? That he couldn't tell. It looked like the casings he used for his reloads, but they were common. He looked around the ground for another but saw none.

He walked around the truck, inspecting the ground for more evidence of what had happened. He saw no more shell casings, but as he walked back toward the driver side of the truck, he saw something that had been concealed previously by the darkness. About ten yards from the truck, close to the corner of the house, there was blood. It wasn't much, but it didn't have to be. He walked over to the spot and inspected the ground around it. At first, he couldn't find anything else. Then he saw another spot of blood. It was at the edge of the sidewalk that led around the corner of the house to the back yard. The sidewalk disappeared into the darkness.

Jack began to worry about what lay in the darkness. Maybe the casing was from his gun, and the intruder was lying dead in the back yard. But it was the intruder's car that was gone, not his truck. He walked down the sidewalk into the darkness. He could no longer make out the trail of blood. He walked quietly along the sidewalk, looking into the darkness before him that was broken only dimly by the light being cast into the driveway.

He walked along the sidewalk to the back porch. When he arrived there, he saw the body. It was leaned up against a corner post, the head rolled forward to its chest.

"Oh, no," was all he said. He stepped over the garden rake and stepped onto the porch. Then he squatted and lifted Laura's head with his hand and looked into her dead eyes. Even in the darkness, he could see the blood now. There was a lot of it. It covered the concrete of the porch, and Laura was sitting in a dried patch of it that spread from where she sat.

Jack took a deep breath and looked up and around.

What was he going to tell his sister?

It was his fault. He shouldn't have been so sure that she would be safe here. He should have insisted that she come along. How could he have been so damn confident? Of course they knew where he lived. But how had they known Laura was here?

The questions and the guilt flowed through his mind as he looked again at the lifeless face of his niece.

Then he closed his eyes, and a tear ran down his rugged face.

He let her head return to its resting place as he ran his big hand across his eyes and stood up. He looked at her one last time. He would call the police soon. From a payphone. Anonymously.

He headed back to the car, where Carrie was waiting nervously.

They couldn't stay here. Jack would have to gather some things and lock up the house. But where could they go?

They could go to Lake Tyler and stay at the cabin that he and his father had built almost twenty-five years ago. He decided that would probably be best for now. A hotel just wouldn't do. There was no telling who might be watching for them. At least at the cabin, they would be safe.

But then he had also thought that Laura would be safe at his home.

As he approached the car, he tried to think of how he was going to tell Carrie about what had happened, and what they would have to do.

But as he stepped into the beams of the car's headlights, she could see his face fairly well, and it told her everything.

6

As midnight approached, Darius prepared himself for the ceremonies.

It was difficult. Too many things had gone badly today. The man who was to be the sacrifice was rotten and barely alive. Would this be acceptable? He didn't know but could think of no alternative. If he had not been so hasty, he could have used Butch, the man he had run his knife through, for tonight. Members of the Family were only used for this purpose if they volunteered or if they were being kicked out. If he had not lost his temper, they would have had a good sacrifice in Butch. Instead, they had a rotting and barely conscious body.

And then there was Slim Tom. That, too, was on his mind.

It was truly difficult to prepare. If he'd had one more night, it would have been much better. But this was the best night for a long time. Tonight, everything would be right—the moon, the stars, everything. It wouldn't be perfect, that only happened once every 121 years. But it would be a good night, better by a great magnitude than the night before, or the one to come.

So, he sat on the floor of his room, facing the encased and preserved body of his Queen. He closed his eyes and again tried to concentrate.

7

The Family gathered around the altar that had been constructed just that afternoon. Trees from the land on which the complex rested had been used to build the altar. The wood was still green, but the piney sap that flowed down the sides of the legs would ignite and burn like so much napalm.

Tonight it was a very large gathering. There were over a hundred people. In the crowd stood the doctor who had repaired Slim Tom, the nervous man who had seen his friend die earlier in the day, the strange girl who was sometimes Darius's bed mate, and Detective Todd Jacobson who was supposed to be bringing the operation down. There were also two lawyers, six salesmen, and a boy who worked at one of Tyler's newspapers. There were two hairdressers, one a pretty woman, the other a gay young man. There were also five warehouse employees, a couple of city and county officials, a couple of grocery checkout clerks, four bums, a florist, and a Baptist minister. Tonight they were all here for the ceremonies of the resurrection. There were countless others who serviced the Family but were not members. These were the people who accepted the money of the Family to further their cause, or those who volunteered their time or money. In the past four months, the number of people involved either directly or indirectly with the Family had grown by five times. But the past few weeks had seen little growth. The size of the Family was just right. A balance had been reached. This made Darius believe even more that the time was at hand.

The members stood in a crowded semicircle, three people deep, around the wooden altar. Each wore a red robe and held a lighted red candle. It was a black night with only the outline of a moon overhead. The stars seemed to go on forever. A cold breeze was coming in from the north, and on the horizon could be seen flashes of lightning from a storm that was pummeling Sulphur Springs, forty-six miles to the north. But overhead there was nothing but stars and the silhouette of the moon.

One of the members of the ceremonial group began a chant they had all chanted before. It was time to begin.

The rest of the members joined in. All eyes trained with anticipation on the blackness that came from the forest just beyond the altar. The chant continued as in the darkness the men prepared.

Five minutes into the chant, Darius appeared from the darkness to the right of the stage holding a brass spike. Tonight, he would draw the shapes himself. Misty stood close to the altar, watching. Darius wore the long black ceremonial robe that had belonged to his Queen. Nothing more. He walked to the ground in front of the altar and drew a shape into the ground, at which point the members of the Family increased the volume of the chant. The shape he drew was one that had come to him both from memory and from inspiration. He remembered the days when his Queen had drawn these same shapes, though until now he could not remember everything that made them up. In the early days, their leader, Cole, had shown them the shapes that he had found in old books. But his Queen had changed those shapes, corrected and enhanced them somehow, from some unknown source. Darius had known they were right. Now this same source gave him the final answers to the elusive puzzle, and he knew the shapes were complete,

He stood and walked to the side of the altar. He placed the spike upon it. Though the altar was built from the woods around them, the construction was solid, solid enough to support a couple of people.

Six robed and hooded figures appeared from the woods. On their shoulders, they carried a large black wooden box shaped like a coffin. In reality, it was not a coffin, but just a temporary holding place for his Queen. A resting place, but not a bed of death.

The figures carried the large box to a place in front of the altar and laid it on the ground, on top of the drawings that Darius had made. His Queen was visible behind a glass lid. She did not look restful. Her preserved features showed remnants of the turmoil of the final few seconds of her previous life. Her skin looked pale and plastic, but the man who had seen to her preservation had done an excellent job. Certainly, she would be pleased.

Then the wind came. It was a cool wind that preceded the cold front that was coming down from the north and was now dropping hailstones the size of golf balls on Como and Pickton. The breeze bent the flames of the candles to the south. And the breeze carried more than just cold air. It also carried a precursor to something ancient, something that had been at rest these past few years. In the breeze was the force of power that had left his Queen many years ago and fled toward the heavens. He had seen it as it flew upward, as he lay bleeding from a gunshot wound. Now, as it returned, the force inside him helped him to recognize it and he felt the joy of what it meant.

Then Darius screamed out and the Family fell silent. His scream pierced their ears and raced through the woods. It brought a feeling of power to each member of the Family, and a feeling of dread to any human or creature within a hundred miles. An owl that had been observing the curious proceedings from a tree on the north side of the clearing flew over the clearing, heading southward, fleeing the instinctive fear that something huge and awful was in pursuit.

To the north, the line of clouds marched southward. Then suddenly, the whole line illuminated as if one gigantic flash of lightning had exploded within every cloud. Then the ground shook. It was as if a ten-thousand-pound weight had been dropped on the forest floor, just to the north of the clearing, only it was felt for miles in every direction.

Now the storm raged over Yantis, Texas. The sky to the north had become one-third storm, two-thirds stars. The line of clouds approached in an almost perfectly straight line. To the north of that line, the temperature was twenty degrees lower than it was at the site of the ceremonies. A tornado watch had been posted for all of Smith and the surrounding counties. The dead moon was almost directly overhead.

After Darius's scream, he raised his arms toward the stars and began a chant of his own. The words were some German, some Romanian, mostly Latin. He did not know the true meaning of the words, but still, he knew the concepts behind them. Like the drawings, the words had not all been in place before tonight. Each time he had performed the chant, it had gotten longer and more complete. Where before there had been blank places, tonight there were none. He was remembering something he had heard only once in its entirety. Even so, the memory of the words came from some other place inside him, a place stirred by the approaching power.

There was another tremendous shaking of the earth, only this time it seemed much closer. A moment later, there was another, even closer. It was as if some enormous unseen beast were walking through the woods toward them, shaking the earth with its tremendous weight.

Darius paused and picked up the brass spike from the altar before him. He pressed the spike against his wrist until a drop of blood emerged from his flesh. Then he ran the spike up his arm, through years of scar tissue that lay as reminders of previous ceremonies. The blood flowed down his arm and began to drip onto the ground. His eyes returned to the skies as he held the spike out from his body. Blood dripped steadily from his left arm to the ground as he called out once again to the ancient spirits that he knew were nearby.

Another shaking of the ground.

The line of clouds drew slowly closer.

It was magic, he could feel it. So could each member of the Family. It had always been magical, but never like this. The air was full of tangible electricity. A few were fearful. They would die. Most were entranced, staring ahead at the black box and their Queen within.

Out of the darkness emerged two men carrying a cot. On the cot lay the white-robed body of James Lorimar. He was semiconscious and moaning. He had not been sedated. The doctor had recommended against it since the man was probably too close to death already. A dead sacrifice would have been useless. Instead, he was carried to the altar and placed upon it in his delirious state. Then the two men who had carried him backed away from the altar, into the blackness.

All of the participants could now hear the thunder from the approaching storm. The wind that preceded it had become much colder.

As the two men brought James out on the cot, Darius took a chalice from under the altar and allowed the blood from his arm to flow into it while he continued his chant. The chalice was large, and it took a full two minutes for his blood to cover its bottom. But as the ceremonies proceeded it would fill with blood. He replaced the chalice under the altar and the man who was to be tonight's sacrifice was placed directly over it.

Then Darius looked down into the face of his Queen. Already he could see some mystical anticipation on her face. A robed and hooded figure came out from the shadows to assist in the ceremonies that remained. Darius walked to a place behind the altar, facing the crowd of entranced people. In his right hand, he now held the pearl-handled knife, which he held over the chest of the doomed man. The man who was assisting Darius leaned over the altar and opened the white robe, exposing the mostly nude body of their sacrifice. The only part of the body that was covered was most of his left leg. The leg had been wrapped in a bandage to conceal the rot and odor. It was only partially effective on the latter.

Darius chanted magical words for ten full minutes. As he did, the wind grew stronger and colder, and the shaking of the ground became more frequent and more intense. The knife he held in his hand began to hum.

Then he screamed out once more, and the Family joined in. As the scream came to an orgasmic climax, he plunged the knife downward, into the chest of the man on the altar.

The knife danced and moved almost independently of Darius's hand. When the knife had finished its work, there was a deep and gaping hole in the body. Darius reached quickly into that hole and pulled out the prize. In his hands, he held the still-beating heart. In that final instant of his life, James Lorimar was shaken to consciousness by the knowledge that something fatal had occurred. The last thing he saw was his own heart beating before him, its blood pumping out and into his opened chest.

The ground shook. This time, it was accompanied by the cracking and splintering sounds of trees being pulverized.

Darius removed the blood-filled chalice from underneath the dead man and walked back to the black resting case of his Queen. Its lid had been pulled open, and her ornamental robe pulled away from her chest. Now Darius stood before her, looking into the open hole that lay between her breasts. It was clean and dry, as it had been since it had first been prepared almost three years earlier. He kneeled and held the heart out before her, then he whispered to her in words that were of no language at all but were full of meaning.

He leaned slowly forward and placed the still-beating heart into his Queen. Then he poured the contents of the chalice into the open hole, filling it with his blood and the blood of the sacrifice. Then he disrobed and laid his naked body down on top of the cold and lifeless body of his Queen.

He stayed there while the Family chanted quietly. Overhead, the clouds finally blocked out the moon. There was a flash of light and a nearby explosion when a tree became stripped of its bark and torn to shreds by the electricity.

Darius could feel the opening in his Queen's chest as it began to close.

There was another explosion. The trees in the woods directly behind the Family parted, flying in all directions, leaving an odd-shaped depression where something very large and invisible had stepped.

Then an icy wind went through the members of the Family on its way to the altar, touching and dooming the soul of each and every one of them. Most of the entranced members merely shook as it passed through them, but three of them screamed out in terror before something inside them gave out.

Then Darius felt the electricity run through him. It paused briefly as if in recognition of the power that lay within him. It also paused to test that power, to kill if it was not recognized.

But it was recognized, and the electricity flowed through him and into the body beneath him.

Then a great streak of lightning reached down from the sky and set the altar ablaze. Darius was knocked off his Queen by the force, and her lid slammed shut, shattering the glass that covered it.

Steam rose from Darius's hot body as the cold air encircled him and his Queen.

Then the rain began to fall.

It was over.

As the rain fell, Darius rolled to his knees and crawled to the black case that had preserved his Queen for so many years. He looked in at the body that was now covered with the shattered pieces of glass. Her robe was still open, but there was no hole. Blood ran down from where the hole had been and down her side.

"My Queen?" he whispered. But nothing was happening.

The Family stood in darkness. Waiting.

"My Queen?" he whispered again.

The rain began to pour from the sky. The sap kept the altar burning and gave Darius the light by which to see.

But she did not move.

Blood ran down his wounded arm and mixed with the water that was gathering there.

Then her eyes flew open. For a moment, Darius saw nothing but terror on that most recently dead face.

Then she opened her mouth and began to scream.

8

1

Jack was up with the sun. His first instinct was to go out and check on his animals. But he couldn't do that today, since he wasn't home. Before leaving his house last night, he had asked Sam McCutchen to take care of things for him until he got back. Sam was his closest neighbor, and the man had accepted gladly, remembering the many times Jack's father had helped his own dad.

Jack got out of bed and saw a few wet places on the floor. It had been hard to sleep during the night for several reasons. First was Laura. She was dead. Jack had called his sister and told her last night from a pay phone near the lake. The phones at his house were dead, the wires having been been cut. The conversation was awful, as he had expected it would be. She seemed cold, almost indifferent. But that was Kay. The conversation didn't last long before she said she had to go. Jack knew why. She was going to cry, and she didn't want Jack to hear it. He would have to call her back today to discuss whatever details were involved in getting Laura's body to the place where Kay wanted it buried. Right now, it was in the hands of the county morgue, whom he had also called the previous night. They would hold the body for now.

Jack was sure that whoever had killed Laura had come to kill him and Carrie too. But if that was true, why hadn't the killer waited for them to arrive before breaking in? Or better yet, why hadn't he simply hidden Laura's body, cleaned up the mess, and waited for Jack and Carrie to come home? Perhaps that had been his plan. Perhaps something had happened that caused him to change his plans.

There was water on the floor. There had been a pretty vicious storm in the night, and the roof of the cabin wasn't in good repair. Jack hoped there were no major leaks. There had been a lot of rain, and some hail had pounded the roof vigorously. The skies rumbled all throughout the night. Jack could see out his window that though the lightning and thunder had passed, the rain continued to drizzle slowly out of the big gray mass overhead.

He put on a robe and walked to the hallway closet ,where the water heater sat. It wasn't on. There was no pilot light. Then he remembered that he would have to go to the big tank outside the bathroom window and turn the gas on before they would have any hot water, or gas for cooking.

"There's no hot water," came a voice. He jumped. "I'm sorry," Carrie said, "I didn't mean to startle you." She was walking out of the bathroom with her hair in a towel.

Jack was taken back by the image. She was wearing a long, silky robe that was tied around the waist. It hugged her hips and breasts slightly. He tried his best to keep his eyes trained on hers, and it was quite an effort. Her face was smooth, and her pouty lips now stood out even more. She had little or no makeup on, and still was stunning.

"No problem," Jack replied. "I just have to go turn on the gas and we'll have hot water. Sorry I didn't get to it sooner."

"That's okay, I needed a cold shower anyway." Carrie shook her hair vigorously inside the towel. The image was somehow erotic to Jack, though mostly somewhere in the back of his mind.

Jack closed the closet door. "I can't believe you took a shower in that cold water. You're more of a man than I am."

"I certainly hope not," Carrie said as she turned and walked back into the bathroom.

Jack had slept more deeply this morning than he realized. He hadn't even heard Carrie taking her shower.

***

By the time Carrie finished in the bathroom, Jack had the gas on. When she finished dressing, she came into the kitchen, where Jack was cooking on the gas stove. The smell of burning gas reminded her of her childhood visits to her grandmother's house, and an involuntary sigh escaped her.

"Did you find some eggs that you'd left from last summer?" she joked.

"Yep," Jack answered. "I figure all of the bad bacteria will be cooked out of them in another ten minutes or so."

Carrie saw that he really was cooking eggs, which he must have brought from the house. Then she asked where the coffee was and began cleaning out the coffee pot, which was sitting on the counter and had a lot of dust on it and a spider web inside. She walked to the sink and turned on the hot water. It wasn't hot yet, but it was warm enough for washing a coffeepot.

For a moment, it felt to Carrie as if she were playing out some wonderfully domestic scene from an old television program that had run in black and white in her childhood, except that Jack was doing the cooking. In that moment, she was with Jack, and they were happy, and there were no problems. Last night had been only a dream, and this was reality. After they cooked breakfast, they would go fishing, then perhaps make love under the pine trees, which had miraculously not left any sticky needles on the forest floor. It was like playing house, and she wished so much that it could be true.

But it was not. They were being chased now. Her life had gone from mundane to terrifying in a matter of days. Her sister had been slaughtered; Laura had been killed. Carrie had asked Jack how Laura had died, but he wouldn't say. Carrie's mind was then only capable of painting the most gruesome, awful scene. There were bad people, and bad cops, and no way to tell the good ones from the bad ones. She and Jack could only stay here for a little while, because the cops would no doubt be trying to locate them after finding Laura last night along with a conspicuous absence of the owner of the house. Maybe they would be stalled at first, thinking that Jack had been killed or carried off. But the dirty cops would know he had not, and they would push.

Less than a week ago, she had found herself near tears over a lost tube of lipstick. Of course, her period had been on its way then, but still the incident seemed even more ridiculous now. It was amazing how a little bit of trauma could put things into perspective. She wondered where she and Jack would go and what they would do. Most of all, she wondered if they would survive.

Jack reached over and touched Carrie's arm as she stood staring into the sink. She jumped and cried out as she flipped the coffee pot across the counter. It slid gracefully along the edge for a couple of feet before tumbling to the floor and exploding into a thousand tiny pieces and a few large chunks.

She looked at Jack, her eyes wild. She was shaking.

Jack knew what she was feeling. He felt it, too. It was an ominous sense of doom that underlay everything.

He stepped forward, crushing bits of glass under his slippers as he reached for her. Then he held her in his arms.

"We're going to be okay," he whispered to her. But she didn't answer. And he didn't really believe it.

2

Deputy Ben Williams called in sick. It was the first time in his eleven years on the force he had claimed an illness when there was none. It was lucky for him that he did, because Budd's careless chatter at the state troopers' station had alerted some of the wrong people, and they were looking for him.

But Ben didn't know this. When the two officers showed up at his door late that morning to speak with him, he was driving his old blue Mustang across a one-lane bridge in the northeast section of the county.

As he rounded the base of a hill, he could see the big compound in the distance. He brought the car to a stop. The road was narrow, and there wasn't any room for turning around. This made Ben nervous, especially since they could probably see him coming, if they were looking.

He surveyed the compound from a distance but could see nobody on the top or in front of it, though they could be observing him from the trees around the compound, or even from the inside of one of the big, dark openings that served as windows.

He cursed under his breath as he backed his car away from the compound and slowly over the narrow bridge. He couldn't just drive up. Instead, he was going to have to unload and walk from here.

When he got to what he thought of as the safe side of the river, he drove his car off the road. He drove past a large rock about a hundred and fifty feet off the road and parked the Mustang behind some brush that would do a pretty good job of hiding it. The car was blue, and it was a dark, cloudy day. It could rain at any minute, or the clouds could all simply pass by, saving the deluge for Louisiana. There was no way to tell what would happen in the skies, or on the ground for that matter.

As if to compound his uncertainty, the clouds emitted a soft rumble of thunder.

Ben grabbed the sack in the seat next to him and got out of the car. He set the sack on the hood of the car and took out the things he had brought for the day's work. He stuffed the snub-nosed .38 in the back of his belt. He liked a bigger gun, but he would need to be stealthy and quiet today, so he had left his favorite .357 magnum in the case in the back room of his house and had pulled his wife's smaller gun out of the nightstand on her side of the bed. He didn't bring any extra shells. He didn't really anticipate needing the gun—he just wanted to be safe.

He reached into the sack and pulled out a small disposable camera, which he stuck in his shirt pocket. He also took out a small canteen full of water, a compact set of binoculars, and a microcassette recorder. This was to be a reconnaissance mission. He was going to get whatever he needed to convince the right people that there was a real problem up here, then he'd be back with help. Now all he had was the rambling story of a young, unreliable girl. Budd had been the testing grounds for that. Budd was his friend, and he wasn't ready to believe. So, Ben would get pictures. Then they would put a stop to this.

Ben hoped to God this group wasn't related to the one that had come to power in New Orleans a few years back. It was his fear that it was somehow related that pushed him to act now and act quickly. If they weren't stopped now, maybe they would be able to finish whatever terrible work they had left unfinished in the woods outside New Orleans. Ben didn't know exactly what that work was, but he had seen enough of their methods to fear it.

Ben tightened up the laces on his boots. He would have to hike about a mile, most of it uphill. He couldn't take the road, since he could be seen easily from there. Instead, he would have to climb over the big hill that now stood directly between him and the compound. It was covered with pine and low-growing oak, but the underbrush wasn't too bad. He figured he would be able to make the trip in about an hour, barring any major obstacles.

He headed back to the dirt road and crossed the bridge again, this time on foot. Once on the other side, he left the road and headed into the trees.

By the time Ben had made it halfway up the hill, his car was spotted by a young man who was on his normal patrol of the area.

3

Sam McCutchen heard the car as it rolled down the dirt road toward his back field. He wasn't expecting company. Jack had said they might come, so Sam had strapped a knife to his leg that morning. Jack left the previous night in an awful hurry. And then the cops had been crawling all over his house. Sam wondered just what Jack had gotten himself into.

The car stopped on the small road, about fifty feet away. A man got out of the car. Were they cops? Sam didn't know for sure. Jack hadn't said very much.

"Good afternoon, Mr. McCutchen." The man who spoke was tall and stocky. His hands were huge.

Sam lowered his wrench and leaned against his big Farmall tractor. "What can I do for you fellas?"

A second man got out of the car as well. He was not tall, and he was more fat than stocky. They both looked clean-shaven and business-like. They wore ties and jackets, despite the humidity.

The big man flashed a badge. "We're looking for Jack Macon."

Sam watched the men as they approached through the corn. He kept a tight grip on his wrench. "He isn't home?" Sam asked.

The other man spoke. "He left last night and hasn't been back. Some of the things he's taken seem to suggest he might be planning to be away for a while."

Sam looked back toward Jack's house. "That's odd. I could have sworn I saw his truck out front this morning."

The man with the big hands spoke. "He's left with a woman. They took her car."

"Is Jack in some kind of trouble?" Sam grew uncomfortable as the men continued to approach.

"Maybe," the man with the big hands answered. "We just need you to be a good citizen and tell us what you know."

The men now stood just a few feet away. Their positioning and stance concerned him. He supposed that this was what they intended. Sam had always considered himself a good citizen and resented this cop's remarks. But inside he was very nervous. He had no intention of telling these guys that Jack had come to him the night before acting oddly. Jack hadn't said where he would be going, but Sam knew of a few places where they could probably find him. Had Jack done something wrong? It wasn't likely. Sam had known Jack all his life. They had played on the old tractor behind the barn together, seen their first *Playboy* magazine together, gone fishing together a thousand times. As adults, their lives had separated some. But Sam still felt like he really knew what Jack was all about.

"Well," Sam began, "the first I knew there was any trouble was when I saw you guys looking around last night."

The two men looked at each other as if they were deciding what needed to be done. Sam watched them closely. Something didn't seem right. Their approach was awkward. They seemed unprofessional. They didn't act like any cops he had ever known. He began to wonder if perhaps they weren't cops at all. Jack had said that people would come looking for him. And he had said to trust no one. Suddenly, he felt as if the knife in his boot was not going to be enough.

The short, fat man spoke. "We saw you talking with Jack late last night. Tell us where he went."

He was fishing. Obviously, if they were the police, and they had in fact seen Sam talking to Jack last night, they would have visited Sam last night. But in the split second before Sam realized this, his flinch and his eyes gave away a hint of panic.

"You must be mistaken," Sam replied as the big man took another step toward him. "I haven't seen Jack in over a month." But Sam felt the warmth in his head, and he knew the men could see the coloring his cheeks had taken on. They had to know he was lying now. Then Sam hoped that they were the police. Then he would be safer.

The big man got close enough to grab Sam's left wrist. "I'm afraid we don't believe you. We're going to have to take you in for questioning."

The man reached into his jacket. Sam grew nervous as he watched the shiny handcuffs emerge.

He had to make a decision. If these men were not police, he didn't want to be handcuffed and taken somewhere his screams could not be heard. If this was the police, he did not want to ruin his life by doing what was in his mind.

As the cuff clicked over his left wrist, he decided.

As the big man pulled at his arm to get him to turn, Sam brought the wrench around high and fast. The big man obviously hadn't been expecting this, and his eyes grew wide as the wrench crashed against the side of his head. There was a snapping sound, and the big man went to his knees, his right hand still holding onto the end of the handcuffs.

Sam pulled free and rushed toward the short man. He could see the man fumbling inside his jacket, presumably for a gun. But Sam closed the distance quickly and tackled the man to the ground. The gun emerged and Sam grabbed the man's wrist, pointing the gun away from himself. The fat little man had not been expecting the attack, and he was panicking. In the back of Sam's mind, he made final confirmation that this small pistol was not police-issue, and he reached down into his boot with his left hand.

As the short man concentrated on the struggle over the pistol, Sam brought his knife up and into the man's stomach. At first, the man didn't realize what had happened, then a burning sensation got him to look down and he saw the blood. He knew it was his own.

"I didn't mean it!" he shouted as he lost his grip on his gun.

A second later, the fat little man's own gun was ejecting a small brass casing as the hollow lead projectile pierced his man's skull and mushroomed inside his brain. And the lights went out.

Sam turned quickly to face the big man. Before he could get turned around completely, he heard an explosion and felt a burning pain in his neck. He fell back to the ground and brought his left hand up quickly to stop the flow of blood. He still held the dead man's gun in his right hand. But it was of little use now.

The big man was standing over Sam, pointing a larger gun at Sam's head while blood trickled down the left side of his own face. There was no way Sam could bring the gun in his hand up quickly enough.

"Throw the gun away," the big man said, "and you might live."

Sam knew he wouldn't live. But he had to play along for now. He let go of the gun but did not throw it away. It lay near his hand where he might be able to get to it at the right moment.

The big man looked nervously at the gun, then back at Sam. "Move your hand away from it," he said, "over there."

Sam moved his hand a little.

"I want you to cooperate a little better than that," the man said.

"Screw you," Sam replied.

The man fired a shot that went into Sam's left leg. Sam cried out and grabbed his thigh where the bullet had gone in. Now he was rolled on his side, away from the gun. One hand held the wound on his neck, the other the wound in his leg.

"You're running out of hands," the man said, "and I've got ten more bullets."

Sam didn't respond. He lay on his side, his eyes closed, the pain tearing at his thoughts.

"Where is Jack Macon?" the man asked. Sam didn't respond.

"I'll blow your head off," the man explained. Then he fired a shot into the dirt beside Sam's head.

Sam wanted to believe that if he told the man what he knew, then the man would let him live. But he knew this was not true. It couldn't be. Not now.

"He went to his sister's house in Oklahoma City," Sam replied. "He's only going to be there for a couple of days."

Sam opened his eyes now and saw the grin on the big man's face.

"Good boy," the man said. "We didn't even know he had a sister." The man aimed the gun again at Sam's head.

"He doesn't," Sam said. The man frowned. "He really went to his brother's house in Des Moines," Sam continued.

The man fired another shot. This one went into Sam's right leg. Sam curled again as the pain ripped through him. He clenched his teeth against the pain and tried not to panic. Death was on its way. He wanted to go out dignified, not like some tortured rat.

After a few moments of silence, Sam opened his eyes again. He could feel the warm blood seeping through his fingers and down his neck.

Then he looked over his shoulder, toward his tractor. "Jack, don't!" he shouted.

The man's eyes grew wide again, and he turned away to look.

Sam rolled back quickly and grabbed the gun that was still lying on the ground.

The big man realized what was happening and turned back just in time to see Sam bringing the gun up from the ground.

"Shit!" the man shouted as he fired four shots at Sam. The first shot hit the ground by Sam's head. Sam brought his pistol around toward the big man.

The second shot hit Sam, smashing through his cheek and coming out the back of his head, taking pieces of flesh and brain along with it.

Sam's gun went off, firing wildly into the air above the big man's head.

The final two shots obliterated what remained of Sam's face.

The big man stood looking at the two dead men lying on the ground before him.

He had lost a man, and he had gotten nowhere. This was not going to rest well with Darius.

4

Jack looked across the table at Carrie. It was late afternoon and, despite the clouds, had turned out to be a warm day. They had spent the better part of the day discussing what they should do next. Carrie had pushed for the extreme. These people had made a mess of her life and terrified her and many others. They would kill her in an instant if they could find her. Carrie wanted to take the battle to them, find their hideout and start shooting. Jack wanted to lie low for a while, leave the state, and travel under false names until things had a chance to settle down.

But Carrie was adamant. She insisted that if Jack didn't come with her, she was going to go on her own. Jack knew she wasn't thinking rationally, but he also knew that she meant it, and he couldn't let her go alone. She refused repeatedly Jack's suggestion that they let things cool off, even for a couple of days.

So, Jack agreed that they would go to the compound, but only to gather information. He knew it was a stupid thing to do, but Carrie was prepared to do something even more foolhardy on her own. This way, he could be with her and give her advice, help her avoid detection. And he would give her a better chance at survival.

Carrie made one concession. She would wait until the morning and let Jack get in touch with his deputy friend to see if he would help them.

But if he couldn't get hold of him by the end of the day, they would go on without him.

"I think you're right," Jack agreed. "We've got to assume that it's some kind of underground thing. It might be big, but it's still underground. It has to be."

"I just wouldn't know what to tell you to do if you saw a police car pulling up here."

"I've thought about that one," Jack answered. "I'm afraid I don't know yet what I'd do, and I'd better figure it out because if the wrong people do find out we're here, they'll have to know we're watching for them and it's very likely that they would send out a police car."

Jack turned his face up and breathed in the breeze as he looked off, a slight smile suggesting fond memories appearing on his face.

Carrie saw the wistful look in his eyes. "Remembering?" she asked.

"Kind of," he replied. "Just thinking in general about the times I came here with my dad."

"You were close to your father?" Carrie asked.

"Yes. We used to do a lot of hunting and fishing together, and I helped him take care of his farm almost my entire life. We had our disagreements, but in the long run, we were good friends."

"That's nice," Carrie said, looking into Jack's distant eyes. "My father was too busy to be my friend. Unfortunately, my mother was too concerned with my spiritual well-being for me to relate to. I'm not sure how my father put up with it for all those years."

"She was strict?" Jack asked.

"Strict and a little on the odd side. If it weren't for Dad, I think we girls would have ended up marrying preachers and doing housework the rest of our lives." Suddenly, Carrie remembered that her sister was dead. Jack saw the sharp turn of her mood.

"Would you like to go fishing?" Jack asked. "There are some old poles out in the pump house."

"I don't know. I'm not sure I'm in the mood for that."

"What are you in the mood for?"

Carrie took a deep breath and let it out slowly. What did she want to do? She wanted to get revenge for her sister. She wanted to stop this horrible thing that was killing people and ruining lives. But that was going to have to wait. So, what did she want to do right now?

"Let's go for a walk," she said. "You can show me around."

"Okay," Jack agreed. "I can show you the trees I used to climb and my best fishing holes. How's that?"

Carrie smiled. "Let's do it." It seemed like a good diversion. An escape. A place to pretend that things weren't quite as awful as they really were.

9

1

The body of Darius's Queen rested amidst red satin sheets on a stone table in the center of a large room. Despite the warmth outside, the room was cool and damp. The table was surrounded by candles that burned dimly and slowly.

Darius's Queen lay still. Her face remained ghostly pale. Her eyes remained open in a wide stare that looked at nothing and never wavered. Everywhere her skin was visible, it was the same dead-looking pale it had been for the past three years. The only real differences between the woman who lay on the stone table now and the one who had lain in the glass coffin were her open eyes and her slowly rising and falling chest.

Darius sat on a stool at the side of his Queen. He listened to the sound of the air moving through her nostrils. Her breaths were slow and shallow, but they were there. After all this time, she was breathing. But he had waited through the night and half the day for something more. For now, there was nothing but the breathing. There were no other signs of life. There was no movement of the limbs, no looking about of the eyes, no blinking or coughing, or movement of the fingers. For over twelve hours now, she had been like this. The only sound that had passed her lips was the blood-curdling scream she had loosed at her revival.

But he had seen the magic, and he still believed. Something was happening. She was going through some kind of healing process. The body had been dead for three years. He'd kept it preserved as much as possible, but still, there was the inevitable decay of time, as well as the decay that had set in before he had been able to dig her out of the ground in the first place. So, she was resting, and she was healing. Then she would come back to him.

Then they would rule together.

Then the real terror would begin.

2

Ben topped the big hill he had spent the last two hours climbing. The hill wasn't that steep or that tall, but getting through the brush had been more of a chore than he'd expected. He had risen about five hundred feet to get to where he now stood, but only had to descend about a hundred on the other side to get to the level of the compound. The top of the hill was relatively bare of trees and was covered mostly by low brush. He took another drink from his canteen, then looked out beyond to the compound. From this vantage point, he could get a much better view of the layout, and it was a much larger place than he had originally guessed. The roof was basically flat with only a slight slope to shed the rain. Most of the windows he could see were large, but either they were opened, or the glass had been broken out of them. Ben supposed that at one time, this had been a magnificent place. But now it was old and rundown and reminded him of a haunted house from an old movie.

He took out his camera and clicked off a shot. Then he pulled out his binoculars and had a closer look. Though he could see more detail on the building, he could not see any people. In fact, he hadn't seen or heard anybody since his arrival. He still believed Laura's story, but wondered if perhaps the group had decided that it was getting uncomfortable and had moved to a new location.

He turned and faced the direction he had come from. He could see the river and the one-lane bridge below, as well as the dirt road that wound its way off into the direction he had driven from.

Then he realized he could not see his car. He had hidden it well from the road, but he should have been able to see some of its blue metal through the brush below. He raised his binoculars to his eyes again and searched the brush. The tops of some of the fuller oak trees could have been hiding it, but he was fairly sure of where it should have been. He spotted the large rock he had driven around, then followed the path he had taken after that. When he came to the place where the car was supposed to be, there was only bent brush and broken tree limbs.

Apparently, somebody was around. Had they seen him, or just his car? There were only a couple of times that he had been so preoccupied with his climbing that they could have started his car and driven it off without him hearing. Either that or they had gotten a number of guys to push it back to the road.

Ben quickly put the binoculars back to his eyes and looked around the brush for people. If they knew he was in the area, maybe they were trying to find him. Then again, they could just keep his car and then guard the compound. It was a very long walk to the closest store or gas station. They could be counting on him to try to get into the compound. Without his car, this was exactly what he would have had to do. But he had the advantage. They probably did not know he was armed. He would have to keep that advantage as long as possible. As soon as he fired a shot, they would know, and there would be no advantage. Laura had said that they were well-armed. Everything she'd said about the place had made it sound like a drug operation, only she swore that aside from a couple of joints, she hadn't seen any drugs at all.

Then he was reminded of Jonestown and the people who had followed that madman to another continent and eventually to their deaths. And that had been for promises of salvation in the hereafter. This cult, if it was what he suspected, offered nothing for the hereafter, only power in the here and now.

He heard a noise to his right and turned quickly in that direction. Through his binoculars, he could see some movement in the brush. Then a man emerged. He was carrying a machete and was using it to clear out the brush that was in his way. If the man had looked up at that instant, he probably would have seen Ben. But he did not. Instead, he was concentrating on making a path and kept his eyes turned toward the ground. Ben knew he would look up eventually, so he put the binoculars in his pocket and ran over the top of the hill, avoiding the brush as much as possible and trying to move quietly. He dropped from the peak of the hill and slid down the rocky slope that started out steep but became much flatter about fifty feet down. He slid until he could get a foothold, then headed for the first grove of trees. Once hidden in their shade, he turned back to the hilltop to see if he had been seen.

A few moments later, the man appeared suddenly at the top of the hill, looking frantically in either direction. Ben knew from the man's actions that he had been seen, probably as he topped the hill. The man turned back and shouted something to someone. Then he made a motion with his hand as if they had not heard him and he was not going to repeat himself. Instead of shouting again, he looked quickly around the area again, then headed in the direction that he thought Ben had gone.

Ben sat still and watched the man who was looking for him. Now he wished he had brought a whole box of ammunition, and some prepared speed loaders. Or better yet, his Glock 9mm (not his favorite, but it held a lot of bullets) and a couple of loaded magazines. But none of that mattered now. Now he just needed to be quiet and unnoticed. He watched as the man walked through the brush, the dried grass crunching underneath his boots. Suddenly, Ben had the terrible urge to pee, and he remembered back to his childhood how this had always cursed him during games of hide and seek. Only this time, he would go ahead and wet his pants if it came to that.

The man looked right in his direction.

Ben froze. In the shade, behind the big branches, he knew he could not be seen. But the man seemed to be staring directly at him. Ben stood still and watched as the man squinted. The man then looked over his shoulder to see if any help was nearby. Apparently, he had decided that Ben could be in the grove of trees, and he was going to check it out.

As the man approached, Ben quickly considered his options. If he shot the man, then the rest of them would head in the direction of the shot and he would be killed or captured. He didn't want to be captured. Not after what he'd heard about the human sacrifices. They would have to kill him. But he wasn't ready for that yet. There had to be a way out. Ben remained still as the man approached. If it had been a sunny day, it would have been almost impossible to see him in the dark shade of the trees. But it was overcast, and soon he would become visible.

Ben pulled his gun out and slowly raised it toward the man, who was very close to the first tree that made up the small grove. The man suddenly seemed to realize the danger he had put himself in, and he moved behind the tree, looking hard into the darkness of the small grove. A man with excellent sight could have made out Ben's dark silhouette behind the small scrub oak. A few small streaks of light sliced through the leaves and ran across his shoulder and back. But this man apparently still did not see him.

The man looked over his shoulder again, apparently concerned that he didn't have any help. "Shit," he muttered to himself. Ben knew what that meant. He was coming in.

"I know you're in there," the man said. "Why don't you come on out, so I don't have to come in there after you?"

The man stood still and listened. The leaves rustled gently in a slight breeze that covered the sounds of Ben's breathing. The urge to pee was back and stronger than ever. The man squinted and looked, unsure if Ben was there, unsure if Ben might be armed.

Then the man aimed his pistol into the grove. "I'm going to start shooting if you don't come out," he warned. "And I'll hear it when I hit you. Then we'll get you anyway, unless I happen to kill you."

If the man began shooting, the others would come. Ben aimed carefully at the man, waiting for the first shot. If the man fired his gun, he would be killed instantly with a shot to the head.

But the man didn't fire. Instead, he left the cover of his tree and entered the grove.

At first, he headed to a small clearing to Ben's right. As he walked, he looked carefully around in all directions except up. Ben wished he had climbed into one of the trees, though most of them were too small to support his weight. If the man continued on his current path, he would pass within a few feet, if he didn't see Ben first. Then Ben knew he could disarm the man and render him either dead or unconscious quietly.

As the man approached the ideal spot for Ben to spring his attack, he turned suddenly in Ben's direction. Ben could see by the look on the man's face that he had been seen. The man's eyes widened, and he began to raise his weapon, when he saw Ben's gun pointing directly at him. He stood still, his gun partially raised, his mind obviously racing, covering his options.

"Drop your gun now, or I'll kill you," Ben instructed the man. The man lowered his gun, but he didn't drop it. "I'm quite serious," Ben continued.

"I'm sure you are," the man said. He spoke loudly, too loudly. "But as soon as you do, a hundred men will be on you. Then you'll be dead."

"Perhaps," Ben said softly, "but you'll never know since you'll die first."

The men stood facing each other, waiting. Ben didn't blink. He didn't waver. He stood still, his gun pointed directly at the man standing before him. The man held tightly to his gun, thinking.

Then the man fired his gun. He fired a shot directly into the ground. The sound surprised Ben, and he almost pulled his own trigger. Then the man did drop his gun.

If he turned and ran, this man would pick up his gun and probably kill him. If he didn't run, the other men would eventually come and capture him.

"You don't have any options," the man said dully. "Put down your gun, and you might live."

Ben heard voices. He was running out of time.

He lowered his gun a little and fired. The man went to the ground as blood seeped through a fresh hole in his leg. Ben hurried forward to the man and struck him firmly on the back of the head. The man fell face-first into the dead leaves, the side of his face brushing a small barrel cactus. Ben quickly snatched up the man's gun and checked him for any additional ammunition. The man had only one spare loaded magazine, and no extra ammunition. He stuffed his own gun into the back of his pants and headed through the grove of trees. The voices were becoming louder, but they all seemed to be coming from behind him. He emerged from the back of the grove. The compound was less than a hundred feet away. Instead of heading into the trees, he ran as fast as he could to the closest window and leaped.

The window had no glass and he flew through, his foot just barely striking the stone base of the opening. He landed hard on a cold stone floor, but the room was empty, and the door closed. He got quickly to his feet and noticed that his left ankle burned as he slid quickly against the nearest wall. He listened, but the voices had grown distant, and he heard no shouts. He waited, ready to fight, but nobody approached. He had made it through the window unseen.

But they would have a description. Before, he might have had a chance to blend in, but now there was no chance of this. Should he have killed the man? Probably. But years of training had forbidden this, and he knew if it happened again, he would probably do the same thing. Hopefully, it had been dark enough and the man's vision had been poor enough that they would only have a very rough description. Still, there might not be many Black people in this cult, and this would certainly end up working against him.

He slid to the floor, breathing deeply, but quietly. He moved his ankle around and discovered that he had incurred a light sprain. He would have to keep it moving or it would stiffen up on him, and he couldn't afford that right now.

The room was cold. Even though there was no window, it was as if the warmth of the outside air stopped at the opening where the window had once been. It was not a comfortable coolness, but a damp coldness that reminded him of the caverns of south-central Texas, where the limestone formations clung to the ceiling and grew from the floor. And the room smelled bad. It was an odor of decay. It was not the smell of freshly rotten things, but more the smell of things that had been dead and decaying for many years.

He walked carefully across the room, holding his arms out in front of him as he went. The room was empty of furnishings, and he made his way to the door. He felt for a knob but found instead a small handle that wiggled back and forth but seemed to be stuck. He tugged at it firmly, and it popped off the door. Outside, something metal clanged to the floor. His heart leaped into his throat, and he listened. Still, there was only the dripping sound. He felt for the place where the hardware had been attached and found a small hole. He remembered seeing a latch like this in an old house once before, and he got out his pocketknife.

A minute later, he pulled the door slowly and looked out into the dark and empty hall.

3

Jack and Carrie sat at a small table in the spacious living room of Jack's cabin. Jack had shown Carrie around the property and taken her fishing as the day passed. Now, as the sun set, they sat playing their fourth game of gin rummy. It was a game that Carrie had learned from her father and had taught to Jack late that afternoon. He was winning again at the game she had played probably hundreds of times. She could tell he liked winning, but each time he did, he was quite apologetic about it. But he wouldn't give her any ground. He didn't try to throw any games but played each one at his best. She liked that. She was tired of people making concessions, men making concessions because she was a pretty woman. She didn't like losing, but she hated worse to win when it was undeserved.

"Sorry," Jack said.

"You're supposed to say 'Gin'," she reminded him.

"Gin," he said. "I'm sorry."

"Don't be sorry," she said as she laid her cards down to count the points. "You're supposed to win. That's the point of the game."

"It's beginner's luck," he said.

"That was believable two games ago," she said. "I think you're just very lucky, and you've got a computer in that country-boy head of yours."

Her mind seemed temporarily distracted. A smile played at the edge of her lips. It was good to see. She was a strong woman. Jack had watched her closely throughout the day and found her to be a very attractive woman. He had known in the first instant that she was physically attractive. But as he had gotten to spend more time with her, he found that the attraction went deeper, and that her beauty was not in fact a facade for a vain and thoughtless and quite ugly inner person. The combination had a powerful effect on Jack, but he had done his best to be polite. Despite the horribly poor timing, he didn't like to make any woman feel uncomfortable. If this woman needed anything right now, it was a friend. If there was something she didn't need, it was a man drooling down her dress.

"Seventy-five," she announced. "That's the game."

Jack threw his hands up and shrugged as if to signify that it wasn't his fault.

"Don't give me that innocent crap," she said. "It's an old act. You'd beat me every time if you could."

"It looks like maybe I can now," he said then.

"Is that a challenge?" she asked.

"If you like," he said. "I just want to give you another chance if you're up to it, not that it'll come out any different."

She showed him a full smile and he felt his heart sink.

"Okay," she said as she began to shuffle. "But I'm not taking it easy on you this time."

She didn't, and an hour and a half later, she eked out a ten-point win.

Outside, it had grown pitch-black. The clouds had passed, and the stars were thick like they can only be in the countryside. The small lamp in the living room was the only light in the cabin but tonight it was not eerie. Tonight, the danger seemed far away. But tomorrow, it would be time to jump into it all again. These thoughts passed through Jack's mind, but he tried not to let it show.

"Come outside with me for a minute," he said.

Carrie stood from the table and followed Jack across the living room to the front door. He held the screen door open for her and she stepped outside. It was cool out, and there was a nice breeze. Jack came out behind her and walked down the three small steps to the yard that was mostly dirt and pine needles. She followed and stood beside him when he stopped and looked skyward. She looked too, wondering what it was he wanted to show her.

Then she knew. The stars were everywhere. Had it been so long since she had stood outside away from the city lights and looked into the night sky? Had life really become that frantic? There were so many more stars than she remembered. And she had even forgotten what that powdery white streak across the black canvas really looked like.

"That's the Milky Way?" she half stated, half asked, pointing to the powdery streak.

"Yea, and that's Orion over there."

"Where?"

Jack showed her what Orion looked like, and where it was. Then he showed her Cassiopeia. Those were the only constellations he knew outside the big dipper. He had learned the names and positions of dozens of constellations in the fifth grade. These three had stayed with him for some reason.

Then a shooting star streaked very briefly across the sky.

The crickets were singing, and it seemed so peaceful.

"Jack," Carrie said, still looking skyward.

"Yes."

"You don't have to come with me."

"I know."

She looked at him and was surprised to see he was already looking at her.

"You wouldn't be going if it weren't for me," she said. "I don't want to be responsible for you."

"You're not. I'm a grown man. I know what I'm doing."

"Are you doing this for me?" she asked.

"Partly for you, and partly for Laura, and partly because I think it's the right thing to do."

"But you wouldn't go in there tomorrow if it weren't for me."

"No," he answered.

"Why not?"

"Because I don't see what we can do, just the two of us, that'll make any difference."

"You don't think we can put a stop to this?"

"Not really."

"Then why?"

"Because if you go by yourself, you'll probably end up dead."

She stood in silence for a moment. "So, if you go with me, I'll be okay?"

He couldn't lie. "Probably not."

"So, you don't think we're going to live through this?"

Jack sighed. "I really don't know, Carrie. I hope we do. But I'm not going to let you go off by yourself."

"Because you'd feel responsible if I got killed?"

"Yes," Jack answered simply.

The stars were so beautiful. Something like a whippoorwill sang in the distance.

It all felt so right, yet so tragic.

"I'm an adult too and am fully accountable for my own actions. It wouldn't be your fault."

"I know, but I can't let you go alone. It wouldn't be right."

"And being right is more important than being alive?" she asked.

"Sometimes doing the right thing is more important than saving your own skin. That's all I'm saying."

They listened to the peacefulness of the night. It was such a contrast to what lay ahead. It was life and peace in the midst of turmoil and death.

"Are you still determined to go tomorrow?" Jack asked.

"Yes." There was no uncertainty in her voice.

After a few moments of silence, Jack suggested they go back inside.

"I want you to do one thing for me," she said.

"Okay."

"I want you to hold me tonight."

Jack looked into her eyes and felt his heart sink again.

Then she leaned forward and kissed him.

And that night as midnight approached, they lay together in the soft bed that Carrie had slept alone in the night before. As if to affirm the life that seemed to be slipping away from them, they moved quietly and gently toward that physical ecstasy that eventually came to them both like fire and electricity.

And they escaped their fears together.

10

1

Darius lay sleeping in his chair at his Queen's side.

In his dreams, she was as alive as she had ever been, only now it was him she was loyal to, not Cole. Now he was the center of her world, and it was he with whom she would rule the new Kingdom.

Then he saw something in her eyes that frightened him. He looked deeply into them, but at the same time tried to look away. He did not want to see what was there. Her eyes were deep and black, and they grew as he watched. Deep inside the blackness, there was fire, and soon her eyes were so large that he fell into them, and he was running but the fire was catching him.

Then he was burning, but he was lying on the floor of a large room and his Queen was there with him, only it wasn't his Queen. And she laughed as he burned.

Then he saw a dim fire very far away, and his Queen was looking at her hands, turning them first one way, then the other.

He felt the coldness of the stone table against his cheek, and it took him a moment to realize he was no longer asleep.

He sat up and saw his Queen lying amidst the satin sheets, regarding her hands.

She was alive, and she was awake.

"My Queen," he said. It came out rough and his voice squeaked. His vision was still blurred, and only two of the candles continued to burn near their ends.

She looked slowly toward him, her eyes wide. They held an eerie emptiness, like the emptiness in the dream. Her eyes looked at his face carefully, and he sat in anticipation, waiting for her to speak, wondering what it was she would say.

Her lips moved, and the voice that came out was deep and rough, much deeper and rougher than it had been before her death.

"Dirk."

It was his name, his old name. The first thing she had said upon reviving was his name. Surely, this was a good omen.

***

"Yes, my Queen?" Darius replied.

She turned away from him and looked slowly around the room. She had been conscious for almost thirty minutes before Darius awakened from his dream. In that time, her thoughts and memories had slowly leaked into place, though they were distant and fuzzy and incomplete. Her brain held much, but much had been lost to decay. Inside her roared the fire of her ancient Power. The Power was alive. Her body, however, was only somewhat alive. This Power looked through her brain too as she tried to remember who she was and found only hints of her former self.

But the Power understood itself, and it was the weakness of the body and brain that gave the Power even more control.

She did not remember her name. She knew that it was not Queen. But she remembered Dirk. And she remembered Cole. And she remembered Saul.

Then she remembered again what had happened before her re-awakening. She remembered the ceremonies, and the altars, and the stage. She remembered the glory that had been, and that which almost was. Then there had been the pain, and at the pinnacle of it all, death had stripped away the Power and left her a bleeding mess on the stage, that stage that had been intended to bring her to the ultimate power. It was these memories of her death that had brought the screams to her lips at her revival. Her own death was at that time the only memory she had. It was something that had just occurred, and it had seemed as if it was the only thing that had ever happened.

The Power was strong now. It was stronger than the memories.

"Where is Cole?" she asked.

The question cut into Darius's heart. "He's dead." He did not know this to be the truth, but it was very likely. The last time he had seen Cole was the day after the terrible tragedy, and he had been an awful mess.

She looked around the room again. There were no memories of this room. How had she gotten here? Where was this place?

"Where are we?" she asked.

"We're in an old mansion," Darius replied. "I brought you here and have watched over you, waiting for your return."

"How long have we been gone?" she asked, her voice sounding like more than just one.

Darius looked confused at her use of "we" instead of "I". He answered anyway. "You left almost three years ago."

Three years. Her memories had lain frozen in death for three years. The rotted mind remembered only the yesterday of death, and the today of the awakening. But the Power remembered much more. The Power remembered the three years it had waited, and the hundreds that had preceded it. The mind was a vessel. The body was a vessel. But both mind and body were in a state of decomposition, and one that had gotten too strong a hold.

The Power knew the truth.

"Cole is not dead," she said. "Saul is dead."

"Yes," he answered.

She had killed his friend Saul. Darius knew this, and he had forgiven her. But was Cole alive? He supposed that she knew. A long time ago, when they had first been a Family, Cole had died once. She had brought him back. But the death had been in a bad place, and she had not had all of the tools necessary to bring him back completely. So, he had rotted over the years. When she had died on that stage, Cole had been in a terrible state of decomposition. Darius had just assumed that he would be dead by now. But apparently, she thought otherwise. Perhaps he would still be alive when his body had completely rotted away and nothing remained but a deflated corpse with eyes that rolled and lolled and a mind that continued to scream for death to come.

"I will call Cole," she said. "He will help me." Then she looked at Darius. Her eyes softened a little. "Dirk," she said, "you have brought us back and we are grateful. You will help me too."

This odd mixture of "we" and "I" appeared to disturb Darius. "I am called Darius now," he explained.

"You are Dirk," she explained to him. "I will call you Dirk."

"Yes, my Queen."

Her own name eluded her, but she could accept being called Queen. It was a good name. But Darius was not a good name. Darius was an ancient name, one that had a meaning she could not recall, but did not approve of.

***

Darius looked closely at his Queen. Her features remained pale. One of her eyes had become wet, but the other had not. Her breathing seemed odd and hollow. He began to believe that perhaps there had been more decay than he had suspected. But he was confident that over time his Queen would be able to overcome even this.

She turned on the table and her legs fell limply over its edge. Darius took a step back, his eyes wide in awe and wonder. He had hoped for this day. He had worked for this day. Now that it was here, it seemed unreal. It was like a dream.

But what now? It was as if his life's task had been completed. He had reached that goal he had spent all his energies pursuing. In his mind, he had made plans for this moment, but these plans were overshadowed merely by the life in his Queen. She would have her own plans. He would be her servant. Her Power, along with his, would bring back the old order, only now it would be better. Even if Cole did come, it was he, Darius, who had brought life back to the Queen. Cole would be weak now, and powerless as always. The things they had left in place three years ago were still in place. The Queen had been revived. Now it was simply time to return to New Orleans and revive the old ceremonies.

She pushed herself off the edge of the table and crumpled to the floor. Her head hit the side of the table with a dull thud. The event took Darius utterly by surprise and he rushed to her aid. He pulled her up to her feet, and still, she could not stand on her own. He could see the place where her head had struck the table. A thick, blue fluid seeped from the wound. Where was the blood? Was she still filled with nothing but embalming fluid? He was filled with questions, but they were questions he didn't dare to ask. Perhaps later, when his fear had subsided some.

Suddenly, he realized he was afraid. He was very afraid. What if she didn't get any better than this? What if her plans were different than his? What if Cole did come and take his place again as the head of the Family? Then Darius would again be no more than Dirk, no more than a minor actor in the main scheme. There were so many unknowns now. For three years, he had been in control. Now that control had been stripped away, and with this came the fear. He did not want to lose control. He wanted to be strong, to appear strong. But already he felt the weakness and uncertainty of the former days coming back. She was too strong for him. Even in this state, she was too powerful. It wasn't just his Queen; it was the ancient power that resided in her.

She turned her head and looked at him. Her lips formed a weak smile as if to reassure him. "Help me back on the table."

Darius lifted her back onto the table, where she remained in the sitting position. He stood back and looked at her. She stared at her legs and her feet. Her face did not show fear. It didn't even show a hint of the uncertainty that had clouded Darius's mind. Instead, she simply looked a little annoyed.

"I want you to leave me," she said to him. "I want you to prepare them for me, and I want to be alone until I know what I can do and what I can't."

Suddenly, her eyes and head rolled oddly, and she laughed out. Just as suddenly, she stopped and was looking directly at him again, her eyes deep and burning.

"Prepare them for me," she continued. "Come back at sunrise and I will tell you more then."

"Yes, my Queen." Darius bowed. Then he walked around the table to the door of the room, his eyes glued to her the entire time. "Call if you need anything."

"Don't disturb me until sunrise. I will be resting, and I will be thinking. I won't need anything until then, and I will not be disturbed until then." She turned away from him and looked ahead at the wall. "Go now."

Darius replaced the spent candles with fresh ones and lit them before leaving the room.

As he walked away, he heard again the hideous laughter.

2

The Queen sat in her dim chamber and regarded herself.

The body was not in good shape. An odd mixture that was not blood flowed through her veins. The heart that was not her own pumped the blue fluid throughout much of the body, though many of the smaller blood vessels and capillaries had deteriorated. Some of the fluid seeped into places in her body where it had not reached before. Some other fluids seeped from the body back into the bloodstream.

She raised her arm. It did not respond to electrical impulses from her mind but to the ancient forces within her combined souls. It was an act of faith (and more) that moved her arm. Faith can move mountains, indeed. But just an arm for now. And soon it would move the legs and hold them more firmly. Hopefully, by sunrise, she would be able to move in a somewhat normal fashion.

But even then, there would be problems.

The mind was not good. Though the mind did not control, it did influence. She felt the voids and rotten places within it, and the madness, oh the madness pulled so strongly, so strongly and it made her laugh...

She laughed out again and it was a powerful release.

Then it was gone, but she knew the madness would return, and she feared that it would grow. She looked again at her hand. It moved at her command. She reached forward and held a finger out over the flame of the nearest candle. After a few seconds, she could see the end of the finger blackening, but she could not feel it, nor could she smell it. But she could sense it. She knew what was happening. She would have known if her eyes were closed.

And the madness pulled at her again and she laughed.

She pulled her finger away and looked at it closely. She wiggled it and it moved. She had known it would move. It would have moved if it had been stripped of all its flesh. That little bone would have wiggled in the air just as if there were nothing wrong.

"Nothing wrong," she said. Then she laughed and rolled her eyes. They had worked on the body. They would work on it some more. But would it get away? Would the body get better, or would it stay this way?

Or would it get worse?

Dirk had brought her back. (Had brought Regina back?) From some corroded portion of her rotten mind, the name popped loose. It meant little to her, except that it had been her name before, and that it too meant Queen.

And her eyes rolled.

She closed her eyes and reached out.

The madness was distracting, but it did not take away from the Power. The Power was preeminent over the mind. She reached out and she found Cole. The Power did not need Cole.

But she did.

Regina needed Cole because he always had the answers, and he would know where to go from here.

She found him and she called to him.

And somewhere in the backwoods of Louisiana, the rotten man awoke from his dreams and headed westward.

3

In the quiet hour before sunrise, a man awoke within the compound. He was a member of the Family and had been for over a year. Although he had not risen to any position of power, he was regarded as useful since he had connections at the newspaper.

Tonight, this man, like many within the compound, was curious. He had heard the scream of their Queen when she awakened at the ceremonies. Much of what had happened right before that was a blur, a dreamy image with lots of dead space. But he remembered the scream.

She had been taken away that night and no one had seen her since. There were rumors running wild. They ran just under the surface and were spoken only in whispers by a few brave (or foolish) souls. What if the ceremonies had been faked? There had been concern that some of the Family members were becoming discontent and that some were considering slipping away. He knew that his own faith had waned in the past few months. In fact, he had made the decision in his mind that when the spring came, he would be leaving the state if (when) nothing happened.

But something had happened, hadn't it?

His cloudy memories seemed to cry out that it had not been a hoax, that it really was the face of the Queen that had shown its terror and let loose that awful scream.

But what had happened after that? Why had she been taken away? Another rumor was that she had awakened, then immediately died again. Another was that she had awakened but was not normal at all (whatever normal might mean under these circumstances).

Tonight, he had been able to get to sleep, but the eerie dreams and the unanswered questions had awakened him shortly after midnight. Now, almost two hours later, he lay wide-awake pondering again what might be, and thinking again that it might be worth the risk.

Unlike those others who lay awake wondering, Travis had a plan to find out what was and what was not. As it had all throughout his life, his need to know once again outweighed his common sense. This quality that had made him a good beat reporter also ruled much of his destiny. He rolled out of his cot and pulled on his jeans as quietly as he could. Two of the five other people who shared this room were awake and aware of what Travis was most likely up to. But they remained silent. They wanted answers too.

Travis grabbed a small flashlight from the shelf near the door. It was the community flashlight for this room, mainly intended to help those who had needs during the night. Travis took the light and exited the doorless room on silent, bare feet.

He made his way through the compound toward the room where, rumor had it, Darius had been spending all his time. As he came to the hallway of that room, he saw a man sitting in a chair, his head lolled forward in sleep. This was supposed to be a guard. The guard would be lucky if Darius did not find him this way. Otherwise, he could be dead.

Of course, Travis knew he was risking his life at this moment, too. But right now, it didn't matter. He would worry about that only if and when it became necessary. He walked past the guard, down the hallway. The rooms in this hall still had doors, and all of them were shut tight. At the end of the hallway was a set of large wooden double doors like those on Darius's room. Travis walked quietly up to them.

Travis smelled a heavy, bittersweet odor coming from the room. It was like old rotten rose petals sitting in a bucket of stale water. The doors were shut tight. He looked them over for a hole or crack and found a place at the bottom where something had apparently chewed its way into (or out of?) the room. He looked back down the hall to make sure he wasn't being watched, then he got down and lowered his head to the floor.

The hole was big, but not big enough. He put his head completely against the ground and looked upward but could only make out some chair legs and the bottom portion of a table. It wasn't enough. He closed his eyes and listened. He heard labored breathing, but that was all. He opened his eyes and got to his knees.

The door was open. When had that happened? It was not open much, just a crack. He pushed softly against the door, and it opened easily and soundlessly. As it did, he turned off his flashlight and pulled back into the shadows of the hallway. The door stopped halfway open. He could see into the room. It was plainer than he had imagined. The walls were stone and bare, just like most of the walls in most of the rooms in the compound. But there were lots of candle holders and quite a few lit candles.

And he could see the Queen. The door blocked everything from the waist down. She looked beautiful to him. She was lying on her back with her eyes closed. She was naked, her clothes lying on the floor next to the table. Her black hair flowed to the sides of her head, just covering the tops of her shoulders. Her complexion was pale, yet smooth. Her breasts rose and fell gently with her labored breathing. So, she was alive.

Then he realized he had entered the room. It was not as if he had decided to do it, he just found himself doing it. He did not resist. Instead, he looked with awe at the nude body of the Queen. It was both lovely and erotic.

As he approached her, she opened her eyes and looked at him.

At first, he felt a great fear and wanted to run. But then he saw that her eyes were inviting, and her lips showed a soft but beautiful smile. For just an instant, he thought her eyes rolled away from him and danced a jig of their own, but now they looked into him again and it seemed unimportant. He continued to walk toward her, and she raised an arm toward him. He felt entranced, and he came to his Queen. His excitement was building. Something very important, very very important was about to happen. He had been chosen. He had been called. All this time waiting had paid off in a big way.

When he came to the table, his Queen spoke. "Kneel," she whispered.

He did, and this brought his face close to hers. Her breath was sweet, and it was sour, like the rose petals. She put her arm around his neck. Her hand was like ice, and it sent chills down his back.

Then she was pulling his face toward hers.

She was going to kiss him.

But as his face approached hers, she suddenly turned his head away.

She was going to whisper some dark secret or desire to him.

His eyes flew open wide as the pain brought him out of his trance. He stood quickly and saw his Queen, her grinning face covered in his blood. A piece of his flesh dangled from her mouth. She was laughing at him, and her eyes were wandering all over the room.

Travis ran to the door, but it was closed now. He tried to pull it open, but it would not come. As he tried to escape, his blood poured quickly out of the artery in his neck, across the hand he held pointlessly against the gaping wound. He looked back at her as he tried frantically to open the door.

She had risen from the table and was walking toward him. That evil and crazy grin was frozen on her face.

The door would not open.

His blood was flowing fast.

Then the room began to turn in odd ways, and he felt her hands upon him.

Her hands and then her teeth.

And the room faded to black.

11

1

As the sun rose that Sunday morning, Jack came out of a deep and comfortable sleep, unaware that the Queen had awoken, unaware that Ben Williams was hiding out in the compound where the Queen was preparing to meet her followers, unaware that the rotten man named Cole was driving through east Texas toward a dream that had called to him in the night. For the moment, Jack was aware only that he was lying next to a beautiful woman, and that for that moment, he was very happy. The fact that the events of the coming day would certainly be full of danger and uncertainty made the moment even more precious. Where would they be twenty-four hours from now? Who knew?

He reached out and stroked Carrie's soft brown hair. She stirred. He pulled his hand away as she moved around under the covers, turning to face him. Then her eyes opened slowly, and she smiled. She whispered his name, and he nodded as if to confirm that she was right, it really was him.

Then her smile faded as she noticed it was light outside. "What time is it?" she asked.

"It's pretty early."

"I think we should get started," she said. "The sooner we get on it, the more daylight we'll have."

Jack reached out and touched her face. She did not shrink away. Instead, she held onto his hand and caressed it.

"Wouldn't you rather stay here one more day, spend it with me? We could stay right here and be lazy until noon. Then we could walk down to the store for supplies and have a picnic." He winked at her to urge her on.

But she was not to be persuaded. "Maybe when this is all over, I'll take you up on that. Maybe we can come back here and spend a weekend at your cabin when there aren't people trying to kill us."

It sounded like a good offer, but he wondered if they would ever have the opportunity to come back. Jack took a deep breath and sighed. He wasn't sure he was ready for this. But Carrie was right. There was no better time than the present.

He looked one last time into her eyes, then she leaned up and kissed him. He felt her warm body against his and it excited him. He kissed her back, and she put an arm around him and ran it down his back.

And their departure was delayed one more hour.

2

An hour before sunrise, messengers had hurried throughout the compound waking up the members of the Family, telling them of the gathering that was to take place in the ballroom at sunrise. Nothing was said about the reason for the gathering, though most of the members knew that something important was about to happen. They were about to receive some answers to the questions that had been plaguing them all since the ceremonies two nights ago.

Since it was a weekend, many of the members who had been there for the ceremonies that had awakened their Queen had stayed at the compound. Those who had not stayed had been contacted by phone, the first of them was arriving as those at the compound were being awakened.

By sunrise, all the members of the Family—except two who could not be reached and one who had gone missing—were standing in the large old ballroom near the center of the compound. The rising sun dimly illuminated the room through the windows that faced the courtyard. There was no other light except two torches that burned at the front of the room, near a doorway that led to a dining hall.

Standing amidst the crowd was Ben Williams. He had watched carefully for a limping man, or for anyone who eyed him suspiciously. But he did not see the man he had wounded, and the rest of the people were too preoccupied with what was about to happen to take notice of him. There were over a hundred people in the room. Many of them had never met. Many of them could have been strangers. Records were kept of their names, addresses, and occupations, but roll call was never taken, and nobody had ever left and lived to talk about it. In fact, only three had ever even tried to leave.

So, Ben entered the room unnoticed, his hand in his pocket, loosely gripping his gun. They did not seem to be looking for him, so they must have assumed he had run off into the woods. That was their mistake, and he was glad they had made it.

The room was full of people, but there was no talking. Then all movement seemed to freeze when the door to the dining room swung slowly open. Ben pushed the button on his cassette recorder and began recording.

***

The doors opened slowly outward, toward the dining room. After a moment, Darius emerged. He walked to a spot between the two torches and stood looking at the Family.

But this wasn't just the Family, it was *his* Family. He couldn't help but feel that he was about to give control of his people to his Queen. It was a moment he had longed for, but now that it approached, he felt his power slipping away, and it frightened him. He would never turn against his Queen, but he wanted to play a role, an important role in the new order that would come now that she had returned. He had lain awake all night wondering just what part his Queen had in mind for him.

Then he had gone to tell her that she would be addressing her people. He had found her in her room with the partially eaten body of Travis Clayborn. At first, he hadn't quite understood what had happened. Then, after seeing the blood-covered face of his Queen, he had known.

A piece of the man's leg lay on the floor next to the table on which she had been resting. She had turned to him and smiled. "Being dead gives one odd and new appetites," is what she'd said. Then he vomited.

Now he stood before his Family, unsure what future waited for them all. For years, he had told them to prepare for this moment. He had told them that power and glory awaited them all when their Queen awoke. Now he wasn't sure what was awaiting them.

The silence was deep and still. Darius stood looking out over the eager faces as he had many times before, only now there was something new in those faces. It was something more than hope—it was eagerness and anticipation. Darius had no doubt that his Queen would find them to be loyal subjects.

"Fellow Family members," he began. "Two nights ago, you were all party to a magical ceremony that saw life come to our Queen. Since then, she has been recovering. Her body was in need of repairs after such a long sleep, and so she has spent her time resting, repairing herself, preparing to take her place as your goddess and leader.

"You have all been waiting. Some of you for months, some for years. This morning, your patience will be rewarded. The most faithful of you will receive the greatest rewards, and all will become a part of the new Kingdom. Our Queen will take us beyond this compound and beyond these hills that surround us. We will take our battle to the cities and beyond, with a power none shall be able to resist."

Darius paused and looked over the eager eyes of his Family. The moment had come. For this brief instant, they were his, and he wanted to enjoy this moment. He felt that he would never be this important again, not to the Family nor to anyone else.

"I present to you, your Queen."

***

Darius stepped aside and turned to his right. Eager eyes rushed to the doors that still stood open. At first, nothing happened. Then there was a cool breeze that rushed through the room. A light, gold-colored dust rose from the floor and began circulating, touching all the members of the Family, touching Ben as well. He felt the coldness of that dust and sensed great evil. Then he felt his arms and legs going numb and he realized he could not move. His eyes remained fixed on the doors, as did those of everyone else. His inability to move terrified him, and he wondered if this was happening just to him. If it was, then perhaps he had been discovered.

But it was happening to everyone. They all stood paralyzed as their Queen emerged from the dining room.

She wore a long, flowing sheer blue gown. This had been her choice from the clothes Darius had stored for her. She had cleaned herself and there was no sight of the blood that had once been inside Travis Clayborn's body. Her gown flowed behind her, as did her black hair. She walked slowly, and though no one noticed, a bit unsteadily. She walked to the place between the torches where Darius had stood and faced her subjects. She held them still. They stared in awe and terror at her.

"My subjects," she said. Her voice was rough and deep, not at all what might be expected from her appearance. Ben heard the voice, but it seemed to come from somewhere inside his head rather than from the woman standing before him. "You have all been faithful, and you shall all be rewarded in time. Dirk has brought us back with your help. Now begins the true test of your loyalty. Now begins the trials that shall determine which of you shall be worthy, and which of you shall not."

Darius flinched at the use of his old name. Nobody in the Family had ever heard it before, but all knew who their Queen was referring to. It was just a step, one step to bring him down in their eyes. Darius's face bore the resentment he felt for the first time since her arrival.

When Ben heard the name Dirk, he knew. Dirk Gash had been one of the central members of that cult in New Orleans. And this woman before him must be Regina.

But she was supposed to be dead. As he began to understand what had happened here, he grew fearful of what lay ahead.

The Queen continued. "Dirk has brought this group together. For that, I shall be forever grateful." She turned and looked at him, then returned her gaze to the Family. "But now you are my subjects. You will follow my orders and my edicts. You will pledge your allegiance to me and do my bidding, or you will die."

"Yes," the Family replied. Ben felt his mouth move and heard the word escape his own lips.

"I am your leader, there is no other," she claimed to them.

"There is no other," they replied.

"You will do as I command, even to death."

"Even to death," they responded.

She smiled and looked over her people. Ben felt her hold soften a little, then thought he saw a moment of uncertainty as her eyes darted oddly about the room. But then her control returned, and Ben felt it tighten around his entire body.

***

"There must be no opportunity for confusion," she said to them. It seemed an odd statement. Then she turned again to Darius. "I must thank you one last time for your faithfulness," she said to him. "And in front of my subjects, I must swear to you my eternal love."

She stared hard at Darius, and he felt the warmth of her words. It tingled throughout his body. It ran from his toes to his head. And then his feet started to burn.

Regina turned back to her subjects. "There must be no opportunity for confusion," she repeated. "You will all be loyal to me, and none other." She turned back to Darius. There was a confused and terrified look in his eyes. His whole body burned. He felt warmth coming from his arms, his legs, his head. He wanted to run but could only stand frozen in his place.

"You understand, Dirk?" she said.

"I love you," he answered.

Then he burst into flames.

At first, he stood in his place, still frozen by her trance. Then he shook free of it and began dancing about. But he did not scream. He ran in small, odd circles waving his arms around, then he ran into the stone wall with a sick thud and fell back to the floor. The place where he had hit the wall was smeared with black soot. The sick smell of his burning flesh filled the room as the members of the Family watched the spectacle in utter terror.

Darius lay on the floor in a heap, no longer aware, but not yet dead. Regina walked slowly to the burning mass and held her hands out before her. After a few moments, there was a soft explosion, and cold air rushed through the room. Ben watched as a brilliant white light exploded from the burning heap. It was like a small fireball surrounded by a white cloud of magical dust. The fireball leaped from the flames and rushed toward Regina. In the next instant, it pounded into her, disappearing into her chest.

"We are home! We are home!" she cried out.

Ben felt a new completeness that everyone felt as she marked them with her brand. And in that instant, he fully understood the Power that he was up against.

The fire slowly went out of the lifeless body, leaving a black, un-identifiable mass behind. Regina stood staring skyward as the flames subsided, her subjects still held motionless by her spell.

Then she began to laugh wildly.

3

An hour later, a man drove up to the compound in a rusted-out 1962 Rambler. The car was deteriorating into nothingness, which was appropriate considering its owner. It seemed that he too was deteriorating into nothingness.

He presented himself at the front entrance and eyed the compound with a mixture of awe and disgust. When he demanded to see Regina, he was led there by a man who seemed both honored and terrified at having been chosen for the task.

The rotten man was led to Regina's room and left there alone to knock.

When she opened the door, she smiled. He could not believe his eyes. She really had come back.

After a short reunion, Cole fell quickly into his place. He began by blessing Dirk for his faith and perseverance, then cursing him for his stupidity. The whole idea of a compound and such high organization was foolishness waiting to be found.

Regina did not think it mattered, but Cole did. So, she called another meeting.

4

Jack and Carrie drove toward the compound. Carrie had a piece of paper on which she had written down the instructions as Laura had given them to Ben. Jack had only been to the northern part of the county on a couple of occasions, and really had ventured nowhere near where their journey would take them.

In the trunk of Carrie's Thunderbird was a small box with their supplies inside. Jack drove on nervously, trying to project an air of certainty for Carrie's sake. He knew he was failing miserably. They had only known each other for two days now, but already she could read him. He felt as if he had known her much longer.

After just under two hours, they reached the second one-lane bridge. The compound was just across the bridge and up the hill now. Instead of crossing the bridge, they drove off the road and into the brush. Jack wished he had driven his truck so they could have gotten farther off the road. As it was, they were able to find a dry riverbed that did a good job of hiding the car from the road. They pulled unknowingly into a spot about twenty yards from where Ben had parked his Mustang.

They got out of the car and got the equipment they would need for their trip. Both of them carried guns. Carrie knew how to use one, and Jack had briefed her on the features of the .380 he gave her to use. He had brought his dad's .45 service revolver for luck, and because it was the largest caliber pistol he owned.

"You ready?" Jack asked.

"Ready as I'll ever be."

They took off together toward the hill that separated them from the compound.

On any other day, they would have been sighted in minutes. But the confusion that had overtaken the compound that morning gave them the edge they needed.

They reached the top of the hill just after noon.

They looked over the compound. It was much larger than either of them had expected. There were a couple of people outside the building, inside the gate at the front. Other than that, there were no signs of activity.

Jack looked over the land between where they stood and where they needed to go. "If we stay in the brush, we should be able to get close enough to the compound to get in through one of the windows or doors in the back, like Laura said."

"Okay," Carrie agreed. She wasn't thinking about how they were going to get in; she was thinking about their plan once they got inside. Laura hadn't known exactly where Darius's room was, but she knew the general vicinity. Once inside, they were going to head that way. Then they would look carefully for the right room. And when they found it...

Well, Carrie had agreed with Jack that they would kidnap Darius and take him off the compound. She had agreed that they would take him away and question him, then expose the cult to the press. But that would be too risky, and too difficult. Darius had overseen the death of her sister, as well as Jack's niece. He had set up an evil cult that sacrificed animals and people. She had no doubt that all other kinds of atrocities and perversities took place within that compound. She had agreed with Jack because he would not agree with her. But when the moment came, she would do what was right, and Darius would be dead.

Jack led the way down the hill. Carrie followed closely. They used the trees and shrubbery for cover, and there were only two places where they had to cross bare ground. They had crossed those quickly and had not been seen.

In about fifteen minutes, they reached the back of the compound. There were no guards out, and the search teams who had been looking for Ben were no longer looking in light of recent events. Jack and Carrie got in through a back door that opened easily and led them into a small entry chamber. Beyond the chamber was a damp and dark hallway.

"We'll use just my light," Jack explained.

Carrie agreed and followed Jack as he walked through the hallways and a couple of small rooms. Finally, they came to the area where Laura had said Darius's room was located. According to Laura, he would be there most of the time. And even when he wasn't, a young, dark-headed girl was. Either way, Carrie was ready to do what had to be done. She had taken the safety off on her gun.

They came to a number of small rooms that turned out mostly to be storage rooms, though a couple of them stank terribly and showed evidence that they had been used to store people. Jack imagined that Laura had been kept in one of these rooms before she'd escaped. And he imagined that Carrie's sister had been kept in one before she had been killed. Jack knew that Carrie was thinking the same thing but felt no need to bring it up for discussion.

They walked on together, quietly and carefully, until Jack saw a large set of double doors at the end of the hallway.

"I'll bet that's it," he whispered. Carrie nodded.

Jack led the way to the set of doors, then stood outside them listening. He could hear sounds coming from inside. He nodded to Carrie. They had discussed this. Laura had not said anything about Darius having a bodyguard or being armed. So, they had decided that the direct approach would be the best.

Jack turned the knob on the door. It turned easily. Once he had turned it all the way, he looked at Carrie one last time. She nodded again.

Jack threw the door inward and pointed his gun into the room. There was a man inside, but it was not Darius. The man turned quickly toward the door and was holding something in his hand.

As the man went to the floor and reached behind him, Jack recognized Ben. The deputy recognized Jack as well and relaxed his grip on the pistol he had grabbed onto.

"I almost killed you," Ben said. Then he got back up, picked up his camera, and walked across the room to them.

Jack grimaced at the joke and lowered his gun. Ben had been the one who had almost been shot. Carrie came into the doorway since she recognized Ben's voice.

Ben looked at Carrie. "He let you come, too?" he asked.

"I let *him* come," Carrie corrected.

Ben looked at Jack with raised eyebrows, awaiting an explanation.

"She was coming here with or without me. I decided I'd come, too," Jack whispered and kept looking over his shoulder.

"You don't have to worry about being discovered here, so relax. What did you plan on doing here anyway? Killing Darius?"

"Kidnap him and blow his story to the press."

Ben looked at Jack in disbelief. Then he looked at Carrie. He could see from the look of hatred and disappointment on her face that she had come to kill, not kidnap.

"Well, either way, it doesn't matter," Ben explained. "Darius is dead."

Carrie's eyes widened. "How? Who did it?"

"The girl they were trying to resurrect."

"Come again," Jack said.

"They did it. She came back to life, then she took over the cult. Part of her deal was to get rid of Darius. Some gratitude, huh?"

Carrie still looked stunned. "Wait a minute. You're telling me that a girl came back from the dead, and now she's running the show."

"I wouldn't have believed it if I hadn't seen her myself. I didn't see her come back from the dead, but from what I saw and felt, I wouldn't doubt that it was true." Ben told them his story from the moment he had gotten into the compound until the first meeting that had taken place that morning. Carrie listened carefully, trying to understand, but having trouble believing. Jack believed but wanted to just get away from it all. But he knew that getting away simply wasn't an option.

"So, where is everybody?" Carrie asked.

"Not long after our first meeting, somebody else arrived on the compound. I've been spending my time mostly in the shadows, listening to the talk and observing, taping what I could get on this tape." He tapped the pocket on his jacket where he had hidden his microcassette recorder. "Nobody seems to know where this guy came from, but I'm pretty sure I know who he is from the stories I've heard. I think his name's Cole, and that he's come here from Louisiana."

"So, this *is* related to the cult in New Orleans like you thought," Jack observed.

"I'm sure of it. As much as I wish it wasn't so, it just has to be them. This guy showed up, then another meeting was called. Regina stood up and told everybody that they would all be abandoning the compound, that it was foolishness to stay here and be organized, that one leak or one intruder could spoil everything. My guess is that the guy who showed up here advised her on all of this. If it's like before, then she is the power behind the cult, but he will be calling the shots."

"But she killed Darius?" Carrie asked.

"Yes. In front of everyone. Apparently, she didn't want any confusion over allegiances. She must have figured that after three years of Darius as their leader, there would be some pretty strong allegiances, and from the talk afterward, I'd say she was right."

"So, how's she gonna keep the group together?" Jack asked.

"Pretty much the same way Darius did—promises of power to those who stay, threats of death for those who think of leaving. Only, I think her threats are more feared than his ever were. I get the distinct feeling she could find anybody if she set her mind and her power to it."

"So, where did they go?" Carrie asked.

"That's where we're screwed. She just said that they would return to the traditional ways of meeting in the woods only. There would be no central living place. Selected messengers would make contact when meetings were to be held. She made no mention of where meetings would take place, or where she would be staying. Most of them have been gone for a couple of hours now."

"So, now we're never going to be able to find them." Disgust showed in Carrie's voice.

"And looking for them would be extremely dangerous," Ben explained.

"What do you mean?" Jack asked.

"She's different from Darius. She's got some kind of power he never had. Even Laura's stories are pretty tame compared with what this witch can do."

"Did you say she's a witch?" Carrie asked.

"That's what I think she is. At least, that's the best word I can find for it. When she killed Darius, she absorbed something from him. I think it was something like his power. I saw it leave him and enter her—everybody saw it. When she spoke, there was some kind of power that held the room and flowed through everybody in it. I know this is going to sound crazy, but afterward, I saw everybody else in a different way, like there was some kind of light in their eyes. I think she made that happen."

"Light?" Jack asked. "What do you mean?"

"Well, I feel funny even saying this, but when I look at a member of her cult, I see a soft glow in their cornea. I guess it's some way for them to be able to identify each other now."

"How do you know you just don't see everybody that way now?" Carrie asked.

"I thought I would until just now, when you two got here."

Jack pondered this. "This could be just what we need to keep track of them."

"I'm not sure that's what needs to be done," Ben said.

"Then what do you think we should do?" Carrie asked, the hostility showing in her voice.

"I've got pictures and I've got tapes. I can deliver copies to the right people in the department and blow this thing wide-open."

"You'd trust the police to handle this?" Carrie asked.

"I'd know who was in on it and who wasn't."

"Even if you do," Carrie went on, "the police are going to try to capture Regina and Cole and charge them with criminal offenses. How far do you think that's going to get? Where do you think they can hold them until a trial? How do you plan on getting them there? These people will kill and die for those two. The police can't handle it with all their pat procedures and by-the-book attitudes. They'll be trying to deal with the supernatural in a totally earthly manner. It can't be done, they'll just get away, and lots of people will be killed in the process."

Ben had thought about this. But his years in the police force had taught him to trust the system and had shown him the perils of taking justice into private hands. Still, her points were valid. What if they did break the cult and take Regina and Cole in as its leaders? Then what? He had seen just a hint of her powers and knew that it wouldn't be enough. But that left only one alternative, and it was one he wasn't comfortable with.

"I know what you're thinking," Carrie said to him. "You can't condone killing the two of them. But it has to be done. If you can't do it, I can. Just don't get in my way and don't try to stop me."

Jack knew she was right, and he agreed that it was the only way. Ben agreed to help, but swore that when the time came, he would not be the one to pull the trigger. That was good enough for Carrie.

The three of them left the compound together. They walked out the front door and down the dirt road to Carrie's car. They only ran into two members who were still hanging around the front. Carrie and Jack looked away so as not to reveal their unmarked eyes. Ben made eye contact to get them through.

Taking the dirt road around the big hill instead of the brushy path over it was much easier and much faster. By a little after one o'clock, they were heading back toward Tyler.

12

1

Regina and Cole sat in a dirty motel room on the interstate near Tyler. It was time to discuss the new plan.

Cole had spent the last three years in the woods near the small towns of southern Louisiana, hoping that he could build again what he once had in the Family. He had formed and disbanded numerous groups of young kids, high school kids whom he lured with drugs and mystery, the feeling that they belonged, and the lure of evil. But no matter what he tried, he could not find the power he had possessed once before, when he and Regina had ruled the most powerful underground cult in New Orleans. He did not know where the power that Regina commanded had come from. Some pieces of that power had also nested within Saul and Dirk, but their power had been nothing compared with the power that had come to Regina. She had been his jewel, the centerpiece of his new dynasty, which was to begin when the world was brought to its knees.

Something had destroyed those plans. Something they should have seen but did not. But now, they would have another chance.

Or so he hoped.

Something about Regina was not right. In many ways, she was the same, but in most ways, she was different. Death had changed her somehow, and he didn't know just how much, and what it would mean. She was prone to fits of laughter and a crazed look often came to her eyes. She seemed to be aware of these fits but paid them no heed. He had heard the story of how she killed Dirk. That frightened him. Could she do the same to him?

But she had called to him. In the old days, he had been in control. Would she yield that control now? Would she let him call the shots, or would she have her own ideas? So far, she had been cooperative, but so far his ideas had all made practical sense. Soon they would come to issues that might be disputed. He would have to tread carefully. The girl who sat before him was not the one he had known before. She was something even darker.

And he was not in such good shape either. Ever since he had been killed back in 1982, then brought back hastily by Regina, things had not been quite right. At first, it had just been an odor problem, much like the one he noticed Regina was beginning to have. Then, as the years passed, he realized that parts of him were actually beginning to rot. It had been a terrible feeling, watching himself deteriorate this way. After Regina had been killed, his deterioration had sped up. Her life and presence had somehow slowed the decaying process, but after her death, he had begun to rot quickly. In three years, he had lost an eye, which was now just an empty socket that occasionally leaked pus, his knee bones had deteriorated to where they actually creaked when he walked, his teeth had all fallen out, and his gums had rotted back into a soft mush that didn't hold his dentures very well and made him talk with an awful lisp. His neck was covered with open sores and one hole that was the result of an accident with a screwdriver. His stomach was sunken deeply, and he had stopped eating when his lower intestine burst last fall. Now he drank liquids mostly, though they seemed to be more absorbed by his drying insides than anything else. He had not bled in over a year, and the cuts and gashes of every collision or fall remained open and festering.

His heart had stopped beating three months ago.

He had thought many times about death. He had reasons to continue to live. The main reason was his memories of the power he had held, and the hopes that it would return. He had considered suicide, but was too frightened to try, frightened that he might not die, that he might simply mutilate himself to the point that he could do no more than lie in a putrid heap and rot in his own hell. Fire was the answer, and he had prepared himself for that day. When all hope was gone, he would give himself over to the flames.

But this day had come first.

He wasn't sure yet if his hopes had been realized, or if they were being destroyed.

***

Regina had, of course, spent the last three years dead. The experience had certainly changed her—she could feel this herself. In the old days, she had been Regina, and she had held this tremendous power that had come to her in her youth in the woods outside Hammond, Louisiana. Now it was more like there was simply a tremendous power that was using this shell that had once been Regina's body. The Power was the main influence. Regina was still there, but not like before. It was still her wants and desires that influenced the direction that the Power would take, but that was more dangerous than anything else. Regina's body and her mind were rotten. Furthermore, Regina had made a terrible discovery. The body and the mind could not be healed. In fact, now that they were no longer being held in a vacuum-sealed and fairly sterile environment, the deterioration that should have taken place over the past three years was playing catch-up. The Power knew that the body and the mind of the vessel were getting worse, and that knowledge was passed on to Regina. The knowledge that she was rotting added to the insanity. It made her furious. Regina knew she was going to pieces. Oh, but there was so much more she wanted to do before she was reduced to a pile of rotten flesh and bones. The fury ran through her and controlled her, and it directed the Power. She wanted to bring Dirk back so she could kill him again. But she could not.

Cole had come. It was Regina who had called to him. Before, he had been the leader, the director of the plan. They had come so far with him, and he was like a father to her. But since she had seen him last, his body had become much worse. He was a walking corpse. He was a constant reminder to her of where she was headed. How long would it be until she too looked like this? Cole saw her revulsion, and it was clear that it pained him.

Of course, there were the healing ceremonies. They had worked in the old days. They had brought Regina back from the brink of death once before; perhaps they would do some good now. Of course, there was a difference between the injuries she had sustained back then and three years of death. They would have to try the ceremonies.

"We should go back to Louisiana," Cole croaked out through his remaining vocal cords.

She had always agreed with Cole. He had always been right. But the rage was so strong. "Is everything still in place?"

"As far as I know, it is," he answered. "We could get the word around pretty quickly. We'd have a lot of the old members back in a short time, plus we could take the group Dirk put together with us."

Regina stifled a laugh. "Why can't we do it here?"

Cole wasn't sure. It just didn't seem right. They had built the Family and their small empire in New Orleans. It just seemed to be the place to go. "It's home," he said. "If there's anywhere that your power is more focused, it's back there."

Her eyes rolled. She considered the idea.

But it didn't seem important. Going back to New Orleans seemed like a waste of time. She had a good group of faithful people here, and they would serve her purpose just fine.

But what was her purpose? There was a reason to all of this, but what was it? There was supposed to be a grand plan. That was what Cole was here for.

Cole saw the confusion in her eyes. "We need to get back to New Orleans and resurrect our first Family and merge them with this new Family. Then we can resume the old plan. It wouldn't take long. We could finish the ceremonies we started. We could bring the fire of destruction down on this place and then rule what remains." *But only,* Cole thought, *if Regina remembers all the details of those ceremonies.*

Regina could remember bits and pieces of the plan now, but most of those pieces had been irretrievably lost in the destroyed portions of her brain. Besides, what good would it do to build the new empire if she could only rule for as long as her rotting body held out? "We have to try a healing ceremony before we decide," she said. "If it works, then we can go."

In the old days, Regina would never have offered any conditions to Cole's decisions. But now she did. Was this just the beginning? Did she really need him anymore? For years, he had tried to rebuild that former glory. Now he was as close as he had been since that terrible day when Regina was killed. Only it seemed like he was further than he had ever been.

He agreed to her condition, and they made preparations for the ceremony.

2

"So, where do we start?" Carrie asked.

They sat in the living room of Ben's house. They had been there for a little over an hour. When they had first arrived, Ben checked his answering machine and found fifteen messages. The first seven had been calls from Detective Jacobson asking where he was and telling him to call in as soon as he could. The next two had been from the sheriff himself and were along the same lines. The last six were dial tones, someone checking to see if he had returned. Ben had not called in yet. He thought that when the time came, it would be best to go to the office in person.

"We've got to get to them somehow," Ben explained. "To do that, we've got to get a hold of the right people."

Jack sat in a big chair; his hands folded in his lap. "They didn't say anything about where they would be?"

"Not a word. All she said was that we would be contacted for the next gathering."

"How do you suppose they're going to contact everybody?" Carrie asked.

"If they're operating the way they did in New Orleans—and with Cole in the picture, I have every reason to believe they are—then they already have some kind of network set up. A few key people will begin spreading the word through a series of cryptic messages. The word will spread until everyone has been contacted, usually twice as a backup."

"So, they'll be getting in touch with you, then," Jack concluded.

"I don't think so. I'm afraid that just because my eyes glow doesn't mean I'm a member. I'm sure somebody has a roster of some kind with a list of everybody. They'll be using this list to make contact."

"So, we've got to find out from somebody who is a member," Carrie pointed out.

"Right."

"Why don't you find somebody who's in the cult, and then we can follow them around until they lead us to Regina and Cole?" Carrie suggested.

"That's what I was thinking. I could start at the department."

Jack leaned forward. "I thought you said they were looking for you there."

"They are. But hopefully, when the right people see my eyes, I'll be able to convince them that I've joined up."

Jack sat back. "If you're wrong, you could be killed."

"I think I can pull it off. The only catch will be if somebody at the department is in charge of the list, and I think that's unlikely."

Jack and Carrie looked uncomfortable.

"I'll also be able to call in some favors, get some help from some officers who aren't involved, maybe even alert the sheriff to what's going on. Then at least we can put a little pressure on these guys, regardless of whether we're successful at getting to Regina and Cole. It might also give us a chance to get to them another way."

"How's that?" Carrie asked.

"I think I should go ahead and play the tape for the sheriff and show him the pictures. If they start an investigation, maybe they'll catch these guys."

"We've already discussed this," Carrie pointed out. "That's pointless."

"Maybe not," Ben explained. "If we can get some help locating them, I can see to it that you are given access to them. Then you can do whatever you think is necessary."

Carrie and Jack looked at each other. Jack liked the idea. Carrie was not as convinced.

"We can't do this all by ourselves," Ben explained.

Carrie knew he was right. She glared at him. "You should have killed her when you had the chance."

Ben just looked at her apologetically. Carrie suddenly felt bad for saying it, but she was so terribly angry.

"Ben's right," Jack explained. "We're going to need all the help we can get, and he's got an advantage we don't have. I think it's a good plan. He can work it from his end, and we can work it from ours. If he gets any information that might be helpful to us, he'll pass it along, right, Ben?"

"Of course."

"So," Jack continued, "you and I will find a place to wait, and Ben will get to work."

"I hate the waiting," Carrie complained. "But we really don't have anywhere else to go right now, so I guess it'll have to do."

"You're welcome to stay here," Ben offered. "From the messages on my answering machine, I'd say someone is suspicious of me, but I think I can convince him that I'm no threat, that I'm part of the Family."

"What if you can't?" Carrie asked. "This wouldn't be such a good place to stay then."

"If you'd feel more comfortable somewhere else, and you have somewhere else to go, please go."

Carrie looked at Jack. "We could go back to your cabin."

"There's no phone, and I think we'll be needing one."

He was right. "Well, we can't go back to your place, either," Carrie said.

"Let me put you up at a friend's house," Ben suggested. "I'll be able to keep him quiet, and no one will be looking for you there."

"What if he's in on this, too?" Carrie asked.

"Then I'll know," Ben said, pointing to his eyes.

"I keep forgetting."

Jack and Carrie agreed that it was the best plan, so Ben gave Budd Holloway a call.

3

Cole sat alone in a dark and musty hotel room. Regina had left to get the supplies for the healing ceremonies. She had left him alone.

He was not in charge. In the moments of preparation for the healing ceremonies, their discussions had continued, and it had become clear that he was no more than a security blanket for her, one she was unsure whether she needed. He was not in control of the situation. He had waited so long for this moment of salvation, but there was no salvation here.

He should never have come. He should have given up long ago.

He looked down again at the gun in his hand. For many years, he had wondered if a bullet in his brain would stop all the noise. In a moment, he would know. In case it didn't, he had set a candle in the middle of a blanket that had been sprinkled with gasoline. He sat on the edge of that blanket, facing the candle.

He looked at his hand. One finger was missing. It had been damaged a long time ago and simply rotted off. There had been no pain. There never was.

What he had hoped for was more than the power and control; what he had hoped for was life. But he knew now that it was a foolish hope. What had she done for him before, when she had brought him back from death? Then he had rejoiced at the life he had been given. But now, he saw that it was not life, but a curse of living death. What more could she do now? Even then, she had not been able to stop the rot.

So, what if she was able to now? Then how many years would he spend in this condition? How long could he stand the gradual removal of his body parts?

And even if there was some healing, it would not be enough. Even then, he would not be in charge. The power he had held in his hands had escaped him. Regina was not what she had been before. Now she was some terrible force that could not be reined in, not even by him. Before, she would listen to him, then it was he who controlled the Power. Now it was the Power that controlled what little there was left of Regina, and it was trying to control him as well.

He placed the gun to his head and pointed it downward so that it would go through as much of his brain as possible. Then he pulled the trigger.

The gun exploded and the bullet tore into his fragile skull, blowing almost half of his brain out the other side. Rotten gray matter splattered the floor to his left. The impact of the bullet threw him to the floor, into the mess his brain had made.

Cole lay on the floor, his legs twitching, his arms limp, but his good eye open. He couldn't move, but he could see the room that lay before him.

"Well, that answers that question," he said. Then he started to laugh.

He lay still, unable to move, while the candle burned slowly down. He was glad he had cut it down to two inches. Otherwise, he would have had to lie waiting for hours.

His body jerked with his dry sobs, though no tears would fall from his dead eyes.

Then there was another explosion, and he was in the warmth of the fire.

He watched as it spread across the blanket toward him, then began to burn his legs. The fire spread across the floor to the bed and began to climb the walls with the help of an old painting. He could hear the sizzling of his flesh and whatever was inside him as the flames worked their way up his body.

And for the first time in years, he could feel. He felt the warmth of the fire as it consumed his neck, then his head.

And for a few brief moments, there was excruciating pain.

4

She knew before she reached the hotel what he had done.

A part of her had brought him back to life ten years ago. Now that part of her knew that he was dead again, and this time, he wouldn't be coming back.

"NO!" she cried out. Her fury and her madness enveloped her all at once and the inside of the blue Mustang grew hot with her anger.

She would not go to New Orleans. That was unimportant. She would not pursue the plans she and Cole had discussed. That too was unimportant.

Now she had a hunger, a great hunger and a fiery rage that would not be satisfied without destruction. Fire and destruction.

Suddenly, there was a jolt, then an impact as she first clipped a Geo Storm, then ran into the back half of a Monte Carlo, spinning that car. Her body flew forward and her chest hit the steering wheel hard, cracking two ribs. Her head bounced off the windshield, leaving a wet blue smudge.

Her disorientation lasted only a second. The world around her came almost instantly into focus. She eyed the blue smudge on the windshield and felt her forehead. It was wet, but it was not running. She pulled her hand away and saw more of the blue fluid on her fingers. She wasn't bleeding—she was seeping.

"Hey, Lady!"

She looked quickly to her left. A young kid stood staring at her through the glass.

"Are you okay?" he asked.

She didn't answer. Instead, she tried to start the car again, but it wouldn't respond.

Her fury grew.

"HEY!" came another shout, this one from straight ahead. It was a tall man wearing worn-out jeans and cowboy boots. His Red Man Chewin' Tobacco cap was set crooked on his head. He had climbed out of the old Monte Carlo and was pointing at her. "Hey! You stupid bitch!" he yelled. "What the fuck were you thinkin' about?"

Her lip rose into a slight snarl. She looked at this insignificant creature and wondered who or what he thought he was. When he got to the Mustang, he pounded both of his fists on her hood hard. She didn't flinch.

"I just got that thing out of the shop, and you go and fuckin' smash it all to hell, and I bet you ain't even insured!"

She stared at him. "Fuck you!" she shouted. "Fuck you! Fuck you!" The cowboy took a step back, a little surprised at her response. Then he saw that she had started laughing.

Then his feet felt warm.

She screamed at him again, then she let loose her fury. His legs literally exploded from under him, and he fell to the ground as if he had been standing on a rug and it had been yanked away. The boy standing beside her window watched in amazement as pieces of the man's legs splattered against the car and the road, and a piece of calf muscle grazed his cheek. The cowboy lay on the road screaming, flailing his arms, and looking at where his legs were supposed to be. His Red Man cap lay on the pavement three feet away.

Regina got out of her car. As she did, the woman who had been driving the Geo got back into her car and drove away, not wanting to lose her own legs. The boy who had been standing next to her door stepped back as she got out. He stood staring in shock at the man on the street. There was blood from that man on his shirt, and he was in shock.

"What's wrong with you?" Regina shouted at the boy. "Haven't you ever been to a rodeo before?" Her eyes rolled.

"Huh?" he asked, stunned, still staring at the screaming mess that just moments before he had thought was a threat to the girl.

"You chicken shit!" she shouted. Then she pushed him away and he fell back to the pavement hard, his head smacking on the asphalt, knocking him unconscious.

John Freeman and Joe Piscitelli spotted the scene from their patrol car that was headed west down the loop. As they approached the scene, the blood and bodies lying on the road became visible to them. Regina stood in front of her car, facing them.

"Good God," Piscitelli said. "What's this mess?"

"Better call an ambulance," Freeman responded.

Piscitelli got on the radio as they arrived on the scene. Officer Freeman pulled up near the Monte Carlo and got out of the car.

Regina saw the officer get out of the car and glared at him. Then she saw his eyes and she smiled.

As he gave the information to his dispatcher, Piscitelli watched his partner talk to the girl while the cowboy lay bleeding to death on the pavement. The man had passed out and was definitely losing fatal amounts of blood, and the condition of the kid lying next to the Mustang was unknown. But his partner stood talking to the girl. Something was very wrong.

When he finished with the call, Piscitelli got out of the car. As he did, his partner turned and began to walk back to the patrol car, the girl following him.

"What the hell's wrong with you?" Piscitelli shouted at his partner. "That man over there is dying, and that one could be seriously hurt!"

"I've got to get this girl somewhere important; you take care of them."

"What?" Piscitelli couldn't believe what he was hearing. What had happened to his partner? He looked at the girl. She had an odd blue liquid smeared across her head. Her eyes were deep chasms, and he found it difficult to look away. But he did. It was no time to argue, as a man lay dying. He forgot his friend and rushed to the bloody mass on the pavement.

"I don't want him helping that guy," she said quietly to Freeman. "Stop him."

John Freeman turned and drew his gun. They were only about fifteen feet away, so it was a good clean shot right through the back of the skull. Joe Piscitelli's brains flew out the front of his head and mixed with the blood on the pavement as he fell forward, lying across the man with no legs.

"Now take me to your house," she commanded him.

"Of course," Officer Freeman agreed. He smiled and held his head up at the honor of their Queen having chosen him.

They got into his patrol car and sped away from the scene.

Seven minutes later, the ambulance arrived to find two dead bodies, one unconscious concussion victim, and about twenty witnesses.

5

Ben headed for the office. He had left Carrie and Jack at Budd's place after making sure that Budd was clean. On his way to the office, he stopped at the one-hour photo lab and picked up the pictures he had taken at the compound. When he picked up the photos, he noticed that he was being watched by one of the lab technicians. The lab guy had probably seen the pictures and wanted to check out who was picking them up. The man smiled slightly when Ben caught him looking and winked one of his glowing eyes. Ben wasn't sure if this was good or bad.

Once Ben got to the station, he packed the pictures and other evidence into a small briefcase and went in.

"Hey, Williams!" someone shouted to him. He turned to look. It was Paul Beck sticking his head out of a doorway. "Sheriff's looking for you."

"Headed that way now," Ben replied, then turned.

"Where the hell you been?" Paul called after him. "Not like you to call in sick, then disappear."

Ben stopped and turned again. "I wasn't sick, and I didn't disappear, I just went hiking. It's nice to just get away from all this crap once in a while."

"Since when did you take up hiking?"

"Since I realized the office couldn't reach me in the woods."

Ben turned away and headed down the hall, toward the sheriff's office. As he approached the doorway, he passed the office of Detective Jacobson, the man who had been assigned to the cult case. As he passed the door, he listened and heard Todd talking on the phone in his unmistakable Yankee accent. It seemed he was putting in extra hours these days. Ben began to wonder if perhaps Todd had in fact been put in charge of the list and communicating between the members of the Family. If so, this plan was shot.

Ben knocked on the sheriff's closed door.

There was a hesitation, then Sheriff Walsh shouted through the door for him to come in.

Ben walked into the office and closed the door. The sheriff was on the telephone, talking to someone about the extradition hearings that were coming up on that guy who had killed two girls in the woods in Smith County and then had been caught two years later stealing glow-in-the-dark condoms at a convenience store in Arkansas. The sheriff motioned for Ben to sit down. Ben sighed in relief as he sat, knowing from the sheriff's eyes that he could be trusted.

A minute later, the sheriff hung up the phone and stuck a toothpick in his mouth. It was a habit he had picked up when he quit smoking three months earlier.

"So, Ben," he started, "we've been trying to get a hold of you. It's not like you to go off where you can't be reached."

"I was doing some work on my own," he explained, "and there weren't any phones where I was."

"Working on your own? On a case?"

"Sort of."

"I wasn't aware you had been assigned to work with one of our detectives. Who are you working with?"

"Nobody just yet."

The sheriff looked surprised. "Ben, you're a deputy, and a fine one at that. But we've got detectives here, and they're the only ones authorized to work on our cases. What the hell have you been up to?"

Ben reached into his briefcase. First, he removed the pictures and handed them to the sheriff. As the sheriff looked through them, his eyebrows furrowed.

"What is this place?" he asked as he looked at a picture of one of the rooms that had been used for storing prisoners.

"This is the compound where the cult that's been stirring up so much trouble was staying."

The sheriff lowered the pictures and looked at Ben. "You knew where they were, and you went and took pictures? Why didn't you give the information to Jacobson, let him handle it? Are you trying to get points for breaking this information? This isn't a newspaper, Ben, it's a sheriff's office. We work like a team here. What if you'd gotten in trouble? Who would have backed you up? If you'd disappeared, you would have taken this information right along with you."

"I got a tip from an unreliable source," Ben explained. "I had to get evidence before I told you what she said."

"Again," the sheriff interrupted, "why not just have her talk to Jacobson, and let him handle this."

Ben got straight to the point. "The girl is dead, and Jacobson is dirty."

"Todd Jacobson is dirty? He's been with this office longer than I have, and he's always been a good cop. I promoted him myself. I have a lot of trouble believing that he's dirty on this one."

"There were some things this girl told me about people in this office, including Jacobson. She was very specific. And she had good information on the people inside the cult, and the location of the facilities. I couldn't bring this to Jacobson, especially since she mentioned him by name."

"So, why come to me with it now? I put Jacobson on this case—how do you know I'm not involved, too?"

"I saw a list," he lied. "Your name wasn't on it."

"But others in this office were?"

"Yes."

"Who else?"

"I can't tell you now," Ben answered.

Surprise again entered the sheriff's eyes. "What the hell's gotten into you, Ben? You're acting damn peculiar."

"There's some pretty serious stuff going on here," Ben explained. "And I'm going to tell you everything I can."

Ben explained about his visit, about the compound and the people he had seen there. He told him about the meeting and the sheriff's eyes widened again when Ben explained how the man called Darius had exploded into flames. When he finished talking, the sheriff just sat looking at him, not sure what should be said next. Ben took the opportunity to play the tape he had made of some random conversations and of the last gathering. There was a lot of static from the point where the girl had appeared in the room, but the words were still understandable. The sheriff listened intently to the sounds of the burning man, believing then what Ben had told him. The tape lasted about thirty minutes, and ended with the sounds of shuffling feet as they left the chamber.

Ben turned off the tape player and sat waiting for the sheriff's response.

"Well," the sheriff finally said, "I guess I'm going to have to let you run on this one. I'm not sure why you've got to do it the way you say, but you've done a hell of a lot in a short period of time. Normally, I'd chew your butt out and put you on suspension, but I think it might be best if you keep working on this. I have to tell you that I don't like the way you've taken things into your own hands, but I can't say as I wouldn't have done the same thing myself given your situation." He chewed nervously on the toothpick. "I want you to let me know what I'm working with here. I want to know who's dirty and who ain't. You're going to have to put together your own team for this, so pick out two men you want to work with and get on it. I expect you to keep me a little better informed of what you're up to than you have been."

"Yes, sir." This was better than he had hoped for.

"What do you think we should do about Jacobson?"

"Don't let him know about any of this. Let him think he's still the only one working on it. He'll come down with the rest of them when it's over. If he asks you to let me work with him, turn it down. I may be able to convince him I'm part of this thing, and he'll probably want me working with him on it when he is convinced."

"Hmph." The toothpick twitched and flipped. "I guess so. And how soon can you get me that list?"

"Give me twenty-four hours," Ben said. He knew he couldn't tell the sheriff about how he really knew who was involved and who was not. But he figured he would be able to make up that list by tomorrow after he had taken a look at everybody.

"Get on it and do it right. I'm going to want some answers when this is all over."

"Thanks for trusting me on this one."

"Don't make me regret it."

Ben packed up his pictures and tape.

"You better make copies of those for me as soon as possible," the sheriff suggested, "in case anything happens."

"Yes, sir."

The sheriff wished Ben luck as he left his office. Then Ben walked two doors down and knocked. Detective Jacobson called for him to come in.

Todd put his cigarette down as Ben walked in. "Well, I've been wondering where you were."

"Busy," Ben replied.

Todd saw Ben's eyes. They glowed, like his own. Then he smiled and offered Ben a chair.

13

The day had passed, and the sun was setting. Clouds spread over the horizon and cast their purple glow.

Budd Holloway drove his four-wheel-drive truck down Highway 110 toward Mount Sylvan. Jack and Carrie rode with him. The three of them had spent the evening discussing the situation and making plans. Budd had offered his help. Jack and Carrie had been grateful but leery. They had discussed whether they should risk someone else's life on their problem. But it hadn't taken long to decide that what was at stake was worth risking many lives.

But what was at stake? What was Regina planning to do? They had simply assumed that whatever it was, it had to be terrible based on their experience with her people. But what was the exact plan?

They decided that it didn't matter. Enough people had died. There was no question that whatever the intent of Regina and her people, it could be no less than evil at its roots.

Two hours after Ben had left them at Budd's house, he had called to say that a meeting would take place that night a couple of hours after sunset, and that he knew the exact location. He had given the information to Jack, who had shared it with Budd and Carrie. They were on their way now to the heavily wooded area between Mount Sylvan and New Harmony. Jack knew the area well as it was only a few miles from his house. In the back of the pickup were a couple of loaded rifles and a shotgun.

As the sun disappeared below the cloud cover, they came to the old dirt road. It was right where Ben had said it would be. The recent rains had made the road muddy, and there were ruts where at least one vehicle had passed recently. But they had arrived early, at least an hour and a half before the ceremonies were scheduled to begin. This would give them time to set up and hide themselves well. If someone had already arrived, they would just have to take care of the situation when they got to the clearing. Budd switched his truck into four-wheel drive and drove onto the muddy path.

The trees quickly grew thick, and Budd had to drive slowly following the old logging road that wound through the countryside. The meeting place was a few miles back, in a clearing that had been made by the logging company two years earlier when they were harvesting in the area. The wilderness was working at its best to reclaim the area, and as a result, the road was very narrow. Tree branches occasionally raked the sides of the truck as Budd drove past them. The sound was an eerie one and it brought images to Carrie's mind of long-clawed hands trying to get at them. A light rain began to fall.

As they rounded a corner, Budd hit his brakes hard and his truck slid off the road into the brush. Lying across the road was a fallen tree. It was too large to drive over, and much too large to move.

"Shit," Budd exclaimed as his truck slid to a stop. "I guess we're going to have to go the rest of the way on foot."

"How's anybody else going to get back there?" Carrie asked. "Won't they just move the ceremonies?"

"Well, they're certainly not going to be able to haul that tree out of the way without some heavy equipment."

Then there was a crack of glass and a loud pop.

Jack knew the sound. He had heard it many times before. He grabbed Carrie and pulled her quickly to the floor of the truck. There was another crack of glass and another explosion, then a third.

Budd didn't get down with them. Jack looked up and saw the man slumped over the steering wheel.

"What's going on?" Carrie asked.

"Someone's shooting at us." Jack felt under the big seat of Budd's truck. He found an old map and four old soft drink cans before his hands ran across the small leather pouch he had hoped to find.

Carrie lay at an odd angle, her shoulder pushed against the dash. Her arm was pressed between her leg and Budd's. She looked up at the man and knew that he was dead. "What are we going to do?"

Jack unzipped the leather pouch and pulled out the small gun that Budd kept in it. It was a .38 special with a snub-nose barrel. It would only be good for close-range shooting, but that was all he needed for now. "Just get down on the floorboard as low as you can. Push Budd's legs over and get down under them."

Carrie did as Jack told her. She felt safer down in the darkness of the floorboard. Next to her, Jack was staying low and looking out the windows. The headlights lit up the exterior of the vehicle well enough that he could see a few feet out. The inside of the truck was dark. That was just one advantage.

The two of them stayed still and listened. They heard voices. Then they could hear someone walking through the brush toward the truck.

2

Ben rode in the car with Todd Jacobson as they headed toward the ceremonies. The car was full of smoke as Todd lit up another cigarette. Another man, one he hadn't met before, rode in the back. The afternoon had been spent checking out the men at the office, writing down the names of the ones with glowing eyes. That list, seven names long, now rested inside an envelope on the sheriff's desk, awaiting his return in the morning.

Ben's plan had turned out to be a good one so far. No one had even suspected what he was really up to. The glowing eyes had put him in the good graces of all the right people. He had learned that the meeting he now went to had been called by the Queen so that she could communicate the plan to her Family. The members of the Family would all be given their special tasks, and her goals would be revealed. It was a cool night, and Ben had worn his bulky jacket. Inside the jacket, he had once again hidden his tape recorder. Already he had two tapes with enough evidence to put three police officers and a banker in jail.

Ben still didn't feel that simply killing Regina was the right thing to do. He knew she was evil, but he struggled with his own definitions of right and wrong. He knew that they couldn't capture her. He knew that if she was allowed to live, there would certainly be more death and destruction. He knew for a fact that this had been the case in New Orleans three years ago. But still, he grappled with his doubts.

Inside, he knew that when the time came, if it became necessary, he could do it. But he also knew he would feel the guilt of it for the rest of his life.

"You're quiet," Todd commented.

"Just thinking."

"It's wonderful, isn't it?"

"Yes," Ben went along, adding just a touch of false wonder to his voice.

"Being a part of this thing, this glorious thing. It's wonderful. You can't know what it's like."

"But I do," Ben replied.

The car slowed and turned off the main road. But it was too early. The turnoff wasn't supposed to be for another two miles yet.

Then Ben heard the sound of a gun being cocked behind him. Todd turned to Ben. "I don't think you do."

3

The tall thin man with the patch over one eye looked at the pickup. It was still running, but other than that, there was no movement.

"Go check it out," he said to one of the men who had come with him. The man muttered his agreement and headed toward the truck; his rifle held out in front of him.

The man approached the truck as carefully as he could. He could see the driver of the truck slumped over the steering wheel. He had gotten him on the first shot. He didn't know if he had gotten either of the other two, but they were not visible from where he stood.

He decided to approach the truck from the driver's side. If the other two were inside, they would be huddled on the floorboard of the truck. He aimed at the base of the door and squeezed off three rounds. The bullets pierced the door of the truck, sparks flying from the metal as the bullets tore through. He stopped and listened. The engine of the truck made it difficult to hear any quiet noises, but he was becoming confident that there were no quiet noises to hear.

He walked slowly to the driver-side window of the truck. First, he raised the barrel of the rifle to the window, then he peered inside.

4

Detective Jacobson must have been in charge of the list. That was all it could be. Or maybe this was just a test.

Ben turned his head and looked at Todd as he drove down the dark road. "I don't understand."

Todd put out his cigarette. "Did you think that just because you have the mark means you can fool us all? We're not stupid as you might think."

"I don't get it, Todd. What have I done?"

Todd smiled and glanced at Ben. "We've got to be very careful around here. Your little discussion with the sheriff was not very helpful. Now we're going to have to do a little scrambling to clean that mess up."

Ben couldn't believe it. He had never thought once that the sheriff's office might be bugged. Now it made perfect sense, and he felt the fool for not having thought of it earlier.

"Ah, I see it makes sense to you now."

Ben didn't answer. Instead, he sat in silence, thinking of how he was going to get out of this. The metal of his own gun felt warm against his side. He would have to get to it somehow.

They rounded one final corner and came to a large clearing that was full of cars. There was everything from a rusted-out Buick LeSabre to an Infiniti Q45. At the entrance to this large parking area, two men stood carrying assault rifles. Their eyes seemed to glow in the dark. They looked inside the car, then let them pass through.

Todd drove to the end of the rows of cars, where he parked. From where they sat, Ben could see to the opposite end of the clearing. There they were, all the people with the glowing eyes. They all stood facing a hastily constructed wooden stage with some kind of table on it.

Todd limped around the car while the man behind him kept his gun pointed at Ben's head. Todd opened Ben's door and told him to get out.

As Ben got out of the car, he realized what the table was. It was an altar. They were going to sacrifice somebody tonight.

"Turn around and place your hands on the top of the car."

This was it. In a moment, he was going to be disarmed. If he was going to make a run for it, this would probably be his last chance. He glanced inside the car as he turned. The man in the back seat was still watching him, still pointing his gun right at him. Ben knew that if he gave up his gun, it would be over. He tried to think fast.

As he raised his hands to the top of the car, his jacket opened slightly and his tape recorder fell out. Both Todd and the man inside the car looked down to where it had fallen.

Ben did not. This would be his best chance.

5

Carrie and Jack listened as the man approached from outside the truck. Then the footsteps stopped. Just as Jack got ready to rise and look, three shots rang out.

All three bullets came through the driver-side door. The first lodged in Budd's limp left leg, about six inches from Carrie's head. The second bullet grazed Carrie's cheek as it flew into the padded seat of the truck. She flinched and brought her head up into the bottom of Budd's leg. The third shot was even lower, and it dove into the seat where Carrie's head had just been.

"Are you okay?" Jack whispered.

Carrie felt her face. The pain stung, and she wasn't sure whether the bullet had gone into her. But Jack needed to concentrate on his task right now. "I'm fine."

The footsteps resumed and a moment later, there was a rifle barrel at the driver's window. A second later, there was a face.

Jack aimed at the face and fired.

The sound was deafening inside the truck. For a moment, everything was silent as their eardrums reacted to the impact of the sound.

There was a hole in the window, and the face had disappeared. After her ears recovered, Carrie could hear the screams of a man outside the truck.

There was another shot from outside the truck. It did not come from the wounded man's rifle as it sounded too far away. Another hole appeared in the driver's window.

Carrie reached up and put the truck in reverse. As the truck jerked backward, she pressed her hand on the accelerator. The truck jumped away, throwing both of them forward. Jack was not expecting the move and he fell against the dash, bruising his shoulder. The truck backed quickly away from the downed tree, backed across the dirt road, then bored into the brush until it collided with a big pine tree. In all, they had moved over a hundred feet and had placed a few trees between them and their attackers.

It was a good move. But there would be time later for thanks. Maybe.

Jack threw his door open and rolled out. "Come on!" he called to Carrie. He fired a shot across the road into the brush beside the fallen tree to give her time to get out. She pushed Budd's legs away and crawled across the floorboard of the truck to the open door. Then she jumped out, landing in the wet brush and cutting her hand on a blackberry bush.

A shot came from the brush across the road. Steam began shooting from under the hood of the still-running truck.

Jack helped Carrie up. "Get into the woods," he told her. She got to her feet and worked her way past the brush and trees that lined the road behind her. Another shot rang out and this time, the truck began leaning to the front and left as one of the tires exploded.

Jack went to the truck and pulled the back of the seat forward. Lying amongst the old Coke cans and beef jerky wrappers was the flashlight he had hoped to find.

He grabbed the flashlight and got away from the truck as another shot came through the driver's window and was stopped on its way to Jack's head only by Budd's heavy neck. Jack walked into the woods.

"Over here," he heard Carrie call.

Jack made his way to Carrie until he saw her outline against a tree. Behind him, there was another shot, but now there were too many objects between them and their attackers. Jack grabbed Carrie's hand and led her back farther into the woods. He worked his way slowly through the darkness until he felt safe turning on the flashlight. Behind them, the gunshots stopped. Jack didn't know if this was good or bad.

6

As the man in the car returned his gaze to Ben, he realized the mistake he had made. His eyes widened and he tried to squeeze off a shot, but Ben fired first and hit him right between the eyes.

An instant later, Todd had him in a bear hug from behind. His arms were pinned to his sides, and he could only point the gun in front of him. The men who had guarded the entry had heard the shots and were coming across the parking area. It was quite a distance, and escape was still a possibility.

Ben stepped down hard onto the top of Todd's foot. He heard a crack of bone as Todd cried out, but his tight squeeze loosened only a little. Ben stepped down again, this time grinding the broken bone against flesh. Todd turned and slammed Ben against the side of the car. Ben's shoulder hit the top of the car where the door to the back seat remained open. He held tightly to his gun. The men were getting closer.

Todd swung Ben back around and tripped him to the ground, landing firmly on top of him, his legs spread out for balance. He wasn't trying to defeat Ben, but just to subdue him until help arrived. The side of Ben's face was covered with pine needles and small rocks where it had hit the ground. He struggled to get up or roll over, but Todd had the advantage and it seemed there was no way out of this.

He struggled fruitlessly until he felt the barrel of the assault rifle against his cheek and heard the command of the man to drop his gun.

7

Slim Tom swore as he watched the man and woman disappear into the woods. This was the second time they had eluded him. This would not play well with the Queen. "You go after them," he told the man next to him. "I've got to get to the gathering."

The heavy man next to him was a gunsmith by profession. That was one reason he had let the other man go up to the truck and get his face shot off. Without speaking, the big man walked through the brush, stepped over the writhing body of the wounded man, and headed toward the truck. Then he realized that the wounded man might start calling for him and ruin everything. He turned and placed the barrel of his rifle against the man's chest so that the noise of the shot would be muffled. But then he found he couldn't do it. As much as he knew he should, knowing the man would die anyway, he couldn't just kill him. It was a weakness that Slim Tom hadn't seen and would never have suspected. He left the man to his pain, telling himself that he would come back and help him when his task was done, knowing in the back of his mind the man would be dead anyway by then.

He looked at the truck. The gusher of steam that had been rising from the hood had slowed, and the truck's engine was beginning to overheat. In any case, he would have to walk around the back of the truck to ensure that he wasn't seen, as its headlights were still on. As he walked along his side of the road, the black Cutlass he had ridden here in started up and pulled out of the bushes. He watched it as it rolled away into the darkness, and he hoped Slim Tom hadn't seen his moment of weakness.

He would have to be very quiet. With any luck, the man and the woman would think they had all left and would come back to the truck.

Then he would kill them. This would put him in good with both Slim Tom and the Queen. Better things would be in store for him.

The truck's radiator blew itself dry, then coughed its last as the engine overheated. The gunsmith made it past the truck and crossed the road behind it. He looked into the woods. In the distance, he could see the occasional glimmer of a dancing flashlight. Then he stepped in after them.

8

"You son of a bitch," Todd yelled in his face. "You're going to be more than a little sorry for that stunt." Todd pulled Ben to his feet. The gun Ben had used to put a hole in the other man's head lay on the ground about five feet away. But it might as well have been five miles away.

Todd threw Ben back up against the car while the other man held his gun on Ben. Then Todd reached inside the car and fumbled in his glove box. A moment later, Ben felt the steel of the police-issue handcuffs as they were locked around his wrists, a little too tightly.

Todd turned Ben back toward the clearing and gave him a shove. Ben stumbled forward and lost his balance, falling to the ground and landing mostly on his chest and face. The gunshot had grabbed the interest of the people and they had turned to watch the spectacle.

"Get up, you worthless shit." Todd kicked at him with his good foot.

Ben rose first to his knees, then to his feet. His head throbbed, and a trickle of blood ran from his lower lip. Todd walked beside him with his new, more pronounced limp. The man with the rifle walked behind them. This way they marched Ben across the clearing and up to the altar.

When they reached the altar, they took Ben to a spot a few yards to the side of it. Todd found a small tree nearby and handcuffed Ben's arms around it. Then they stepped back and waited.

Ben looked over at the crowd. Their gaze was fixed on him. Then he looked back at the altar.

Then he understood what was to become of him.

9

Jack led Carrie slowly through the woods. The clouds covered what moon there was, so it was extremely dark. Carrie followed Jack, one hand on his back for guidance. Jack picked his way through the brush, using the flashlight from Budd's truck. In the daytime, the tall pine trees blocked out most of the sun, so the underbrush here was fairly limited. This made it a little easier to walk, though it was still quite a challenge. They had made their way about fifty yards from the truck.

They heard another shot coming from far behind them. A moment later, they heard a car drive away. Jack stopped walking.

"Are they giving up?" Carrie asked.

Jack listened as the car drove away from them, back up the path to the main road. "Maybe for now."

Carrie felt her face with her free hand. The blood was still running from her wound. She wondered just how close she had been to death.

Jack listened as Budd's truck began first to sputter, then died completely. Then the woods were eerily silent.

"What do we do now?" Carrie asked.

"Shhh," Jack whispered. The thought had just occurred to him that they might not be alone. He listened carefully but could hear nothing. Still, he was uneasy. He turned off his flashlight, then got as close to Carrie as he could and whispered in her ear. "Maybe we should just stay here for a while to make sure that we're alone." Her hand remained on his back in the darkness.

The woods were silent, oddly silent. It didn't sound as if anyone was coming after them. They could make their way back to the road, though it sounded as if the truck had overheated and wouldn't be of any use to them. Jack was also worried that someone might be sitting near the truck, waiting for them. The best plan would be to wander through the woods toward the main road. It would not be an easy journey, but it might be the only way to stay alive.

"Let's keep walking," Jack suggested. "We'll head back toward the main road. It'll take us a while, but it's the safest thing to do." Before

Jack started walking again, Carrie tapped him on the shoulder with her free hand. Jack turned to face her. Even in the darkness, he could sense her closeness. At least in this, there was some comfort.

"Jack," she whispered.

"Yes?"

"I want you to get us out of this."

He could hear the frustration and fear in her voice. These were things he felt too, but for now, they would have to take a back seat while he tried his best to get them to safety. "I'll do my best."

"Jack," she whispered.

"Yes?"

"I love you, Jack."

This took him by complete surprise, but once it had been said, it seemed so natural and felt so good. It gave him strength that moments before had eluded him. She felt for his face with her hands. When she found it, she pulled it to her and kissed him.

It was warm and good, and he knew that if life ever became normal again, if there was any way the two of them could return to the routine and mundane, they would be spending a lot of time together.

Then there was the snap of a twig. They both heard it. Jack turned and began making his way through the woods in the darkness, being as silent as he could. Carrie kept her hand on his back and followed.

There was definitely somebody in here with them. Jack could sense it. There was something about the new silence that was wrong, some subconscious rustling of leaves behind them, something taking up space and moving toward them.

10

The crowd stood waiting for their Queen. Ben remained handcuffed to the small tree. Moments earlier, a tall thin man with a patch over one eye had arrived and Todd Jacobson had left. The man had looked Ben over quickly, then turned his gaze to the woods just beyond the altar.

Then there was a rush of sudden coldness. It wasn't a breeze of any kind, just a sudden change in the air. The people fell completely silent as the woods already had. Now there was virtually nothing to be heard except the approaching footsteps.

Regina emerged from the woods. She was clothed in the black ceremonial robe that had first been hers, then Darius's, and was once again hers. In a small pocket on the inside of the robe was the silver dagger that she had used years ago in those magical ceremonies, and that she would use again tonight.

She walked over to Slim Tom and looked into his eye. Slim Tom felt the coldness slice through him, and he smelled the odor of her slow decay. "Is this the one we will be sacrificing?" she asked.

"Yes," Slim Tom answered.

She looked at Ben, looked into his eyes. For a moment, she was taken aback. This man's face reminded her of Saul, her good and true friend whom she had been forced to kill years ago. "He has the mark," she answered. "If he is one of us, and he is to be sacrificed, he must come forward of his own free will."

"He's not one of us," Slim Tom explained. "He's a cop who'd infiltrated the compound and was at the ceremonies where you marked us. But he's not one of us."

Regina returned her gaze to Ben. An evil grin crawled onto her face. "But he will be," she explained. "He will become one of us, and he will be invaluable. He will help us maim and destroy, and it will be a sweet torture for him, much worse than mere death."

Slim Tom did not understand her intentions, and he did not know where they would be able to find someone at this hour to serve as their sacrifice.

Regina looked deep into Ben's eyes, and he shifted uncomfortably as her Power pulled at his soul. She spoke to him, but her lips did not move. "You have spent your days trying to destroy us," she said. "From tonight on, however, you will stand by my side. You will be a part of us, and you will help us wreak the revenge that is mine and mine alone. You will love and despise me. You will worship and blaspheme me. You will be both alive and dead, much like me." Then she laughed and her eyes rolled.

The words were hypnotic. Already Ben felt some part of himself slipping away, never to return. It was not a test of wills; it was merely a destruction of his will by sheer power. But there was much more of him to be destroyed before any of what she said would be true.

"The night is young," she answered him as if reading his thoughts. "And you have seen only the beginning of what you will become."

Regina backed away from Ben and walked up onto the platform where the altar stood. Once there, she looked over the crowd. In a section near the back, she spotted a young couple who did not carry the mark. Their eyes seemed dull and dead to her. She motioned to Slim Tom to come to her. "See the young couple near the back," she whispered. Slim Tom looked but saw many young people. "The ones who do not have the mark," she clarified.

"Yes," he answered. "They are new to the Family. They're friends of the Perrys. We checked them out, and they're fine."

"We cannot sacrifice anyone who has the mark here tonight, not for these ceremonies. Walk around to them and bring them forward. They will be our sacrifice tonight. Tell them to come forward to be initiated. I will handle it from there."

Slim Tom grinned his yellow grin and stepped down off the stage. He walked to Todd Jacobson and had him bring a couple of men with him in case there was any trouble. They walked around the crowd to the young couple, who gave no resistance and in fact, seemed quite eager when told that Regina had requested that they come forward. They walked in front of the men to the stage. As they approached the stage, fear showed on their faces. This woman had risen from the dead. Witnesses had confirmed it. Some of the witnesses were quite reputable people. So, the couple had decided to join this new and powerful cult, in search of the riches and glory its followers promised. Now that they faced the woman, their eyes showed that they too felt her awesome power as it pulled at them, beckoning them to some deep crevasse that seemed to lead to the center of the earth.

"Come forward," she said to them both.

They did not intend to resist, but their bodies seemed to respond on their own nonetheless, not waiting for them to get over their hesitations. They both stepped onto the stage and faced their new Queen. She smiled at them, and it seemed like both an inviting and a threatening smile.

"You are about to become members of this great and wonderful Family," she told them. "Lie together on this table so that we may initiate you."

Fear gripped the woman and she tried to resist her body as it walked to the altar and lay down upon it. Her resistance was futile, however, and moments later, she lay by her husband. They lay together looking into the starless skies. Suddenly, it seemed very peaceful, and they felt a kind of waking sleep grip them, paralyzing them from head to foot.

It didn't matter. What time she had left was going to be hell for humanity. And it was all going to start here.

Tonight.

14

1

The crowd of people stood in awe and silence as they became hypnotized by the Power of their Queen. The rain that had been falling lightly stopped, but they all felt chilled to the bone as if they had been soaked. She raised her hand. The headlights that lit the gathering area were turned off, leaving them all in absolute darkness.

Ben felt the paralysis that had gripped the crowd as it took firm hold of his brain. What did this woman have in store for him? What did she mean by both living and dead? How was he going to become instrumental in her plans?

Even in the pitch-black darkness, he knew exactly where she stood.

But then he noticed that it was not completely dark. His eyes had adjusted somehow and now he could see her, though it was more a ghostly image he saw than the actual woman. From where he stood, he could also see the crowd, though it was only their faces that were visible.

Then he knew. It was their eyes. They were all seeing with their new eyes.

Regina moved around to the front of the altar. Her feet were not visible, and she seemed to float rather than walk. When she reached the front of the stage, she took a shiny object from her robe and began etching the odd ceremonial shapes into the soft wood. The silver spike cut through the wood almost magically, and the shapes she drew glowed red, though the young couple could see none of this, as they had not been marked. These were ancient shapes that she had drawn before and that came from some place not within her rotten mind, but from within the unaffected and whole Power. It was that Power that guided her hands as she drew the stars and the triangles, the multi-pupiled eyes, and cryptic symbols.

There was Power here like there had never been before. Now that there was less of Regina to interfere with the Power, the Power was even purer and less constrained by its human host. Regina gave herself over to this Power, which knew and obeyed her goal.

With all the shapes drawn, she stood again and faced her Family. Their softly glowing eyes looked up at her, their gazes inexorably fixed on her own. She opened her mouth and began to speak. The words were not English. Some were Latin, others even more ancient.

Ben listened to these words and understood. It was not so much sentences and statements as concepts. The words evoked images of old and terrible Power; Power so old that eternity suddenly seemed to be something comprehensible.

As she spoke, the golden dust began again to flow between the members of the Family. Ben watched as it wound its way out from the center and moved toward the edges. As it passed through the people, something about their eyes changed, though Ben could not tell exactly what it was. He watched as the dust made its way toward him, and he feared what was waiting for him.

Then it touched him.

At first, there was a numbness that started at his head, then raced through the remainder of his body. He found there was absolutely nothing he could do to move any part of his body. Then a new numbness began to creep through his brain. He felt his thoughts being somehow restrained, confined, and controlled. There was something foreign inside him, something that was not only him but everybody here, and especially Regina.

She regarded her Family as they became a part of her and the Power. She opened her mouth again.

This time, Ben heard the words as they emerged from his own mouth. He felt an odd duality as if these were words that came from his own mind and soul, yet they were also deeply foreign. He struggled to stop speaking but found himself unable to do so.

As he spoke, his eyes followed Regina. She floated slowly back to the opposite side of the altar. As she did, the bodies of the young couple again became visible under the glow of her body. They lay perfectly still now, except for the quick rising and falling of their chests that indicated both life and panic.

There was a rumbling sound like thunder and the ground shook, only the sound came not from the skies but from the ground. Then Regina began to rise from the stage, floating slowly higher until it looked as if she were standing on the edge of the altar. Her hands moved gracefully, producing in her hand the razor-sharp knife. It appeared there, as if by magic. She held the knife out before her and raised her eyes to the heavens. Words flowed from her and from her people. As they spoke, the ground shook as if being moved by a mild earthquake. The rumbling grew louder as she spoke, and her eyes took on a new fiery glow that seemed to extend upward from her toward the skies.

Then she returned her gaze to her people and terror gripped them all. It did not look like her face at all. They could see face after face, all on top of each other, extending six faces deep. They were ancient and tortured faces, they were the faces of the Power, and they struck terror into the souls of everyone present.

Then the body of their Queen began to tilt forward. As it did, there was a tremendous scream that rose first from Regina, then from the crowd of people before her. The golden dust flowed quickly, rushing around and through the crowd, touching them and chilling them as they both watched and felt. Moments later, Regina's body lay face-down in the air, about two feet above the bodies on the altar. The young couple still saw only darkness, but they felt the shaking of the stage, and felt the icy breath of the faces above them.

Then the knife came forward. It danced and carved, then disap-peared. A second later, Regina's body moved slowly back to the upright position, something wet and pounding dripping redness from each of her hands. Slowly, her feet returned to the stage behind the altar. She returned her eyes to the heavens and spoke once again.

Then Ben could see the stars. It was as if the clouds had disappeared, and the sky had become magically clear. Only the stars looked wrong, as if they had moved around. Then he noticed they were red, and suddenly seemed much too large.

As the stars grew, he realized they were falling from the skies, descending upon them all. He tried to look away, tried to cry out, but could do neither. Instead, he watched as the fiery balls came down upon them.

The fireballs hit with tremendous force. Ben felt their searing heat and saw their blinding light. He felt himself burning up inside them, being somehow taken up and away by them.

The pounding hearts burst into flames in Regina's hands. The crowd before her stared skyward in utter terror as their wills and their souls were stripped away by the ancient fire.

The two bodies on the altar exploded into flame. In the last instant, Regina freed them from her hold, and they writhed and screamed for several minutes as the fire cooked their flesh.

Then everyone screamed as they died a terrible death.

Then they were instantly reborn as something new, something that kept the part of them that was their minds and their memories, but something that was filled with some part of the Power.

Then the fire that burned their souls died down, as did the real flames that had burned the two bodies on the altar.

The glowing symbols on the stage faded.

Total darkness returned.

Then, a few moments later, the headlights were turned back on.

The men who turned them on did not have to be told to do this—they just knew that it was time. The same way they knew exactly who had survived the ceremonies and who had not.

Then Ben understood, though he was now something less than Ben, and something more. He was no longer just one man—he was a part of the Power, and it had invaded him to the core. He could feel a part of what everyone felt, see a part of what everyone saw.

Worst of all, he remembered what Regina had said to him about helping her wreak death and destruction, and he knew that she had been right. He would help. And he would do so as if it was all there was on this Earth to be done.

And in a sense, it *was* all that was left.

2

Jack led Carrie through the woods as quickly as he could. If someone was following them, there was a good chance their pursuer was moving faster than they were since he was most likely alone. Jack hoped that the darkness was enough to keep the man confused. He wouldn't be able to shoot at what he couldn't see.

Then Jack ran into a large tree that had fallen over most of the way the previous winter. Unfortunately, it had never quite made it all the way to the ground and instead was leaning against a limb of the nearest tree, a limb that had grown very weak over the past year. Jack's shoulder provided the final bit of force needed to snap the supporting limb, and the tree rolled from its perch, first pushing Jack and Carrie backward, then jumping from its stump and knocking them both to the ground.

Limbs and branches snapped and broke as the big tree crashed the rest of the way to the forest floor. The main trunk of the tree missed Jack by less than a foot and would have quite easily crushed his chest under its weight had it not.

But a large bottom limb did not miss. It came down hard on Jack's midsection, knocking the wind out of him as it threw him to the ground and then pinned him quite firmly to it. The trunk of the tree knocked Carrie out of the way and into another tree. She lay on the forest floor, dazed from the impact. She tried to sit up, but it seemed as if her body did not want to respond right away. Her left shoulder hurt badly, and she began to fear she might have broken it.

Jack lay pinned under the tree branch. Breathing was becoming a task as the branch of the big tree pushed its weight down on him. His chest felt numb where the limb lay, and he wondered if his ribs had all made it through the ordeal unbroken.

Jack wanted to call out for Carrie but was afraid to make any further noise. He listened carefully and could hear her as she tried to get up.

Then there was a light. It appeared to Jack's left and was heading quickly in his direction. He tried to rise but could not.

Carrie too saw the light, and she knew that it meant something bad, but her circuits were still crossed as she slowly regained her senses. By the time she understood what was going on, the light had grown and enveloped her.

"Don't move," came a voice from behind the light. She could see the outline of a man, though he looked like two men holding two flashlights. Her head throbbed. The man also held a rifle, and it was pointed at her.

The gunsmith looked at the dazed woman and prepared to shoot her.

But something inside him resisted. It would have been much easier if he had found the man, but instead, he was looking at a beautiful woman. He wondered what kind of threat she could be, and then began to wonder if he was going to be able to kill her.

He shone the light around to see where the man was. He found him quickly and saw that he was pinned under the branch of a large tree. Then he looked back at the woman, who was trying to get to her feet.

"Take it easy," he warned her, pointing the rifle again in her direction.

She stumbled to her right once, then was able to stand using the nearby tree for a brace. She looked again at the man. There were still two of him.

"Move over there." The man motioned with his rifle toward the fallen tree.

Carrie walked unsteadily to where Jack lay pinned by the big pine tree. He was struggling to get his free hand behind him to get a hold of the pistol he could feel pushing into the small of his back. But the limb had him firmly pinned down, and he could not rise even an inch off the ground.

"Stop moving around," the man commanded Jack. Jack stopped squirming.

The gunsmith looked at the two of them. It was clear from his expression that he wished Cory had been successful in his attempt at killing these two when they were still faceless strangers in the truck. Now he could see them, and it was likely that their faces would haunt him forever.

It was obvious that he didn't want to kill the woman. But it was also clear that he had seen the terrible wrath of the Queen, and that he did not want that wrath turned upon him. If he did kill them both, he would certainly be rewarded with position and power. But he would never be the same. If he'd been able to kill them as they ran through the woods, even that would have been okay. Clearly it was seeing their faces that had changed everything.

Jack could see the man struggling with himself. "You can't just kill us," he said. "How can we possibly be a threat?"

Carrie still saw double, but she had regained most of her senses and she understood what Jack was trying to do. "Why are you doing this?" she pleaded with him. "We haven't hurt anybody."

"Shut up, both of you." The man re-gripped his gun and the hard look returned to his eyes. The struggle was obvious on his face. Carrie had a soft and soothing voice. Jack could tell that it was going to be very difficult for him to kill her.

The gunsmith walked closer to the two of them and raised his rifle. As he did, Carrie reached down and grabbed Jack's hand. Jack's breathing was heavy and labored. The man swallowed hard and aimed his gun at Jack's head. He didn't want to see it when the guy's head exploded, but there was no way it could be avoided. He closed his left eye to be sure he was aiming right in the middle of Jack's forehead. Then he squeezed the trigger.

Jack did not close his eyes. Instead, he watched as the gun was leveled at his head.

The man was aiming right at the center of Jack's forehead when he fired. The gun was sighted for one hundred yards, not ten feet, so the bullet went high, grazing the right side of Jack's forehead. The man cursed. He had compensated some, but apparently not enough. He lowered his barrel another four inches and fired again.

Then his arm came down. He was trying to fight something. Jack thought it might be a heart attack or a stroke. He and Carrie just watched as the barrel of the gun rotated to the ground and yet another shot went off. The gun and the flashlight jumped out of the man's hands, and it didn't look like he was going to try to pick them back up.

Then there was a rumble of thunder, only it seemed as if it was coming from the ground, not the sky. Carrie took a step toward the man. His eyes seemed locked straight ahead, his stare looking somewhere beyond her. Then the ground began to shake.

Carrie walked carefully toward the man until she was close enough to get down and grab the rifle. As she approached him, his eyes widened suddenly, as if he realized what was happening around him, but was helpless to do anything about it. Her heart raced as she squatted and grabbed the barrel of the rifle. She pulled it toward her until she got a hold of the butt of the gun, then she quickly turned it around, pointing it at their attacker.

The man stood almost motionless, his mouth moving as if he were trying to speak, but no words were coming out.

Carrie wondered what was wrong with him. She backed away from him and returned to Jack. She was going to have to put the rifle down in order to help Jack move the tree. But there was a chance that the man could come out of this odd attack as quickly as he had fallen into it. So, she should shoot him. But she couldn't. Instead, she walked back to where he stood and picked up the flashlight. She brought it to Jack and put it in his free hand. Then she crossed over the branch that was pinning him down and laid the rifle on the ground. This way, if the man did come out of his odd trance, he would not know where she was, or where his rifle was. It was the best she could do.

She walked out as far as the branch went before it split off into dozens of smaller branches, so she could get the most leverage. Then she lifted. The wood dug into her soft hands and at first, she didn't think the branch was going to budge. But then it did. Jack put down the flashlight and pushed with his free hand. The two of them were able to raise the branch several inches, though branches on the opposite side of the tree would allow it to roll no farther.

"Can you hold it?" Jack called out.

"Yes," she answered, unsure if it was true.

Jack slowly released his grip on the tree and began sliding out from under it. His chest burned and his back ached, but he slid as quickly as he could.

The weight of the tree was tremendous, and Carrie felt her grip slipping. She held firmly as the bark tore across her hands, pulling downward. She held it as long as she could, then the branch came out of her hands.

The tree rolled back over, and the branch came down on Jack's shins. The impact smarted but was cushioned by the other branches that had stopped the roll. The tree rolled back some, enough that he was able to slide his legs the rest of the way out.

Then the man screamed. It was a high-pitched, blood-curdling scream and it made Jack jump. Carrie grabbed the rifle.

Then they saw the stars.

They were small red points of light that seemed to be coming down from the skies. They grew as they fell, and they were headed for the ground not far from where Jack and Carrie stood.

The man continued to scream as the fireballs fell to the Earth, lighting the woods with an eerie red glow.

Then they landed.

The earth pitched with one last tremendous rumble and the man grabbed his head. His screaming stopped and for a moment, his eyes glowed a hot white as he fell to his knees. There was a sizzling sound then a loud pop as his eyes suddenly went black, and he fell face-first to the ground.

Then it was once again deathly silent.

3

The ceremonies were over, and the cars were leaving.

Ben now stood without handcuffs. He stood near the stage where his Queen watched as the people departed. She remained in some kind of trance.

Inside Ben's head somewhere was his own independent mind. It tried to lift his hand, but the hand would not respond. Neither would his eyes, which seemed to roam the horizon of their own accord. He felt something new inside him. It was something that didn't belong, something dark and terrible that had come down from the skies with the fireballs. There was also another Ben Williams. This Ben could raise his arm, and direct his eyes, and even think some. This Ben was connected in some way to all who had survived the ceremonies. He was a part of some interconnected community of which Regina was the head.

She felt them all. She could see through their eyes, feel through their limbs. The input was overwhelming, but already she could tell that she was getting used to it. While the people still had their thoughts, they had hers as well, and it was her thoughts that were preeminent. It was her will that directed them. Through them, she would have her revenge, and she would experience it all as if she were actually there.

The clearing became empty except for seven cars. Everyone had left except for Slim Tom, Todd Jacobson, Ben, and Regina. One of the remaining cars belonged to Todd. One was the big black Cutlass belonging to Slim Tom. The remaining five belonged to the people who lay dead on the forest floor, between the altar and the woods beyond the clearing. There were always the few who did not survive. The Power was incompatible with their life forces, thus their forces burst like bubbles.

"Where should we go now?" Regina asked Ben.

Ben thought for a moment. "I know a place where we'll be safe."

Regina smiled. "Good."

Todd looked at Ben. Even though Todd could feel a part of Ben, he did not trust him. Neither did Slim Tom.

Regina looked quickly at them. "Yours is to obey, not question. This man will serve me better than either of you two could possibly hope to. And he will suffer every minute of it."

She was right. Even as Ben decided the safest place to operate from, he tried to keep the information inside, to hold it back somehow. But he could not.

Regina stepped down from the stage. Her robe flowed in the wind, revealing passing looks at her gray but still attractive body.

Ben felt the excitement that she forced upon him, and inside he cried out against it.

They walked to their cars and got in. Todd drove his own despite the pain in his foot, and Ben and Regina got in the black Cutlass with Slim Tom. They drove away from the clearing and headed back toward Mount Sylvan—Ben remembered exactly where the big house belonging to Jack Macon was, and he directed them to it. As they rode, Regina spoke quietly to him. Sometimes she called him Saul. She touched his arm, and he felt an icy shock run through his body, exciting him against his will. But it was what she wanted, and he knew it.

"Tell me," she whispered. "If you wanted to kill a hundred people and not get caught, how would you do it?"

Ben didn't hesitate. "I'd poison the water supply. Probably get a lot more than a hundred if they didn't catch it right away."

She pursed her lips. "That's no good. It's not violent enough. Give me something terrible and bloody, something that will fill me with an awesome sense of destruction."

Ben thought for a moment. Then he remembered some terrible stories from some buddies of his in Temple and he knew that she would like his next idea.

4

Carrie and Jack stood together near the pine tree that had almost cost Jack his life. Jack breathed deeply, then coughed. His ribs hurt tremendously, and he was sure he had at least cracked a couple of them. His right knee hurt too, but he could still walk fairly well. Carrie's left shoulder hurt badly, and although she didn't admit it, Jack could see the pain in her eyes.

"What should we do now?" she asked him.

"I think we should head in the direction that the fireballs came down. I would bet that's where the ceremonies are really being held."

"Are you in any condition to make the trip?" she asked.

"It's either that or back to the road, and I'll bet it's the same distance either way. Besides, the knee will loosen up as I use it." As he said this, he moved his lower leg back and forth as if demonstrating how it would work. It reminded Carrie of the Tin Man. Jack couldn't conceal the grimace that came with the pain. "Can you make it okay?"

"I'm fine. My shoulder just hurts a little, and my vision is a little blurry, but I can see where I'm going if you'll lead the way through the brush."

Jack took the rifle and the flashlight. He took the pistol out of his pants and handed it to Carrie. Then he led the way.

***

It took them almost an hour and a half walking through the trees and brush to make it to the clearing where the ceremonies had been held. It was well after midnight when they arrived. For the final half hour of the journey, Jack began to wonder just how far it was to the place where the fireballs had come down.

They emerged in the clearing opposite the stage. The altar on top of it was mostly burnt up, though its general shape could still be made out. As they walked into the clearing, Jack discovered one of the dead bodies. He looked it over quickly and saw that the eyes were like those of the man who had been trying to kill them, burnt out.

"It looks like not everybody survived the ordeal," Carrie observed.

Jack shone the light around the clearing and revealed six more bodies. "Looks like we missed the party. They've all gone. If we'd been here a couple of hours ago, we might have been able to do some good."

Carrie finally asked the question that had been bothering her the most. "Why do you think Ben told us to go to that other place? Is he really in on this? Do you think maybe they turned him at the compound, and he's been working for them since then?"

"I don't think so. If they had, he would have had plenty of opportunity to kill us on his own. I think they were on to him, and they told him that's where the gathering would be."

"So, where do you think he is now?"

Jack had already asked himself that question. The only answer that made any sense was that Ben was dead. "I don't know."

But as Carrie thought about what Jack had said, she too came to the conclusion that Ben must have been killed by now.

They looked the area over briefly. On the stage were lots of bloodstains and a few burnt bone fragments. The odor caused Carrie to gag once, and she waited off the stage for Jack to finish checking things out.

Jack got down off the stage. "Well, you ready for a little walk?"

Carrie sighed. "We've been doing a lot of that today. I'm going to be sore in the morning." She subconsciously rubbed her right thigh, which already felt worn out. "How far to the road?"

"I think we've stayed pretty parallel with it, so I imagine it's not more than a mile."

"Then we hope someone will drive by in the middle of the night, and that they'll pick up two strangers?"

"I guess."

"What if one of *them* comes along?"

"We're armed," Jack reminded her. "We can walk, but it'll be over five miles before we even get to a phone."

Carrie led the way toward the road. "Let's get started."

It was still pitch-black out, and they could only see as far as the flashlight beam, which was growing quite weak. They almost stumbled upon the first car before seeing it.

"So, we do get some good luck after all," Carrie said.

Jack looked inside. No keys. "I guess the keys are back there on one of them."

"Look around first," Carrie suggested. "Maybe there's another car here."

Jack shone the dim light around the small clearing they had entered and strained his eyes to see. The light reflected off some metal and he walked toward the reflection.

The keys were inside the old Dodge Daytona, and it started on the first try.

"Where to?" Carrie asked as she got in.

"How about a hotel for now."

Carrie agreed and they headed back toward the highway.

15

1

Jack awoke the following morning with Carrie by his side. His ribs were quite sore. He and Carrie had wrapped them with bandages and tape the previous night. The pressure helped some. The aspirin helped more. His arm was still draped across Carrie's stomach and her skin was smooth to the touch. She looked angelic to him, even with the small Band-Aid tacked to the side of her face where the bullet had grazed her otherwise-unblemished skin.

He moved his hand softly across her belly, up to the base of her breasts, then back down. He loved the feel of her skin. He was so rough; his skin was textured like a low-grit sandpaper. But her skin was so smooth and soft, just running his hand over her body like this relaxed him.

She came slowly awake and smiled at him.

Jack looked into her soft brown eyes. "I'm sorry I woke you."

"I didn't think I was going to be able to sleep." Jack continued to rub her stomach as she spoke to him." It took me a while to get there, but then I must have slept like a rock."

Jack moved a little higher with his strokes, including the bottom half of her breasts. They too were soft. "Me too. It's after ten already."

Carrie looked surprised, but she was glad to have gotten the rest. Her body still felt sore from the adventures of the previous night, and Jack's hand felt so good on her. "What are we going to do today?" she asked him.

Jack continued to lengthen his massage in either direction. "I'd like to go by my house and get some fresh clothes."

"Me too," Carrie agreed. She raised her arms over her head and stretched. There was just a twinge of pain left in her shoulder, and her vision had returned to normal. "But let's just stay here for a while and enjoy the rest of the morning." She turned to her side and faced Jack, then put her hand on his left thigh and teased him by scratching the inside of it.

"I'm game," he agreed.

She smiled.

2

Two men in a late-model Mazda pickup truck pulled into the parking lot of the Corral Bar-B-Que at exactly noon. They sat and watched as the popular lunch spot began to fill with people.

Ted fingered the trigger of his AK-47 nervously. The safety was on, or there would have been holes throughout his partner.

"Would you stop that!"

Ted glared at Robby and stopped fingering the trigger. Ted had been chosen because he had been trained for combat, just like the others who had been chosen. There were enough vets and cops in the Family to do the jobs right.

3

A woman sat down in a deep ditch by the side of the road. The pit had been dug a few days earlier when a water line had broken. The pipe had been repaired, but quitting time had come before the hole could be filled back up. Now Karen stood in the ditch, watching the passing traffic. Nobody would volunteer for this job, so it was hers. This was not what she had expected to find when she joined this group, but now it seemed like the best she could hope for. The real Karen would have resisted some, but this woman was only part Karen, and mostly something else.

She looked at her watch. It was a little after noon. She checked her rifle one more time. It was ready and loaded. Twelve boxes of ammunition sat in the ditch with her. Her six-year stint in the Marine sniper unit was what got her this job. In a few minutes, she would see just how much of her skills she had retained.

It would take the civilians on the highway a while to figure out what was going on. It would take them even longer to figure out where the shots were coming from.

4

Not everything would happen at once.

Jed Robertson carefully screwed the threaded cap onto the ten-inch length of one-inch-diameter iron pipe. Two small wires came out of a small hole in the top of the cap. When the cap was securely in place, he set the small bomb down next to the twenty others he had completed so far. By this coming Friday night, the aluminum bleachers at Tyler High would be riddled with these little bombs, tucked neatly under the lip of the seats where they would not be seen, all connected with a fine, silver wire. Nobody would know they were there, at least not until well into the second quarter of the football game.

It had taken most of the morning for him to get a hold of the explosives he needed to build the bombs. The list of ingredients, along with the instructions on how to make the bombs, had been supplied by Ben Williams. Dynamite had been considered, but by Friday, the demolition company on Pine Street would have noticed the missing explosives, and that could lead to problems. Besides, he was enjoying building the bombs, and they were really designed to maim and burn as much as to destroy.

5

The school bus was parked in the shade. That was good because it wouldn't be rolling again for three hours, and Jane would be spending those three hours hiding behind the back seat with the spare tire lying on top of her. She had looked through ten different buses before finding one with a good hiding place, one big enough for her and her pistol.

She was a good shot. Of course, Regina knew that, and that was why she had chosen Jane. Almost anybody could hit a target only a few feet away, but anybody else might lose their nerve. Jane hated children. She always had, and even when she had been one, she preferred the company of adults. Everybody always gave them so much attention, as if being small versions of big people gave them some mysterious irresistible quality. But Jane saw them for what they really were, underdeveloped ignorant menaces for whom nothing was ever good enough.

Jane could have no children of her own, which was fine with her, and even better because while she hated children, she loved sex.

Anybody else might have had trouble walking down the aisle of the bus, firing shots into the bodies of the seventh and eighth graders who would be riding this bus on their way home. But she would actually enjoy it some, and all of the commotion would not take away from her concentration, because she was a good shot. She had even brought her own gun, the one she used at the firing range twice each week.

The real Jane only had a slight distaste for children. But the Power had found this distaste strongest in her and had helped it to grow into the proper magnitude necessary for the task at hand.

6

Ben cried out as his orgasm shook him. It was like fire and ran throughout his body.

Regina felt it too, through what he had become, and it was a moment that was like no other. In that moment, she was only Regina, she was in control, and she was with Saul, and she cried out his name.

Ben felt both intense pleasure and utter revulsion. Inside, he wanted to throw the woman to the floor, to stomp her head flat, and escape this place. Another, more powerful part of him wanted to keep on screwing her, on and on for eternity.

Then she stopped, her eyes glassy and distant.

He could feel something then, some weakening of her hold.

But it lasted only an instant, then she was off him, putting her robe back on and walking across the room to her chair.

They were in Jack's house; they had performed many kinds of sex on Jack's bed and in his bathroom. Regina could not get enough. For her, it was a way to escape into the glorious past. For Ben, it was a terrible torture, yet one that a part of him craved.

7

Slim Tom and Todd Jacobson were still around. She had made them her admirals of sorts, with Ben holding highest rank. The men were downstairs, screening the people who came as she requested them, and organizing the acquisition of supplies. The lists of things they needed to get were usually brought down from Jack's room by the person Regina had summoned. And the lists were all in Ben's handwriting.

It was just past noon, and soon, all the ideas that Ben had given his Queen during the night would take their terrible form. He had told her things that would kill and maim thousands of people over the next week, which was the way she wanted it. She didn't want them all at once, just a steady, building flow of terror. She would feed off this terror, grow off it. As the various forms of death took the people of Tyler, she would draw strength from their suffering and the entire Family would grow stronger.

She sat down in the big chair they had moved up from the living room. It faced the curtains that covered a large window that looked toward the city. The room was dark and cold, colder than it should have been. One reason was that she had turned the air conditioning on high and closed all the curtains in the house. She wanted the cold. Warmth made her feel weak, and it made her rotting odors worse. Part of the coldness came from her.

Steam rose from Ben's weary body, and he struggled to get up off the bed.

"You're mine now, Ben," she said without turning to face him. "You're a part of me, and I a part of you. I know that you are still struggling, but that will only make your suffering worse."

She laughed as he struggled to move, but his body lay still.

Then she closed her eyes and waited for the rush that was about to come.

8

They had stayed in bed too late for breakfast, so they decided to go for lunch. Jack was going to take Carrie to his favorite barbecue place, but it was just after twelve and the place would be packed. Instead, he drove to a deli that was right by Highway 110, on the way to his house. There they ate a couple of sandwiches and planned out the rest of their day. They assumed Ben had been killed, and that they would be virtually on their own.

Neither of them had any idea that regardless of their plans, it would all end for the two of them within an hour.

9

"Let's do it."

Robby drove up to the front door of the barbecue place and let Ted out of the car. Ted carried his gun out in the open. There was no reason to conceal it now. A little girl in the parking lot with her parents spotted the man with the gun and pointed him out to her mommy. She thereby saved the lives of herself and her parents, and her father was the first to call the Tyler Police and tell them what had begun.

Ted walked in the door and took ten paces inside. It really was a perfect layout. He could see virtually all of the tables from where he stood. He also had a clear shot at a number of people, probably fifteen of them, walking through the line and getting their orders. Ben had said to start with the closest people since they would be the easiest targets, and the ones most likely to cause him trouble if he didn't take them out.

A woman screamed as he released the safety on the assault rifle. He had a modified magazine in the gun, and two more in his pocket. He had to resist the urge to just shoot everywhere. Ben had said this would wound a lot of people but kill only a few. So, he raised the rifle to his shoulder and looked down the sights at the man sitting closest to him. Ben had told him to aim just below the chest since most of his shots would rise from where he aimed, and even then, they would be very likely lethal.

The man looked at him wide-eyed, pieces of his salad dangling from his mouth. It was a comical look to Ted; it reminded him of the time he had put a whoopee cushion in his Aunt Bess's seat.

He fired. The shot echoed loudly in the building. A splash of red appeared just in the center of the man's chest. Ted adjusted slightly to his right and fired a shot through the man's heart.

10

Regina gasped as the thrill and power of the first death rushed through her. She, too, saw the man's terrified eyes, and they filled her with a wonderful sense of control. But she also saw something more, something Ted sensed but could not see. She saw the electricity that surrounded the man's fear, and the explosion of colors that came with his death. She fed off this release and awaited the next.

11

The woman sitting next to the now-dead man was frozen in terror. Ted shot her quickly and right through the heart.

The line awaiting their meals had begun to scatter, so he fired into them. There was not much cover for them, and he was able to put seven of them down, killing one and wounding the other six. Then he returned his attention to the tables.

He shot slowly and with calculation. Most of the people were going under the tables. Ben had said they would, based on some stories he had heard out of Killeen. Those who stood up, he shot down. Those who went for the door, he shot down. One did get out the door with a bullet in his shoulder. It didn't matter. There were seventy-three more people who would not escape.

He stood, waiting for those who would scramble for better cover. He picked off three more this way.

Then he squatted to get an idea of how everybody was arranged. When he did, he saw and took two more clear shots. The first went through the head of a man wearing a suit, and the second through the lung and liver of an elderly woman who was having trouble moving away from him.

Then he began working his way toward the people he had wounded, but not killed, in the food line. He would finish them off, then take out the people who thought he wasn't paying attention when they made a run for the door.

Ben had said that a few of them would try. And Ben had been right so far.

12

Joe Ganey and Jeff Kelsey got the call first. They were less than a mile from the restaurant when the call came in. Jeff hit the siren and Joe put the pedal down.

Images of the Killeen massacre came instantly into Joe's mind.

Neither man spoke as they raced toward the scene, knowing that as they drove, people were probably dying.

They pulled into the parking lot near the door. Big glass windows revealed the mess inside the restaurant, and from outside, they could see the skewed tables and a few of the people inside, both alive and dead. But from where they sat, they could not see the gunman.

Joe glanced around the parking lot for the man's vehicle, but no one car stood out. They were all parked properly in their place. There was a car in the handicap spot that did not have a handicap license plate. That was probably the gunman's.

Joe jumped out of the car and squatted. "Cover me," he whispered to his partner. Jeff got out of the car and leveled his pistol across the hood, ready to shoot if the gunman appeared.

It would have been better for Joe to wait for backup, and procedure called for this. But he had lost a cousin in the massacre in Killeen, and in the months since had wondered how many lives might have been saved if the first man on the scene had gone ahead and gone in. Those people inside couldn't wait for his backup, which would be another two minutes in arriving. He could hear the shots inside the restaurant. Each one meant another possible death. He had to try to stop this.

Jeff covered him as he ran low to the door. Since the gunman did not appear, Jeff took his chances without cover and ran to his partner. He couldn't let Joe go in there alone.

Joe could see the gunman. He was sideways to the door, shooting at three men gathered under a table. They were bobbing and dancing as he fired into them.

Then the man paused to reload.

Joe pushed the door open and rushed inside. Jeff came in right behind him.

Ted had heard the sirens and had been waiting for the little bell on the front door to ring. He knew they were here, but he wanted to get a few last shots in before quitting. That was risky, but each death had brought him some strange and muted rush, residual of what Regina was soaking in miles away.

But then the bell rang.

He dropped the gun immediately and raised his hands.

Joe raised his gun. As he did, the man dropped the rifle and surrendered.

This was terrible. Joe looked down his sights at the man, and his hand shook. The man was unarmed. He was supposed to stop now, to take this man in. But nobody would say anything if he killed the man now, quickly. Surely not the people sitting terrified under their tables, surely none of them would tell. And Jeff...

Jeff had aimed his pistol, and he pulled the trigger.

The front of Joe's face exploded as the first bullet emerged. The second came out the top of Joe's head. His legs went out from under him, and he fell forward to the floor.

Officer Kelsey put his pistol back into his holster as Ted picked up his rifle and headed for the door.

Ted hurried past Jeff, who stood watching the disbelief in one woman's eyes. "Get going, fast," Jeff shouted to Ted as he hurried out the door.

The car in the handicap spot had pulled out and was waiting for him. Ted jumped into it and Robby hit the gas.

Jeff took his gun back out of its holster. "What the hell are you looking at?" he said to the shocked woman under the table. Then he shot her in the face.

As Ted and Robby sped away, Jeff left the restaurant and got into his patrol car.

The next officers to arrive on the scene saw Officer Jeff Kelsey's patrol car as it left the parking lot and would not know for almost fifteen minutes exactly what had happened and why the officer was leaving the scene.

By then, Jeff would have already ditched the car and caught a ride to the mall.

13

It was getting warm in the ditch Karen was standing in. She looked at her watch. By now, the massacre at the barbecue restaurant would have begun.

She raised her rifle and picked a car at random, one that was approaching from the west. She waited until the little Hyundai was about a hundred feet from its closest point, then fired at the front left tire. She was using hollow-point bullets and the tire exploded off the rim, sending the car suddenly to its left, where it hit another car. Both cars pulled to the side of the road about a hundred feet past her, which would be perfect. As she waited for the cars to pull over, she fired at two more cars, which drove a little farther before their drivers pulled them over.

Traffic was beginning to slow down and back up as the people passing by looked to see if there had been an accident, and if it was a bad one. A short, fat man got out of the Hyundai and walked toward the car he had hit. As he walked, Karen took a clean shot and blew off the top of his head. He fell to the ground in view of the traffic. Only a couple of people heard the shot and realized what had happened; the rest thought for the moment that the man had been hurt in the collision. The sight of blood and twitching legs caused the traffic to slow down and back up even more.

Now the cars were moving slowly enough, and she began firing at the ones closest to her. Although a few of her shots went wild as they broke through the glass, she was able to shoot two or three times at the driver of each car, until she was sure she had a kill.

It all happened so quickly that she was able to kill ten people before anyone really had any idea what was going on.

14

Officer Jeff Kelsey was a few minutes late getting to the mall. His driver pulled up to a back entrance and let him out.

There were a lot of people in the mall today. That was good. There seemed to be plenty of young attractive girls, which was pleasant, but not what he needed. Jeff walked until he found a middle-aged man who was not dressed very well. For this plan, an attractive young woman would not work.

He pulled his gun out and arrested the man, throwing him against the wall and cuffing his hands. The man protested that he had done nothing, though by coincidence, he was in violation of his parole. The people watched in amazement as the cop took the guilty-looking man into an abandoned store.

Once inside the store, Jeff shut the door behind him and locked it. The son of the mall's manager had given him the key that morning. He pushed the man across the dim room, into the farthest corner.

"Hey, man," the man protested, "this ain't right."

Jeff threw a punch that sent the man to the floor, then he pulled out a long, shiny knife he had brought from home and sharpened just for the occasion.

The man started to cry out for help, but Jeff kicked him in the face and the cry never escaped. Then he knelt over the man, who lay on his back dazed from the kick. Jeff waited until the look of terror returned to the man's eyes before he drove the knife into his chest.

When the scream did come, Jeff held a rag over the man's mouth and no one heard it except the two of them.

Then it was over. Officer Kelsey waited five minutes, then he did it again.

The owner of the shop across from the abandoned store watched the show as it happened over and over. Sometimes the cop found his man quickly, sometimes it took him a while, but he always found his man. It looked like a simple sting operation of some kind, like she had seen on that real cop show on television. She paid little attention to her customers as she watched the Tyler Police officer emerge from the abandoned shop every few minutes and grab another criminal. Some of the men he grabbed did indeed look like criminals, but others really didn't.

But he had to know what he was doing, being a cop and all. And she had always thought there were too many jobless men wandering around the mall during the daytime anyway.

15

Regina sat in the big chair, her head moving slowly back and forth. Occasionally, a moan of ecstasy escaped her lips.

Ben felt it too, though only in part. He felt each death and knew that he was responsible.

He also felt something else. In her ecstasy, something had changed about the Power. She was lost in the glory of the events, absorbing the power of the terror and death. Although there was no question at all that he was still a part of the whole, that he was a pawn to the Power, he felt a slight lightening of the burden.

He tried to close his eyes but could not. He tried to move his leg, but it remained on the floor. He looked around the room, but something else controlled his movements. He tried to cry out but remained silent. He tried to make a fist.

His finger moved.

It lasted only a second and was immediately corrected. But it had moved.

But this was useless. He could not engineer some complex attack on Regina with his simple ability to move a finger. And the Power still dictated his thoughts and his movements. Even now, in the back of what remained of her rotten mind, Regina had noted his small victory and had made corrections to him, and he was completely locked up again. The Power had grown inside him, and it had diminished somewhere else, probably in someone who was quite loyal to begin with.

Inside, Ben screamed in rage. But no sound escaped his lips.

The deaths were coming quickly now, each one sinking into Regina like a hit of some wonderfully stimulating drug. But this was better than any drug she had consumed, better than any pleasure she had ever known. The power of it all raced through her body. She could feel the electricity everywhere, even in places where she had lost feeling.

Another man got a bullet in the head as Karen squeezed off another round.

Another man cried a muffled cry into the rag as Officer Kelsey drove the knife into his heart.

A woman breathed her last as a young man who had broken into her home cut her neck with a razor.

Regina cried out in her ecstasy as the death and terror spread. As the day rolled on, the pleasure would both continue and grow.

16

1

As blood flowed in the homes, streets, and public places of Tyler, Texas, Jack drove up Highway 110 toward home. He passed all the old familiar landmarks, and they gave him a sense of peace he had not felt in days.

Where had this all come from? Where was it all going? Ben had told them a little about the woman who was running the show and the cult she had once run in New Orleans. He talked of terrible evil and dark plans, but he had never been specific. Now Jack wished he had pushed for those details, now that Ben was gone, and they had lost Regina completely.

Carrie thought back to when it had all started. If her sister just hadn't gotten involved in this thing, then she would be at work right now, totally unaware of where her other life would have led her. And Terry would still be alive, still bitching about her job and her friends, but still there.

But the evil would have continued even if Terry hadn't become involved. And there would have been no one to try to stop it. Then again, they really didn't seem to be doing any good. But she had also met Jack. She reached over and squeezed his hand. He was a special man. She just wished she had met him sooner, and under different circumstances.

They passed the sign that warned them that the speed limit was reduced to fifty, just before they passed the old church that Jack had seen the inside of several times in his youth. He slowed after the curve and prepared to turn into his driveway.

He saw the cars. There were three of them.

Carrie saw them, too. She recognized the black Cutlass as the one that had followed her and Laura into the parking lot of the hardware store. It belonged to the tall, thin man.

Jack stopped his car. It was still a good eighty yards to the house. He backed away and pulled the car behind a small grove of trees that hid them fairly well but gave them a view of the house.

Jack stared out the window. "Somebody's in my house."

"I recognize the black car. It's the one Laura and I told you about, the one that followed us."

The front door opened and three people came out of the house. One of them was Detective Todd Jacobson and today, he had a terrible limp.

"It looks like they've taken up residence in my house," Jack observed. "I suppose they thought you and I had either been killed or are on the run. Either way, somebody didn't think we'd be coming back."

They watched as Todd walked with a couple to one of the cars, which they then got into and drove off in. Jack and Carrie ducked as the car passed by them, headed back to Tyler. Todd lit up a cigarette and walked back into the house.

Carrie stuck her head back up and looked toward the house. "Do you think she's in there?"

There were only two cars. One belonged to the tall thin man. At least one person had certainly come in the other car. "I think we can count on the man we saw and the tall thin man being inside. I figure they both came in the black car. That means there's probably one or two other people in there. One of them might be her, but there's no way to be sure."

"There's one way," Carrie suggested.

There it was again. Carrie's aggressive and tenacious side showed. It always came out when Jack was ready to enter the planning and thinking mode. Perhaps this was a good thing; otherwise, they might always be planning and thinking instead of doing.

"Maybe we should sit here and watch the house for a while, see what's going on. I'll bet that within an hour or two, we'll be able to tell whether she's in there. If she is, we can come back at night, cut the power to the house, and get to her."

Carrie thought this over. She didn't like it. "I think the darkness would be to her advantage. Remember Ben's story about her setting that man on fire? If she can do that, what else can she do? I think we should move soon, maybe now."

"But we can't be sure she's in there."

Carrie looked at the house again. Something wasn't right. Then she figured out what it was. "She's in there. Look at the windows."

Then Jack saw it. All the curtains were drawn, every one. No light was being allowed into the house. "I'm not sure that means she's in there. They might just be using my house and they've drawn the curtains to hide whatever they're up to."

"From who?" Carrie asked.

It was true. There were no close neighbors. The house couldn't be seen clearly from the road, at least not by a car passing by at fifty miles per hour. But this still didn't mean she was there, and he had to be certain before risking his life on it. Inside, he thought Carrie was probably right. But it was only a hunch. And he wasn't ready to die, not on a hunch.

"I know she's in there, Jack." Maybe Carrie was right. Maybe not.

Carrie took his hand in hers. "There's got to be a way to find out."

Jack thought. He thought hard. He looked at his house and tried to think of a way they could know for sure.

Then he saw something that answered the question and left no doubt.

2

Regina faced the window, lost in her ecstasy. It enveloped her, enthralled, and empowered her. She was not in Jack's room in Jack's house—she was in a ditch next to the loop shooting people in passing cars. She was in the mall, driving the sharpened butcher knife into men's hearts. She was breaking into houses, slicing women's throats.

She was in all these places and more.

Then the curtain rod holder flipped again, as it had three days earlier. Jack had never gotten around to fixing it. The curtain rod swung down to the side of the window. The sudden change from darkness to light broke her concentration for an instant.

Ben felt it. He tried again, but all he got was again a slight movement of his finger, then the correction and nothing.

Her eyes remained closed, her face showing mainly ecstasy, but also some annoyance at the light that ran across her face and upper body. Ben walked over to the window and put the curtain rod back in place, pushing the rod holder firmly into the wall in the upright position.

When darkness returned, Regina was completely absorbed once again. Ben went to the bed, where he sat down, awaiting her next command.

3

When the curtains fell, they caught Jack's eye. Carrie saw it too. A dark figure appeared briefly and then the curtains were back in place. They hadn't seen much of the person who had fixed the curtains, but they had both seen Regina. Ben had described her to them, and who else would be sitting in Jack's big chair, facing a window with the curtains drawn? Even from where they sat, they could both tell this was the woman they were looking for.

"We've got to go in now, while we know where she is," Carrie demanded.

"We need to have a plan," Jack countered, "a well-thought-out one."

Carrie looked at him. "If we take too much time to think about this, the opportunity will be gone. And what could happen in the meantime? And what will she do if we lose her?"

Carrie was right. Jack looked back at his house. At least it was his house, and he knew it better than those who were inside it.

"I should go in alone," Jack concluded, "through the back door."

"You'll need me to back you up, and you know it."

"We've only got one gun," Jack reminded her.

"We can get another one. It will only take us a few minutes. You can borrow one from someone you know in town, or we can run to a pawn shop." Silence. "I'm not letting you go in there alone. You'll get yourself killed, and then I'll have to go after her by myself."

Her logic was exceptional, and Jack wished for the moment that it was not.

She was right. "Okay," he agreed. "We'll go in together. But we're going to have to get you a gun, and while we're doing that, we are going to make a plan, okay?'

She agreed and they pulled away from their hiding spot.

4

Jack drove to Sam McCutchen's house. As they approached, he noticed the yellow tape that indicated a crime scene. Immediately, he knew that he had indeed gotten his friend in trouble, and he could only hope that he hadn't gotten him killed.

Jack left Carrie in the car and went to the front door. It was locked. Sam never kept it locked, so this must have been done by the police. Jack walked around the house, trying the windows. The police had locked them, too. Finally, he went back to the front door and kicked it in. Sam had never taken Jack's advice to get deadbolts and the door opened easily.

Jack walked through the house. If there had been trouble inside, there certainly hadn't been a struggle. He walked to Sam's back room where he kept most of his guns. Jack pulled open the drawer where the pistols were kept, and he picked out two that had extra magazines. He loaded all the magazines and grabbed a couple of boxes of ammunition as well, just in case. With the two extra magazines apiece, they would each have thirty-six shots before having to reload. He didn't think they would need that many.

He thought about leaving a note, then decided against it, figuring the police might hassle him over it. Especially if Sam...

He hoped Sam had not been killed. But the house was dank and lifeless, and he suspected that it was so.

He returned to the car and handed Carrie her gun. After showing her briefly where the magazine release was and how to quickly put in a new one, he put his own gun on the seat and headed back to his house.

5

Regina felt stronger.

And more was coming. Not as fast as it had been when Ted was knocking off people at the restaurant. That had been a wonderful rush of ecstasies. Now it was a new death every few minutes. But Ted was on his way to another location, and there would be a new rush of souls soon.

Ben watched and waited.

6

They were running a little behind schedule due to the backup Karen had created in the eastbound traffic. They passed in the other direction, on their way to another busy restaurant. They would be there in ten minutes. Being behind put them in some danger since they had coordinated their hits with patrols of the city police, making sure the right car would get there first.

But the task could not be abandoned. That was not an option. And even if it were, Ted didn't think he could stop anyway. The killing was like a drug, each new death bringing him the echoes of some intense pleasure.

They got around the bad part of the traffic and started making good time.

7

Jack and Carrie returned to Jack's house. At first, he suggested approaching through the front door, passing themselves off as members of the cult. But Carrie reminded him what Ben had said about the eyes. They would know he was not a member. Jack suggested sunglasses. Carrie suggested the back door.

Of course, he still had his keys. This made the most sense.

Jack parked the car by the trees again. Then he jogged across the yard toward the back of the house, hoping that for the next minute, they would at least have the good luck of nobody coming out the front.

As Carrie reached the back porch, another car pulled into the driveway. If it had taken them ten seconds more to reach the cover of the porch, they would have been spotted. As it was, this would now work to their advantage.

"We'll wait until they go to the door," Jack whispered. "Then we'll go in the back and hurry around to the stairs. They'll never see us."

"Why don't we take them out?" Carrie asked.

"Because she'll hear us. If she knows we're coming for her, there's no telling what she might do. We don't really even know what she's capable of."

Carrie agreed to the plan, and they waited on the porch until they heard the doorbell ring.

8

Slim Tom answered the door. Two men had come. She had called for them and they had both left work to come. Each man was capable of performing a task she needed done. She knew this because of what they had become, because a part of her resided in them. But Slim Tom did not know exactly who they were. They provided him with their driver's licenses and Slim Tom made sure the pictures matched the men. They did. Then he walked to a small table behind him and...

Was that a noise? For a moment, he thought he had heard an odd noise, but he wasn't sure. And there was a breeze...

But the front door was wide open, so of course there was a breeze. He walked to the small table and picked up the envelope that Ben had brought down ten minutes earlier. On it was a list of things they would need along with a few diagrams and a map. All in all, it was the plans for the deaths of approximately eighty more people, though they were not scheduled to die until tomorrow afternoon.

9

Jack led the way through the small room and to the stairs. The house was cold inside, too cold, and he could hear the air conditioner still running. From the base of the stairs, he could hear the tall thin man as he answered the door and spoke to the people who had just arrived. He assumed the other man was down there with him.

The stairs were wooden, and he walked as quietly as he could, but the bottoms of his boots made some noise. To Jack and Carrie, it sounded as if the sounds they were making were being amplified throughout the entire house. But nobody heard them.

As they reached the top of the stairs, they heard the tall thin man walking across the living room. Jack held up his hand in a signal to wait until he walked outside with the visitors. He thought it would be best to wait until they had driven away. Until then, he hadn't given much thought to Carrie's and his escape. It would be much easier to make that escape if there were only two other people to contend with instead of four. He figured that they would be able to get both of the occupants of the room upstairs before anybody knew what was going on.

10

Robby pulled into the parking lot of their next restaurant and parked next to the door, in a place marked for handicap parking. There was no time for discussions this time around. Ted jumped out of the car immediately and walked quickly across the parking lot to the front door of the establishment.

11

Jack listened as the car doors outside the house slammed shut. Adrenaline flowed through his veins. Carrie too was wired and ready for battle. Her hands were shaking in anticipation.

Then there was an unexpected noise behind Jack.

Carrie's eyes widened as the man came out of the small bathroom at the end of the hallway. Jack turned his head quickly.

Detective Todd Jacobson was still buckling his pants. His cigarette dangled from his mouth, which remained open in surprise as Carrie fired two shots at him. The first took him in the chest and threw him back into the bathroom. The second went high and cut through his throat. He fell dead between the wall and the toilet, his last cigarette smoldering on his unbuckled pants.

It was time to move now, before Regina had any more time to prepare.

12

Ted began shooting at the people in the restaurant. Again, he was slow and methodical, making sure to kill rather than just wound. The place was even busier than the barbecue joint had been, and there would be one more restaurant to go after this one.

A young boy screamed as the first shot only wounded him. But the second shot pierced his skull and came out the other side, lodging in his mother's leg.

A waiter tried to make a run for the protection of the kitchen. Ted fired three shots in his direction, finally knocking him down with the third shot, then firing a fourth and fifth into the upper half of his back.

Ben had said always go for the upper portion of the upper body if you couldn't get a clean headshot.

13

Regina heard the shot that was in the house with her, but it seemed a world away. Fresh, new terror was coming to her, death was taking soul after soul in the restaurant on West Market Street. Each death was a powerful release. The combination of them, one after another, had her caught in its euphoric grip.

Ben heard the shot, too. Against his own will, he stood and walked to the nightstand, where he picked up the revolver he had placed there in case there was any trouble.

Then the door came open.

14

Jack went into the room first. It was even colder in here than in the rest of his house and steam came from his mouth in billows. He had expected to see someone in the room guarding Regina and he aimed at the man standing near his bed.

But then he saw it was Ben. He was alive after all. But why was he here?

Before he could figure any of it out and come to any conclusions, Ben fired at him. It was a good shot, hitting Jack high in the chest. Jack fell back against the side of the door, then spun to the floor.

Regina tried to pull herself away, but she had extended herself too much and the Power did not want to return to that small room when it could roam the city, absorbing with her the death and terror. It was like being absorbed by some powerful drug—she fought to come back to consciousness, but somewhere inside, didn't really want to. But she knew she had to.

Carrie stepped into the room when Jack went down. Her first instinct was to look at Jack, to see how badly he might be hurt. But she knew there was a more urgent task at hand.

She aimed her gun at the man whose attention was still on Jack. He was aiming for a kill shot, in case the first one hadn't done the job. Then he saw her.

Ben knew he had killed Jack. He also knew he was about to kill Carrie. He felt the confusion of his Queen and tried to work against what he had become. But it was a fruitless effort.

Carrie stood with her gun pointed at Ben. When she recognized the man, she too hesitated.

The hesitation was all he needed. He was, after all, a trained police officer. He brought his gun up quickly, aiming for the kill zone.

As he squeezed the trigger, he put forth everything he could to point the gun away.

Regina felt a part of herself slipping away. "No!" she yelled from her chair. Then she began to stand.

Ben fired.

But first, his hand moved.

The shot hit Carrie in the shoulder, sending her back a step. Ben fired again quickly, fighting against himself. This shot went into the wall beside her head.

Then she shot.

She hit Ben in the stomach, and he went down to his knees.

Inside, he was both terrified and grateful. Now he could escape the living hell he had been captured in. But he did not want to die.

He raised the gun slowly, trying to get another shot into Carrie before it was too late.

She would not hesitate again. She aimed carefully and put a bullet in his chest. He dropped the gun and fell back to the floor. He lay almost completely still. Then he blinked once and whispered, "Thank you."

Carrie didn't understand.

She raised her eyes and saw the terror.

Regina stood facing her. Her eyes rolled wildly as she fought for consciousness, fought for just enough control to solve the current problem. Even as it stood, it was not life-threatening, just a menace. If she had not been in her meditative state, both the attackers would already be dancing balls of flame. As it was, it was just a matter of time.

Carrie began firing.

The first three shots went into Regina's chest. They made a terrible sound as they entered her. One went clear through and cracked the window behind her. Blue fluid began seeping through the robe she wore, a robe that had once been Jack's.

Regina came more into focus and took a step toward Carrie.

Carrie emptied the rest of her magazine into the girl, shooting at her body and filling it with holes from which the blue fluid flowed. A hissing, gurgling sound escaped Regina's lips, and her eyes began to glow.

Carrie pushed the button on the side of the gun and the empty magazine fell to the floor. She reached into her pocket for a fresh one.

The wounds brought Regina back. The electricity of the newest deaths in Tyler went unabsorbed. She had cut the line and was nearing total consciousness. As she did, she became furious at what had just become of her body, and her eyes focused on the woman before her.

Carrie popped the next magazine into the gun and racked the first bullet into the chamber.

But then she noticed that the room was no longer cold. In fact, it had become very hot. It felt as if someone had opened an oven, and the hot air hit her hard and she broke immediately into a sweat.

Regina gurgled a laugh at her as the blue fluid seeped into her lungs. Carrie knew the bullets were not going to kill this woman. It was over.

Her feet felt as if they were on fire. She felt it coming fast now.

"NO!" Carrie screamed out as she dropped her gun. The flames started low and worked their way up quickly.

But a second before they came, when Carrie knew what her fate would be, she leaped.

Regina's eyes grew wide with surprise as the woman flew across the room and grabbed her. She wasn't ready for it, and she flew backward with the impact of the attack. The flaming woman grabbed her and pushed.

Regina's back hit the window hard, shattering the glass and breaking the wood frame. They flew out the window together, Carrie screaming and burning, Regina still unsure of what had happened, still drugged with the effects of where she had been.

They hit the pavement of the driveway with a sick wet thud.

Regina hit first. Brains and blue went in every direction. Carrie did not let go, and the dark consuming fire took her flesh as it had been commanded. But it didn't stop there.

Regina's mouth opened into a blood-curdling scream as the fire consumed her ravenously, determined to leave nothing behind but burnt bone fragments.

15

Her screams of death were echoed throughout Tyler.

Ted shot a young girl in the back as she sat huddled in a corner of the restaurant. But something had changed. This death had not brought the rush the others had. He thought perhaps he had not killed her after all and prepared to fire into her again.

But then he suddenly dropped his gun and grabbed his head. There was pain, so much pain, and suddenly his eyes went fiery white. He screamed a terrible scream, then his glowing eyes burst into flames.

16

Cory had found another woman to slice. First, her screams filled the room as he walked toward her with his open knife.

Then his screams drowned hers out as his eyes too went fiery white.

17

The shop owner at the mall was watching the cop as he once again emerged from the vacant store. He had a gleeful grin on his face, as if the operation was going quite well.

Then his eyes, too, burst into white fire.

18

Throughout the town, people who had at one moment been a part of the terror became consumed by it. For the last moment of their lives, they became what they had once been, they understood where they had gone wrong, and then they died in great agony.

They were not quick deaths, the worst of them lasting a full five minutes.

The fire began with their eyes and ate its way slowly through their brains, stopping only when there was no more life. It was their combined life forces that caused their own destruction. It was a massive short-circuit, caused when the main switch had been burned clean through.

It was finally over.

EPILOGUE

The terror had come quickly. It left slowly. For some, it took months to heal, for others, years. Some never did.

No one ever really knew what had happened that day in Tyler. There were no survivors left to tell the tale.

One man had his own story. It was the sheriff of Smith County. Tonight, a week after all the mayhem, he sat alone on his back porch watching the sunset and admiring the beauty of it, reaffirming his life.

He still had the tapes and the pictures Ben had made. He had lost seven of his men that day and had seen two of them when their eyes had done that terrible thing. Their suffering had been tremendous.

The FBI had come in, and they asked their questions and took their pictures. But Sheriff Walsh kept Ben's tapes and pictures to himself. The way he saw it, the government would have just buried them anyway. This way, he would have something to hold onto, some proof that it hadn't all been a terrible dream.

What had driven those people to do what they did? Sam could only guess. They had even found Ben in the mess, but nobody could tell exactly why he had been in that house, and why it appeared that his gun had killed Jack Macon.

Sam admired Jack. He certainly didn't admire his being dead, but he admired what he had done, and wondered what had driven him to do it. He wondered if he would have done the same, and just how bad it would have gotten had Jack just run away from it all.

There was someone else, too. But so far, all they had was too many bone fragments. Two people had burned in front of that house. One had been that Regina woman Ben had talked about. But who had the other one been, and how had she done it?

In time, they would get all the bodies sorted out. Then there would be some answers.

But he knew there would be many they would never have.

Sam sat back in his chair and took another drink of his cool lemonade. Inside, his wife was cooking dinner. The smells drifted out through the open back window.

On the horizon, the storm clouds were building again. They would probably have rain by morning.

In the distance, the whippoorwill resumed its mournful song.